In All *Places*

A Stripling Warrior Novel

In All *Places*

A Stripling Warrior Novel

by

Misty Moncur

Eden Books - Utah

Cover design by Heather Waegner

Published by Eden Books, Stansbury Park, UT

ISBN-10: 0989895912
ISBN-13: 978-0-9898959-1-0

Moncur, Misty Leigh, 1978-
In All Places / Misty Moncur
Summary: Keturah finds it hard to return to civilian life after the war against the Lamanites.

ISBN: 978-0-9898959-1-0

Library of Congress Catalog Control Number

2013951976

To Kaiya

Acknowledgements

A big thank you to Heather and Laura
for all you've done to help me with this series.
It has not gone overlooked or unnoticed.
Sadly, it is going to go unpaid.
Sorry.

And because I think it bears repeating,
Misty is better than Chad.

Chapter 1

"Ouch!" I rubbed my chest where the small, buckskin ball had hit me.

All the boys laughed, and Corban crooked an arm around my neck.

"What's got you so distracted, Rabbit?"

I rolled my eyes when he used my exasperating nickname and gestured toward the city. "My mother. The healers are coming through the gates."

"I wonder if she brought us anything to eat," said Reb as he swept up the ball and hit it over to Ethanim with the outside of his heel.

He said it lightly, as a joke, but it was true that we were on strict rations. We had taken prisoners after the siege on Cumeni, and feeding them had depleted our own supplies. Food in the city was scarce, and most of what we ate, we scavenged from the forest.

After I dropped the ball two more times, Lib offered to take me to find my mother. He bent to pick up the ball at my feet and tossed it to Cyrus.

"Come on," he said, and not needing to wait for my answer, he started to walk away.

"I can't help but remember the battle we fought here," I said dismally as I caught up to him.

Lib didn't say anything, but he gazed at the city square as we approached it. I could see he was thinking about it too.

"This war will be over someday," I said, wistful at the distant prospect of obtaining peace. I was weary of the fighting, the constant attacks on our villages and people, and the unrest in all the lands around us.

Lib's voice held weariness too. "And you'll go home," he said.

"Won't you?"

He lifted one shoulder in a shrug. "Is that your mother, there?"

I looked in the direction he pointed.

"That's her." I turned to him when he slowed and hung back. "Aren't you coming?"

He glanced to where Mother and Kalem unloaded supplies from the travel pallets.

"No."

"Alright," I said, frowning at his refusal. "I'll be back later."

He looked at me for a long moment. His eyes looked sad, but I thought it was just the nagging hunger that caused him worry.

"Try to get Kalem to walk you back."

"Stay," I invited. "Mother will want to see you, too."

He shook his head and gestured me toward my mother.

I went straight into her arms. She waved to Lib over my shoulder, and I turned in time to see him staring plaintively at us. When our eyes caught, he turned abruptly and stalked away, his golden hair glinting in the sun.

Mother pulled back. I could see the questions in her eyes.

"Everyone is alright," I assured her. "But Zeke is—" I looked down and took a breath. "But Zeke lost a lot of blood."

"Will he recover?" Her words were clipped and emotionless.

"The healers think so." I turned to acknowledge Kalem with a small smile. "But I've run out of herbs for him," I admitted. "Everyone has some ailment for which they need treatment, and I've used up all I have."

"It is not right to leave someone in pain when you can help," she reassured.

"I can finish with this pallet," Kalem offered. "Let Keturah show you where the good herbs are here in Cumeni."

I witnessed a smile pass between them, one I had seen many times before and had long ignored the meaning of.

"Are you sure you don't want to stay in camp to rest?" I asked her as we approached the city gates. She had been traveling all day, and I could easily take one of the men with me later to find plants.

"No, Kanina, finding herbs and medicines will calm my nerves. I've known nothing but worry since we got news of the battle. I've wearied Kalem with my fears."

I laughed, and it felt good. "I doubt that very much."

Kalem had been helping Mother take care of my brothers and me for many years. If he hadn't already tired of us, I didn't think he was likely to at that point.

"I know a pretty meadow that has hyptis and sage," I suggested, feeling an unexpected heat in my cheeks as images of the last time I had been in the meadow came into my mind, images of Gideon and moonflowers. The sunlight slanting in from the west. His smile. His lips.

I shut my eyes tight. "There are some cases of stomach pains in the camps," I said quickly. "It will spread."

"Alright." Mother's voice was gentle. "It is wise to be prepared."

I could feel her looking at me. She couldn't know why I

was blushing, but she was seeing too much in my face, things I couldn't conceal, so I turned away and concentrated on the warmness of the afternoon as I led her toward the meadow. Though it was located outside the walls of the city, it was not far, and she barely had time to question me again about my brothers before we stepped into the small clearing.

"You say they are all well?" Mother asked. "They've no serious wounds?"

I shook my head. "Jarom also came through the battle practically unscathed."

"And your unit? Lib, Zachariah?"

"They have their wounds. We were not here when the battle began. We were taking our prisoners to Zarahemla under Gideon's command." I held a branch out of the way for her. "We didn't make it that far."

"And Gideon?"

"He led us back to fight beside our brothers."

The smell of the forest was good. The hot, moist air made it all the more pungent and earthy.

"Keturah."

The way she said my name made me blush furiously.

"I do not want to know his rank in the army," she said. "I want to know what is in your heart for him."

I thought I heard someone else walking nearby. A footstep or a breath. My hand went to the blade on my arm, but though I scanned the area, I did not see anyone. It was probably nothing, but still, my training told me that anyone with good intentions would have let himself be seen. When I did not answer my mother, she tried a different question.

"How do you feel about Gideon's wounds?"

I bit my lip and brought my eyes back to her as I discreetly removed the blade and held it to my side.

"He is strong enough to bear them," I said. "I've been taking care of everyone's wounds. Zeke is the only one that fell unconscious, though some are in a great deal of pain."

She sighed, but did she really think I could talk to her about Gideon?

"Like you?" she asked.

I guessed I hadn't been hiding my limp as well as I thought. "Much worse."

"Tell me about what happened to Zeke."

I didn't want to tell her about Zeke racing across the battlefield to protect me. I didn't want to tell her it was all my fault he had nearly died and still might. She would be disappointed in me, but her high esteem of Zeke would rise all the more—she'd betroth me to him on the spot.

I quickly convinced myself she was only seeking the medical information. "He took one too many swords," I told her. "The final wound, the biggest one, high on his leg, pulsed blood even after he had fainted."

Mother hummed softly. After a moment, she said, "You were there with him."

Not a question. Mother knew that my unit did not fight beside Zeke's.

"Yes, I was there."

She started to ask me more, but stopped when she saw the large tear that rolled down my cheek. Instead, she drew me around to face her and wrapped me in loving arms that I did not deserve. She loved Zeke like he was her own child, and I had nearly gotten him killed.

I willed my tears to stay at bay but let her hold me, even as I held inside all the things I could have told her. How Zeke had sacrificed his life for mine. How it had not been necessary. How my heart belonged to someone else.

Guilt churned inside of me, and I eased from her arms. I moved away from her worried frown, and went about the business of gathering plants and herbs. After a moment we were both snipping it off at the nodes of the branches between our thumbs and our knives, working away from each other across the clearing.

Mother had her little herb knife, but I used my father's large obsidian blade. I had grown comfortable with it in my hand, and because I used it daily, I was confident with it when I needed to be.

The day was sunshiny, and despite having to tell Mother about Zeke and despite grappling with my guilt, I was feeling better than I had since the battle. I was relieved to have Mother there to help with Zeke's care. Her healing hands were the only ones I really trusted with his life.

When I heard a twig break, I glanced up, supposing Mother to be closer to me than I had thought, but two men with dark skin and leering smiles emerged from the trees near me.

"Mother!"

She looked up, and I saw her face register alarm. She dropped what she carried and ran in the direction we had come, but one of the men darted to cut her off.

The other man approached me slowly, a menacing gleam in his eyes.

The Lamanite army had fallen back to Manti when they couldn't recover Cumeni. That was what my brother, Kenai, had said—our army's chief spy. These men looked to be stragglers. I had seen enough enemy soldiers to know what they looked like. They had probably defected from the Lamanite army, perhaps deserted during a battle. They carried no weapons of war, just bows and arrows to hunt in the wilderness.

I sent a quick glance toward Mother, and I was dismayed to see she held her little knife out, pointed at the man.

"No, Mother! Drop it!"

She glanced at me, not daring to take her eyes off the man for more than a second. Would she trust that I could protect her? I had to get to her quickly. I had to keep her from breaking her covenant.

No, I thought, Mother would have to make that decision for herself. I would have to protect her when she did not break her promises to God.

But I could not protect her until I had first protected myself from the man who edged steadily closer to me like he thought he had all day to assault me. Clearly, these men thought Mother and I were easy targets.

I almost felt sorry for the man who reached out to grab me when I took him down with one of my oldest moves, the four count drop Kenai had taught me. Whether it was my training or catching him off guard, it worked, and I made sure he hit his head hard on the ground when he went down. He wasn't unconscious, but it would take him a few minutes to shake off the blow.

I jumped to my feet and ran headlong toward Mother and the other man. His eyes widened, perhaps in surprise, perhaps waiting to see what I would do. I ducked, rolled, and picked up a thick branch that lay on the ground before him. It only took one hard blow to his head, which he failed to defend against, to knock him to the earth.

As I caught my breath, I looked over my shoulder at the other man. He had rolled onto his side, but he was still on the ground. The one at our feet was not conscious. I bent, picked up Mother's little knife from the grass where she had dropped it and handed it back to her.

"Come on," I said as I began to run toward the city walls. "I don't think they will follow us."

Mother and I hurried over the hilly paths back toward Cumeni, but we didn't make it all the way before we ran into Gideon.

"There you are," he said, a faint smile on his lips when he saw me. "Lib sent me after you when Kalem came—" He stopped when he saw our faces. "What happened?"

"Two men. In that meadow surrounded by willows." Surely he knew the one I meant.

His eyes shot in the direction of the meadow. He remembered.

"Did you leave them alive?"

"They had no weapons of war."

As warriors, we had all been trained to kill, but we had been commanded never to kill if there was another option. We were not to take life unless our own lives were in peril. The Lamanite men had not drawn their bows on Mother and me and had likely planned to take us captive and carry us to one of their strongholds. Perhaps they thought they could buy their way back into the good graces of their king for deserting the army. There had been rumors of that happening all over the countryside in the small towns and villages that were not protected by walls or other fortifications.

Gideon grimaced and escorted my mother and me back to the safety of the walls of Cumeni.

Though I had proved I could protect both myself and Mother, I felt immeasurably safe and comfortable with Gideon's warm hand on my back. But even as I welcomed his touch, the guilt tugged at my stomach.

When we were back at Mother's camp, Gideon pointed to my leg. "Leah, she's bleeding through her bandage," he said. Then his eyes lit a little. "I'm going to put together a patrol."

Mother stared after him. I tried not to.

After he had disappeared around a stack of supplies, she leaned forward a little to catch my eye. "He's a good man," she said.

"They're all good men," I returned, avoiding the subject of Gideon, which she seemed determined to bring up. "Are you wounded anywhere?"

"No, Kanina."

I held out my hand. "Can you dig out these slivers then?"

She pursed her lips. "After I see to this wound you've been hiding."

I looked down to see that my bandage had been saturated and my sarong was soaked through with bright red blood. Maybe running headlong toward my enemy had been a bad idea. But then I looked at Mother, safe here with me, and the wound no longer mattered.

As Mother unwound the bandage she said, "Thank you. For what you did."

I laughed a little. "Was there any other choice?"

"I might have protected myself." Mother was firm in her covenant not to do so, but there was frustration in her voice.

"No, when you saw they did not intend immediate harm, you acquiesced. I picked your knife from the grass, Mother."

"I do not like that you put yourself in danger for me, but Zeke was right. You have a warrior spirit."

"Zeke said that?"

She glanced up at me as she worked. "Zeke came to Micah and me long before he asked Helaman to speak on your behalf. He told us of your desires." She smiled as she remembered. "He was so much against them, and he was so worried about you he was sick in his stomach. I had to make him a tea."

I winced when she poured wine over my wound, gritting my teeth against the deep sting, and I kept my eyes on it as she worked. "That sounds like Zeke, managing things that aren't his business," I said, pretending annoyance, but I thought of him lying unconscious in the infirmary station because he had tried to save me, and I felt remorse for my actions, not disdain for his.

"Oh, Kanina. None of us knew about your Gid then, and we all thought your welfare was your intended husband's business."

Your Gid.

My eyes shot to my mother's. "I understand now that Zeke didn't want me to get hurt." I looked back at the wound. Pain like this was only one of the things he had wanted to protect me from. "He asked you to refuse to let me fight."

"No," she said, surprised that I thought so. "He asked us to consider your plan."

My plan. It sounded like a falsehood.

"He has always loved you."

"I love him too," I said, in case she was doubting it.

Mother tied the bandage tight and gave me a look. "I am not the one who needs to hear that. Let me see your hands now."

But I love Gideon too, I wanted to say, to blurt out fast and hot—so I could deal with the betrayal of my heart, so she could help me cope with it.

But I left the words unsaid. They would have cut her, and I would have choked on them anyway.

When my wounds were tended to and Mother's nerves had settled, I took her to see Zeke, which I should have done in the first place. We could have entirely avoided the danger I had placed her in that afternoon.

She knelt next to his pallet. "He's pale," she observed as she put a small, dark hand to his forehead.

"Actually, I think he's gaining color."

She glanced at me, then her full attention went back to the boy who was almost like a son to her. "Tell me what you've been doing for him."

Kneeling with care on the other side of his pallet, I explained what the healers had done to repair his leg. I told her what his unit and I had been doing—getting liquid down him, changing his dressings, and mostly just watching him sleep.

"Have you given him anything for pain?"

"He's unconscious. He doesn't seem to need it, though I have tried a weak willow tea."

"Sometimes when the body is in great pain, it shuts down like this, or the body wouldn't be able to bear it."

"So if we relieve his pain, he will wake up?"

"Not necessarily. You said he also lost much blood?"

I nodded, remembering the pool of it soaking into the soil.

"These things take time, Kanina. Be patient with him. He will heal in his own time."

I remembered the herbs Zach had shown me, and I got out my book to show Mother the pictures I had drawn of them.

"Zachariah says these will ease pain much better than the

willow, and these," I turned over the folds, "will help him make blood. His grandfather was a healer."

"Yes, I know," she said, her eyes on the pictures.

That didn't surprise me. She was very good at getting to know people, a talent I had not picked up from her.

"Will they help? I wanted to ask you before I treated him with anything I was not familiar with."

"You will be a wise healer," she said.

Recognizing it as a compliment, I blushed.

"It is no wonder all the boys love you. You've a pretty blush to your cheeks."

I rolled my eyes.

Mother smiled, and tucked a strand of hair behind my ear. "There is nothing wrong with being beautiful and amazing. Just be considerate of their feelings, hmm?" Turning her attention back to Zeke, she studied his face, and after a long moment, she added, "There is nothing wrong with following your heart if it leads you toward good, my Kanina."

I looked at Zeke's face too.

"Yes there is," I said stonily, but she made no reply.

After Mother had checked all of Zeke's wounds, she said, "You've done well with these. The dressings are clean and the wounds are healing. I have seen other healers using those plants. Can you get them?"

"Yes."

She nodded. "Bring them to me, and we will see if we can get this boy to wake up. And Keturah?"

"Yes, Mother?"

"Take one of the men with you this time."

I grinned, but my heart ached when I stared at Zeke's face again for long moments before I left. He was handsome even lying there so still. He was not a boy any longer. He was a man who had nearly died for his country.

And for me.

Chapter 2

Corban was helping me launder tunics at the river when Lamech appeared from behind the trees. I had no idea how long he had been skulking there and as it always did, his brooding stare unnerved me.

"Zeke's awake," he said finally.

I jumped to my feet, water cascading from the hem of my sarong.

"He doesn't want you."

I felt my face fall.

"Relax," Lamech said with a smirk. "He doesn't want you to see him all crippled, not until he can walk." He looked deliberately around. "Where's Gid?" Was there a note of contempt in his voice?

"Zeke's not crippled, and Gideon's on guard duty with Joshua," I said as I knelt to finish what I was doing. I wrung out the last tunic and handed it to Corban.

"Why do you call him Gideon?"

Because that was how he had introduced himself to me in the forest. Because he had told me he liked when I used his full name. He obviously wanted me to, so I did. He was Gideon to me.

"That's his name."

"No it's not. It's Gid."

"Is my mother with Zeke?"

He didn't answer, only stared at me with dark, unreadable eyes.

I spoke slowly as if I was speaking to old Zequinim back in Melek. "His name is Gideon."

"A name is what people call you, and everyone calls my brother Gid."

"Fine. His name is Gid. Is my mother with Zeke?"

"Then why do you call him Gideon?"

I sent an exasperated look to Corban. "Will you take me to see him?"

He nodded, already gathering up all the tunics that lay drying across rocks.

Lamech smirked. "I said he didn't want to see you."

I stepped to him and poked him hard in the chest with my finger. I had a little brother, two if you counted Jarom, and I knew how to handle annoying little brothers.

"No you didn't. You said he doesn't want *me* to see *him*."

I yanked hard on one of his braids and walked away.

After a few steps, Corban caught up, damp tunics in his arms. When I glanced at him, he was hiding a grin.

I could see Mother fussing over Zeke long before we reached them. His head moved as he watched her, and they appeared to be conversing. Mother smiled and laughed. Sometimes, it was weird, but I thought she was half in love with Zeke herself.

The moment Zeke noticed me approaching, his eyes tracked my face. There were a lot of things I wanted to say to Zeke, but when I saw the guarded look in his eyes, I couldn't find words, let alone the right ones.

"You're awake," I finally said, staying a short distance away. Maybe Lamech was right and Zeke didn't want me there. I wouldn't blame him. I couldn't.

Zeke shrugged. No one else would recognize it, but I knew he was embarrassed. About his wound? We were all wounded. I was flooded with relief when the corner of his mouth turned up.

Corban cleared his throat and spoke up. "Glad to see you're awake. We couldn't keep Ket away from your bedside." He dodged away from my elbow. "I'll go see if I can help with any of the wounded."

I gave him a grateful smile, even though my cheeks were burning.

Mother said, "I'll be back later," and she squeezed my arm as she brushed past me.

"You can come closer." Zeke's smile faded when, after several moments, I did not move forward, just stood staring dumbly at him. His voice turned cool. "I can hardly harm you from this position."

His words startled me into moving, and I stepped toward him, my limp still evident.

"You're hurt," he said, concern darkening the coolness in his eyes, and he shifted as if he would get up.

"I took a javelin in the leg," I said and eased down beside his pallet, effectively hiding my wound from him. I shrugged it off. "It was better than the alternative, and anyway, the wound is not as bad as yours."

His eyes went to his wound which was high up on his thigh, and his cheeks flushed. "It was just that I lost so much blood. The wounds are healing. There are lots of men worse off, or so Leah says."

Zeke hadn't even lost the leg. He was lucky. I nodded absently as I looked him over. He was really awake and healing. He was going to be okay.

"I'm sorry," I said. I did not want to put it off any longer.

The coolness returned to his eyes, already tight against the pain, and his voice held a challenge. "For what?"

I opened my mouth to speak, but I choked on the words. I stared at my hands for a while, and then when I still could not talk through the lump that had formed in my throat, I began fingering the frayed edge of one of the bandages on his arm. He let me. Sometimes, Zeke had amazing patience like that.

Finally, he reached up and stopped my nervous hand by covering it with his. He wanted me to say the words, to say I was sorry for...what? For having feelings for Gideon? I couldn't be sorry for that, and I wasn't going to say I was. I was only sorry that I had hurt Zeke with my expression of them.

"Can you forgive me?" I asked instead.

He wanted the words, but he didn't pretend not to know what I was asking.

"I don't know," he said resolutely, like he had been thinking about it for a while.

I glanced down, swallowing my disappointment. I shouldn't have expected any more than that from him, but somehow I had let myself hope everything I had done to hurt him could be forgiven so easily.

I reached out and felt his head, his cheeks, with the back of my hand. "How is your pain level?"

He shrugged.

"I can give you something that will ease the pain."

He snorted his disbelieving reply. "My leg is fine. The pain is bearable. What happened with your mother?"

I grimaced. "She told you about that?"

"A little."

"We were confronted in the woods by two Lamanite deserters."

"Leah said you were attacked."

I shook my head. "No," I said slowly. "They did not attack us. I attacked them."

The corner of his mouth tipped up again. "My Keturah."

"They didn't carry any weapons," I continued. "So I incapacitated them, and we ran for the city walls."

He stared at me for a moment. I bristled. It probably hadn't been the right thing to say, but I was tired of filtering what I said to him.

"Not many of us get to protect our parents so directly," he said.

I tilted my head and frowned. "No."

"I'm glad you were with her. But what were the two of you doing alone out there?"

He was controlling his voice well, but I could tell he was upset. I wondered if he had chastised my mother this way.

"I wasn't thinking," I admitted, but I wasn't going to tell him we had been gathering herbs to ease his pain. He didn't need guilt on top of everything else. "It was careless of me. I think Lib felt the imminent danger when he left me at Mother's camp." I paused for a moment and then sought his eyes and confided, "But I felt nothing, no warning of danger. It makes me wonder what's wrong with me."

"Nothing's wrong with you." Zeke sounded affronted. "Perhaps there was no danger, since you were easily able to deal with the men."

I certainly hadn't thought of it that way.

"Or perhaps you were just excited to see Leah," he went on, quickly taking back his beautiful compliment. "You were preoccupied."

"A good warrior doesn't allow preoccupation. That's what happened in the battle. When I stopped fighting. The man you fought, the man who did this—" I gestured to his leg. "I knew him, and in that moment, with the battle raging around us, he wasn't an enemy soldier. He was one of God's children, and I couldn't fight him. It was stupid. It was dangerous." I glanced at his leg again.

"Knew him? A Lamanite soldier? How?" he demanded.

My leg was aching, and I shifted my weight. "His name is Muloki. He was the guard at the gate of Antiparah." Then I had to tell him everything about the day Kenai had ordered me into the enemy stronghold in broad daylight. I did not tell him how Muloki had flirted with me at the gate of Antiparah, and I did not tell him I had spent three nights alone with Gideon.

Zeke's jaw clenched as I talked. He was holding back his anger, but he looked as murderous as Gideon had.

"Kenai?" he ground out.

"Don't be mad at him for sending me in," I nearly begged on my brother's behalf. "We needed information, and he did not have to order me. I volunteered. I went with faith, and I was met with miracles for it." I told him about the voice I had heard and meeting my mother's sister and the little girl who looked so much like Chloe.

By the time I was finished, Corban stood over us. "I've got a guard detail soon," he said regretfully when I looked up at him. "Do you want me to send someone else over?"

"No, I'll come with you. Zeke needs to sleep."

I caught the look of worry on Zeke's face when he saw I needed Corban's help to get to my feet, but he hid it well behind a swallow and a nod when I turned to say goodbye.

I smelled cook fires and roasting meat as we walked through the city back to our camp. The hunting parties must have had success that afternoon.

"Well," Corban ventured after a while. "He didn't kill you."

"Reb will be so disappointed," I said dryly. "I think he lost a bet."

Corban shrugged sheepishly, obviously having taken part in the wagering, but I couldn't help a small smile, relieved at Zeke's reaction.

Our unit was already eating when we got back to camp. Corban and Mathoni took their food and left for their guard detail. I got mine and sat between Lib and Ethanim. I had come to feel safe between them, and since the grisly battle a week before, I had found myself seeking their company.

When I finished eating, I was still hungry. So were the others.

"Who cooked?" I asked.

Lib nodded toward Cyrus, who gave a little shrug.

"That's all they gave me," he said regretfully.

"It was good," I told him over the embers of the cook fire. Everything tasted good when you were starving.

Every last one of us could hunt our own food, but doing so was not allowed unless we were assigned to a hunting detail, and then we had to give anything we killed to the army. There was an order to things, and we had to preserve it. Hunting parties went out each day, but they weren't bringing in enough game to feed an army of hungry boys. The grains in the storehouses and supply tents were getting low. Consequently, our rations had been pared down. We had gone to Cumeni to lay siege on the city, but we were the ones who were starving.

After we cleaned up, I asked Zachariah to take me into the forest to pick more of the plants he had shown me. Maybe we could find some roots to eat, too, though much of the forest had already been scavenged for edibles.

The terrain was steep. We had been moving about on it for many weeks, but I had to let him help me over the trickier areas.

"Thanks," I said when he caught my arm to keep me from sliding down the mountainside.

He didn't reply beyond a grunt and a curt nod, just kept moving along with his eyes on the vegetation.

When we came to a small gully, he hopped easily over it and held out his hand to me. I grasped it for balance and hopped the gully too, but not as gracefully. He dropped my hand quickly, when some of the others might have held it for an extra moment or two.

"What's your home like?" I asked him, trying to draw him

out into a conversation.

He shrugged. "Same as everyone else's, I guess."

"Do you have a girl at home?"

"Hopefully."

That surprised me. Though some of the oldest boys in the army were betrothed—some were even married—none of the boys in my unit had any such arrangements, though they frequently talked about girls from their town of Orihah, girls I didn't know and, frankly, never wanted to know.

"Do you think she has gotten married?" I asked him.

It had been three years. She would likely be married, even considering how many of the marriageable young men were away with the armies. There were plenty of older boys, boys who had been old enough at the time of the oath to make it and who had remained in Melek.

He shrugged as he inspected a cluster of leaves. "It's not totally up to her."

Her father might have betrothed her to someone, he meant.

"What's her name?"

"Elizabeth." He took a slow breath and set a handful of stems and leaves into the basket I carried. "Beth."

I wondered if Zeke said my name like that.

"She is the only one," he went on, wiping off his knife on his tunic to avoid my eyes. "I could never love someone else. If Beth is already promised, I'll go to Zarahemla with Gid and become a guard."

It took him a moment to realize what he had said. When he did, he flushed, glanced at me, and then crouched to cut some more stems.

"I know that's what he wants," I said. "Everyone knows it."

He stood. "I know it's not a secret, Ket." He sighed, placed his hands on his hips and set one foot farther up on the incline for balance. "But I know what it feels like to part with someone you love, not knowing if you'll ever see them again."

I imagined this tall, handsome boy saying goodbye, possibly forever, to the girl he loved.

"You'll know it too."

"Zach. It will be okay. God knows our hearts. We might get hurt, but in the end we will find that He has prepared the perfect way for us."

"Say that again when you watch Gid walk away," he said with pain in his eyes. But then he gave his head a shake. "Sorry."

He missed Beth. The ache and confusion were clear on his face, and I had never noticed them. Having to leave Beth had hurt him deeply, but I knew why he had joined Helaman's army. The same reason we all had.

"Come on," I said. "Let's go back. We have enough plants."

Many days passed with small rations and little to do. Some of the troops were deployed to other cities to hold them from the Lamanites, but we stayed in Cumeni waiting on provisions from Zarahemla.

Finally one morning Micah showed up in my camp. He had all his gear strapped to his back, and when I glanced behind him, I saw eight or nine other men prepared the same way.

"Where are you going?" I asked before he could tell me, which was obviously why he was there.

"We're taking a communication to the governor, a petition for more supplies."

I nodded even as I felt my stomach rumble.

At my worried look, my oldest brother put a hand on my shoulder and said, "There's food out there, Ket. It's not a famine or anything. We just need to get it here."

I nodded, melancholy seeping into my smile. "Be safe."

He kissed me on the top of my head and led his men away. It was a comfort, at least, to know the leaders were trying to do something about the problem we faced.

I thought of the way the Lamanite women had looked

when we had let them leave Cumeni after the siege, and I hoped things would not get so bad as that for us.

I was tired of this war, and I was hungry. How I wished for the corn in my satchel each morning, but it never came. Why, I wondered, did God withhold it? We hadn't needed it on the march to Judea, not nearly so much as we needed it then.

But I had learned to trust in God, for He knew all things, and I most assuredly did not. I resolved to leave it up to Him when to distribute His food to the hungry and when to try their faith.

Chapter 3

I was pondering on my hunger one afternoon when Zeke walked slowly into camp.

Delighted to see him up and walking, I went to him, meeting him halfway. But I had hesitated for just a moment, thinking his pride might demand that he walk the full way to me on his own power. His eyes were fixed on me, so of course he noticed the falter in my step, and disappointment showed in his face.

I thought I might insult him by not allowing him to walk to me, by diminishing his achievement, but I had managed to insult him anyway.

Still I knew my delight shone in my eyes. If he couldn't read it there, then he was blind.

"Come for a walk with me?" His voice was deep and familiar. His dark hair was tied back, and he looked so good—clean, strong, flushed with life—that I felt butterflies in my stomach where moments ago I had been wishing there was food.

"I would like that," I said firmly. I thought to suggest we could sit and give his leg a rest, but I had no sooner thought it than discarded the idea. I would let Zeke do and say what he thought was best without second guessing him. He was capable of making his own decisions. He led fifty men! And I led none.

Our wounds were similar, and I had been traipsing all over the wilderness to hunt game and gather herbs and roots. Zeke was strong and resilient. He would recover. I was feeling overprotective of a man who had proved he could protect both himself and me. But was it so wrong to want him to be safe? I needed him to be safe.

Was this the way he worried about me? Tainted with dilemma and selfishness? Constant wavering between caring too much and feeling unable to care at all? I swallowed hard and tried to think of something else, something that wouldn't cause my heart to race or helplessness to rise in my chest.

It was a perfect, beautiful day. The air smelled clean. Fluffy, white clouds drifted in a blue sky. Birds sang in the trees.

Birds sang in the trees.

My hand went to my sling, and I fit a stone into it. Without a word, Zeke placed his hand over mine.

He was right, of course. I was not on a hunting detail.

"Remember when we used to hunt together at home?" I asked, tucking the sling back into my belt.

He winced at the pain in his leg as he swung it over a branch in the path. "Of course I do."

How I hated to see him suffer!

"And you and Kenai would wait to the sides of a path," I hurried on, "while I lured something into your trap."

"You made beautiful bait."

It was a compliment I was accustomed to, but I blushed when he offered it so genuinely.

"We caught a lot of things that way," I remembered with a reminiscent smile.

"Between two men," Zeke said quietly.

For a long time I didn't respond, and his words hung in the air between us. I wanted to ignore them, to just let it go, but I kept thinking about them as we walked on. They wouldn't go away.

We hadn't yet talked of Gideon or of what Zeke had seen just before he had slipped into unconsciousness on the battlefield. It wasn't just that my captain had embraced me. It was the clear show of passion that had accompanied it, and not just on Gideon's part. It was the way he had grasped me tight to him, the way he had kissed my brow as if it was his to kiss and the way he had looked into my eyes.

We hadn't yet talked of my feelings for Gideon or of Zeke's. How could we? It was impossible.

"Don't start that, Zeke," I said at last, trying to keep my voice even. "I don't want to fight."

"Don't start what?"

I bristled at the challenge in his voice. "Don't you think you're taking this jealousy thing a little far?"

He threw me a glare, a look he seldom let me see, and we both stopped walking.

"No. I think I've been tolerant of the time you spend with Gid."

I repeated the word slowly. "Tolerant? It's not as if there is much of a choice. He's my captain. He's in my unit. He—"

"As a captain, he could have chosen any unit," he interrupted.

"But I couldn't. Why do you blame me?"

"You spend a disproportionate amount of time—"

"I do not! I spend equal amounts of time with all the men in my unit. You," I jabbed at his chest much the same as I had with Lamech. "You choose not to see that. You see what you want."

"You think I *want* to see you with him?"

I stared into his cocoa-colored eyes. So familiar. Warm, even in his pain. Beloved. I willed my anger to fall away. He was not the one I was mad at.

"No." I gave him the courtesy of an answer.

"Micah said you sought forgiveness, but he was wrong. You only seek justification."

That stung. "Can't you see I'm trying to love you? You're poisoning it with this bitterness and this jealousy."

"I don't want a girl who has to try to love me."

The words, flung like a stone, hit their mark.

"You don't love me," he pressed on with insistence. "And you," he poked me in the chest. "You are the one who has poisoned it."

I stared down at my chest where his finger had struck. It hurt, and I covered it with my hand. The sting of betrayal welled in my eyes when I looked back up at him. This was not the Zeke I knew.

"Gideon doesn't want—"

"I don't care what Gid wants!" His voice was higher than normal and raw with honesty. He took a breath. "Gid's feelings are not the ones that make me jealous, Keturah."

I glanced around. We had made our way to the edge of the terrace where the army was camped, but we weren't yet in the main part of the city where the buildings would provide us more privacy. A lot of people could see us.

I closed my eyes and remembered Zeke's blood seeping into the soil at my feet. I thought of what my mother had said. *I am not the one who needs to hear that.*

I lowered my voice and said, "I love you, Zeke." And I really thought I meant it. If I hadn't learned what love was by then, it couldn't be learned. "How can you doubt it? My friendship with Gideon or anyone else does not change how I feel about you. It has no bearing. I promised I would tell you if my feelings changed, and they haven't."

I put my hand over my heart because it felt like it was breaking.

"I keep my promises," I finished.

Zeke squinted into the distance as if he didn't like what he saw there. "Maybe your feelings for me haven't changed," he allowed. "But your feelings for him have. Give me some credit. I've seen the way you look at each other, Ket. I saw you melt into his arms." He paused, and when he spoke again, his voice cracked. "And not as if it were the first time. It is not just friendship, and I don't know why you claim that it is. You lie to yourself and to me." He took another deep breath and let it out. "And probably to him."

I was not a liar. I was not a liar!

"You think fighting about this is going to endear you to me?"

Zeke turned on me, and I caught my breath when I saw the fire in his eyes. "Shall I stand down and do nothing? I *will* fight for you, Keturah!"

"You're not fighting for me, you're fighting *with* me!" How I wished we weren't saying these things to each other. "I don't know what you want me to do!"

"What do you want to do?" he demanded.

I couldn't hold his gaze when it turned from angry to pained.

"What do you want to do?" he asked more quietly.

Unable to answer, I turned toward the precipice near which we stood and looked out over the grand square and the homes which were now occupied by families. Behind me stood the army, their tents and their weapons, the young warriors who were probably even now staring at us and hearing every word we yelled at each other. The afternoon winds had kicked up and strands of my long hair swirled around me.

"I *have* poisoned it," I said at last, resigned, but my voice was carried away on the wind.

Unable to bear the thoughts that were racing through my mind, I turned and started to run away, but even on his injured leg, Zeke was quick.

He grabbed my arm, but not with the gentleness he had

always used in the past, not with the gentleness I had become accustomed to.

I looked back at him. He looked like he might apologize, and I was prepared to insist that everything was my fault, because it was. He was right—I should acknowledge it so we could both move on.

But he didn't apologize, and I couldn't acknowledge it.

"Walk with me," he said, his eyes burning into mine.

Zeke and I limped side by side, but we didn't touch and we didn't talk, and that was the last time we spoke of Gideon for a long time.

He came by my camp often and we walked together. "Walk with me," he would say. We didn't fight, which was good, but we didn't talk either. We didn't talk about Gideon, or the fact that I was a soldier, or the problems my selfishness had caused. Our opinions on these things differed so greatly that any talk seemed to end in a quarrel that boiled down to my feelings for Gideon.

But how could I not love Gideon, who understood what was inside me, what drove me? He had a way of making me feel comfortable in my own skin. He never made me feel shame for choosing to be a soldier. I never felt small or incapable in his presence. I could try to explain it, try to rationalize it, but I knew that my feelings for Gideon were more than could be added up on any list of qualities. So very much more.

And yet, Zeke's love for me was rooted deeply in our past. It was thorough and unconditional. Even when we disagreed. Even when I hurt him. He viewed my desire to be a soldier as a flaw, and he loved me anyway. Zeke knew every mistake I had made since I was born, and still he wanted me. To be loved like that—it was more than I deserved.

Gideon loved me because of who I was, and Zeke loved me despite of it. And I had come to know that God loved me in both ways.

The worst part was that I didn't even care anymore

whether or not Zeke understood me. He did support me, and a part of me had always known it. Before the war, I had thought being in love meant we had to understand each other completely and perfectly. But that wasn't it at all. Love was an entirely different feeling than I had thought, because it was so much more complex than just a feeling.

Slowly, as Zeke and I walked together, we healed. Our strength increased, and our friendship, though guarded and different, grew too. He was my best and oldest friend. Our friendship had been tried, but I very deliberately rebuilt it, and I made sure everyone saw. Zeke had nearly given his life for me. I would give mine over to him in return.

When nearly everyone was healed enough to march, Helaman commanded us to prepare to march on the city of Manti.

On the way back to our tents from the council meeting that night, I asked my captains, "Wouldn't it be better to wait until we have provisions? How far can we march with no food for strength?"

"Manti's got provisions," Seth pointed out. "When we take it, we will have its provisions. And we can hunt on the march."

"And if Helaman has no hope of receiving assistance from the government, he has to take action of his own," added Gideon.

The next day, I looked around at all the troops. They all showed signs of hunger—sallow cheeks, dull eyes and hair, sedentary when they were not on assignment. I was becoming worried. Not for myself, but for my brothers in arms. They needed much more food than I did to maintain their strength, and the rations now were even too scant for me. Their wounds were healing, but they needed nourishment to heal fully.

I had chosen life in the army and all that came with it. I was willing to suffer through this grim time myself, but it was very difficult to watch those I loved suffer, even with the faith I had in God. As I watched the men suffer, I understood more fully the anger our prisoners had felt toward us for the unforgivable act of starving their families.

After our meager morning meal, I looked into the azure sky and knew I needed to make peace with the horrible conditions here in the camps. I looked back down and met Gideon's eye as he passed a water skin to Zachariah, and I knew I needed to make peace with my feelings for him too.

I approached Lib, and when I told him what I wanted to do, he placed his hand on my shoulder and agreed to take me. He had a couple conditions, but they were acceptable to me and even welcome by then.

He and Ethanim walked with me to a part of the city that was still deserted. We climbed to the top terrace where the more dilapidated homes sat. There was no poor class of people now. We were all poor, and the army stayed in the areas closer to the city center.

I chose an area behind a humble, abandoned hut. As Lib and Ethanim checked the yard for any hidden dangers, I stood at the edge, overlooking a very small stream that ran through an overrun garden that hadn't seen tending in a good while.

I had my tent for privacy, something I always appreciated, but I seldom had enough privacy to speak aloud to God.

I was so worried and so troubled and confused, I just had to speak with Him.

Ethanim began to walk away, but Lib lingered. He touched my cheek with the back of his fingers and looked into my eyes. "I hope you find what you seek," he said. And then, surprising me, he bent and kissed my temple.

I wanted to throw my arms around him and hug him tight to me, but not more than I wanted to hug Ethanim. I cherished them both. They had been so diligent for these three years, shielding, protecting, warning, and comforting me. How could I ever thank them for doing this? How could I ever let them know that I appreciated their efforts? I knew it had not always been easy or fun for them.

"You know I can offer you only friendship," I said through a tightness in my throat, feeling that I had somehow misled him. We had never spoken of his feelings for me, though we had both been aware of them for a long time.

"I know," he said. "I only want you to be happy. I hope you can find the peace you need."

He looked at me for a moment more, then let his hand drop and followed his best friend away from me. When they were gone, I turned and walked slowly into the overgrown yard. I wondered who had lived in the tiny hut that sat there. A war widow? A mother with children? An old man? Everyone had a story, a life, and everyone's life came with problems and worries, joys and love.

I knelt in the dirt among the plants and flowers. God watered these flowers and gave them nourishment from the earth, and He would provide nourishment for me. I bowed my head, as the flowers did each night, and I began to speak the worries of my heart. I began to pour out my soul in my prayer to God.

I had always thought I had faith. Could I have gone into battle, a weak little girl, if I had no faith? This problem, however, was so much bigger than my faith. In battle I could rely on my training and even my experience. I could sling my stones, brandish my knife, and wield my sword. I could act. But in this problem I could see no path forward. I did not know what actions to take.

I explained this to God, and I did not ask him for anything save peace to my soul. There was so little food in Cumeni, but in truth, I wasn't sure there was an answer to that problem, at least not one that was in my power to fix. It was not my responsibility to fix it all. The answer to that would come through the proper channel, which was Captain Helaman. When I realized this, I felt calmer. The burden I felt lifted from my shoulders when I recognized it was not mine to carry.

I already knelt motionless in the soil while the plants and long grasses swayed in the soft breeze around me, but I stilled inside and listened for the promptings and instructions and peace of the Spirit. When I felt a calmness that edged out my fears, I knew that God would provide for us and determined to spend no more of my energy on worry.

I moved on to the subject that had been perplexing me since the day I had stumbled upon the obsidian in Melek, the day God had placed Gideon in my path.

In my mind, I could see Gideon standing there as he had that first day, sword in hand, his complete attention on me. He had teased me, something I had since come to know was not typical for him. I saw every feature, every expression of his that I had memorized since then. Why did I have such feelings for him when I was supposed to love Zeke?

Zeke was the eldest son of my mother's best and dearest friend. They had looked forward to my marriage to him from the moment I was born. I thought of Hemni and my brothers and Zeke's family. I was betraying them all, and I could not stop it.

I thought of that moment after the Lamanites had retreated when Gideon had pulled me roughly to him, of the sheer relief that we had both survived such a terrible battle, and for the briefest of seconds I let myself wish again what I had wished in the next moment—that Zeke had not been there.

I wept for that. I choked on my traitorous feelings. I said I was sorry, but I received no response. I did not even receive a peaceful feeling. My mind was not at ease and was still churning with questions. Finally, disappointed, I ceased my prayer and bent forward until my head touched the ground. I had wanted and expected a distinctive answer, and I had received none.

As I lay there in the stillness, I noticed the sound of the little stream. I sniffed and turned my ear to hear it better.

The scriptures compared God's love to water, his word to food. I let my mind wander through those thoughts until I found myself thinking that after we took Manti, I wanted to go home. And though I did not see my path laid out before me as I wanted to, I felt hope that I would see it when the time was right. The war was not over, but for me, the fighting was done.

I couldn't fight my feelings for Gideon, but I wouldn't dishonor Zeke or my family.

"Keturah." His voice was gentle and so familiar, and somehow it belonged there in that garden with me.

I uncurled and looked up to see Gideon. At the sight of his face, my mind calmed, my heart unclenched, and I felt traitorous all the more for it.

He went to his heels beside me and brushed some dirt from my forehead. Then he wiped the lone tear from my cheek. Answering the question in my eyes, he said, "I felt like I should come find you."

A bird took flight, and my eyes tracked it upward. The sky was still brilliant blue.

Gideon touched my arm, and I looked back down at him.

"Did you get any answers?"

I shook my head.

"You will. I'm waiting on mine too." After a moment he said, "Do you want to pray together?"

Yes! I wanted our combined faith to carry mine. I wanted to lean on Gideon's strength. Instead, I just shook my head. I could not think of a worse betrayal of Zeke than to pray with another man about our future.

He seemed to understand. He rose and helped me to my feet, and after he held me for a long, long time, he walked me back to camp where I collected my weapons before we started toward the training ground.

I would not let an empty stomach keep me from doing what I knew to be right. I would deliver my countrymen from the hands of the Lamanites. And God would deliver me.

Chapter 4

"Heads up, Ket."

We were halfway to the training ground. Hunger clawed at my stomach, my head ached from crying, and Gideon tossed a ball up between us. He wanted me to hit it back, but I snatched it from the air.

"I don't feel like it," I told him.

"Come on, Ket."

I hadn't even known he carried a ball like the other boys did. He never refused to play when someone else brought out a ball, but he never initiated a game either.

He took the ball from my hand and tossed it into the air again. After he hit it a few times with his knees and feet and elbows, he knocked it back in my direction.

"What's the point?" I snatched it from the air again.

When he tried to take it back, I held it out of his reach—as far out of his reach as I could.

"Life is not meant to be a drudgery, even during hardship. Men are that they might have joy, Keturah."

I stopped walking and put my hands on my hips. "And what about women?"

He made a grab for the ball again, but I quickly put it behind my back. In a playful attempt to get it back that was completely out of character for him, he snaked an arm around my waist and pried the ball from my fingers. But he didn't let go of my hands.

"Women are that men might have joy, too," he said.

A little gasp came from my throat, and I did something I hadn't done in a long time, maybe since I had been at home with Cana. I giggled. I tried not to. I ducked my head so Gideon wouldn't see my smile. He was so close, with his arm still around me, that my forehead rested on his chest, and I could feel his low chuckle.

It was entirely too wonderful.

"Let me go," I said as I tried to wriggle away.

"I don't want to," he said, and he had no trouble holding me in place—maybe because he was strong, maybe because I wasn't trying very hard to get away.

We were both laughing when I noticed Seth and some of his men coming up the path.

"Really, let me go," I said. "They will see."

"I don't care who sees," Gideon said, but he gave my hands a final squeeze and let me go.

In a moment, Seth and the others had stopped before us and we all stood awkwardly staring at each other. I sent a look to Gideon, a reprimand for embarrassing me. Gideon tried to wipe the grin off his face, he really did, but he just couldn't. He raised his brows at me, and I covered my mouth to keep from laughing.

"Are you two going to the training ground?" Seth asked, looking between us.

I nodded and pulled my bow more securely onto my shoulder.

Gideon glanced at the sun. "Actually, no. I have to return to Captain Helaman at the government building." He turned to me. "Have fun," he said. Then he leaned close to my ear and whispered, "That's an order."

He tossed the ball up and caught it as he left.

Seth's kohl-lined eyes were watching me closely.

"You all go ahead," he said to his men.

None of them argued, and they moved away quickly, passing me without a word.

Seth and I stared at each other until the sounds of the men faded.

"You're mad at me," I said.

He sighed and slowly shook his head. "I'm not mad." He stepped closer. "Gid's different than the rest of us."

"I know."

"He could be Chief Captain over the entire Nephite army," he said emphatically.

"So you've told me before."

"If you love him, don't jeopardize it for him."

"What do you care?"

"Obviously more than you do."

I stared at him again, and then turned on my heel and followed the others toward the training ground. It was only a moment before I heard Seth hustling to catch up.

"Ket, wait."

When he was at my side, I said, "I didn't provoke that." I waved behind us. "Back there."

"You provoke it just by being you. You still have no idea what you do to men."

I gave him the dirtiest look I could find, reaching deep inside myself for a scowl that would make him back off. Gideon had been trying to comfort me. He had made a deliberate effort to remind me of the sweetness in life. I wouldn't let Seth make it into something it wasn't, something ugly and common. I didn't know what I did to men?

"I guess you would know."

It was a cruel thing to say. His shoulders stiffened, and I

knew it had been too cruel. I wasn't unaware that he himself had feelings for me, nor was I without feelings for him.

"I'm sorry. Seth, forgive me."

He swallowed. "Not necessary. I shouldn't have said anything. I should have given Gid the credit to make his own decisions, and I should have had more faith in you."

I bumped his shoulder with mine. "I think it was the hunger talking, for both of us."

We entered the training ground. As strange as I knew it was, the familiar sounds of swords and spears and boys yelling were comforting to me.

"Let's put our aggression to good use," Seth said, and he led me across the field.

It had been quite a while since Micah had returned from his embassy to the governor when I saw a group of Kenai's men hurrying through the city toward the command station, which was now housed in one of Cumeni's government buildings.

I recognized them all but only knew one of them. I groaned, but approached them anyway. I hated any interaction with Mahonri. When I fell in alongside him, he glanced at me. I couldn't tell what he was thinking. He was as ornery and difficult to communicate with as Lamech, except Lamech had the forgivable excuse of being young.

"Where's Kenai?" I asked, not really sure what information I wanted from him. I just knew he had some information, important information from the looks of it, and I wanted it.

"How should I know? Kenai doesn't report to me."

"Hmm..." I said. I would have to try a different tack. "Where are you going?"

He didn't answer. The men he was with looked between us with varying degrees of amusement. They had obviously been putting up with him for a while and were probably wondering why the stubborn Mahonri was the one I had chosen to speak to.

"Look," I told him. "The faster you tell me what news you

have, the faster I'll leave you alone."

"Or you could just leave me alone right now."

He was such an irritating person.

"You will find out soon enough," he added, giving me a dismissing once-over that clearly implied he did not think I was anything special. He wasn't going to tell me just because I was pretty.

Instead of being insulted, I felt a respect for him blossom inside me. Still, I was about to argue when my eyes flicked to movement beyond Mahonri. One of the other boys appeared to be pantomiming the eating of food, bringing his fingers to his open mouth. Another boy pushed him playfully, and someone else laughed.

When Mahonri turned to see who dared to laugh in his presence, I inserted a note of dejection into my voice and said, "Nevermind. I will go find Kenai myself."

Could it be true? Provisions were on the way?

I went to Kenai's camp. He took one look at my face and said, "How do you hear these things?"

"So it's true?" I exclaimed, already planning my first meal.

"Who told you?"

"Nobody told me."

He groaned. "Well, thanks to your wiles, I'm going to have to reprimand a unit of men."

"Nobody told me."

"Listen, Ket, if word gets out prematurely, it could cause problems." He made sure to catch my eye. "We've got to get everything in and secured and organized for distribution."

"Nobody told me," I repeated, but I had trouble keeping a sly smile from my lips.

He glanced heavenward and then gave me a stern look. "Just when I thought you had grown up. Don't breathe a word of the news yet."

I thought it would be the kind of news they would want

to shout from the highest tower, but when the first of the provisions were distributed in the still small rations, I could see what Kenai had meant.

Everyone was in a panic for more food—it was all I could think about too—but the rations were still very small.

"We wouldn't be able to hold it down if we gorged ourselves on food," Lib informed me as we fixed our meal together.

"And besides that, there are now two thousand extra men to share the provisions with," Ethanim pointed out.

That was true. I had only thought of the troops who had guarded the provisions to us as a blessing, not a liability.

"Remember how we put the Lamanite prisoners on a small ration?" Lib went on.

"I thought that was because we don't like Lamanite dogs," said Reb.

"It was because their stomachs weren't prepared to process food again," said Lib.

"And because we didn't want them at their full strength," added Gideon.

I thought about this as I portioned out the meal to my unit brothers, about sharing food even with those we didn't like, about not being ready to receive it, about needing it in order to be at full strength.

"Let's pray," said Lib, and we all knelt while Corban offered up a grateful prayer.

And then, on Lib's advice, we tried to eat slowly.

With time, our rations increased little by little as we became ready.

A few days before we planned to march on Manti, Zeke came to my camp to take me for a walk. He had long since stopped asking me to walk with him, and he just waited patiently while I got ready. I had been sitting with the others checking over all our weapons, and I thanked heaven I was sitting between Lib and Ethanim and not next to Gideon.

The day was warm, though the breeze was cool and carried with it the first hint of the change of seasons.

"What are you thinking about?" Zeke asked me as we left the camps and walked out onto the terrace.

He probably assumed my mind was on the upcoming campaign, the march on Manti. We still did not talk much when we walked together. Talking gave us too much opportunity to disagree.

"I was thinking about the word of God."

"What about it?" he asked.

"Well," I began, a little uncomfortably. "When the provisions were low I asked Lib to take me to a private place so I could pray."

Zeke remained silent, listening.

"I wanted so much to find strength in my hunger, to find the meaning in it all."

"And did you?"

He asked this so casually. I had nearly forgotten how comfortable he was talking about the things of God, and I remembered how knowledgeable he was too. Perhaps if I had approached him earlier, he could have helped me to see my way.

I took a breath. "I had this impression about the living waters. You know? How they are a representation of the love of God. And I remembered how Nephi said to feast upon the word of Christ, as if it were food, or sustenance. I guess my mind was really on food."

His brows knit together as he considered it too. "But that was meant to describe the way we must approach the scriptures—feasting, eating heavily from many courses and varieties, taking it into ourselves and making it a part of us."

"I know." I shrugged. "It was only that if water is the love of God and food is the word of God, wouldn't His love and His word sustain us in difficult times?"

He searched my face as if he were looking for something familiar in it.

"What?" I said a little defensively.

He only shook his head. "I'm glad you received an answer to your questions."

I thought of the other questions I had asked that day and tried to keep the heat from rising in my cheeks.

We had entered the woods, and I loved the familiarity of it—the smell of the pine, the shadows, the softness of spongy ground. It was almost as if we were back home together in Melek.

In the coolness of the trees, I searched Zeke's face. He was my oldest friend. Trustworthy in every way. Deserving of the truth.

I licked my lips. "There is something else. When I was praying, there in the garden, I wanted very much to know how to stop hurting you."

"Is it so hard to figure out?" he asked quietly. "I wonder that you had need to ask the Almighty."

I ducked under a branch, even as the ground became steep. "It is hard for me, yes. Sometimes it doesn't seem to matter what I do, you get angry. You take it the wrong way. We've no trust between us anymore. I don't want it to be like this between us when we are married. I hate that it is like this between us now."

He glanced down at me. His quiet words seemed to bring the forest to utter stillness. "I have not asked you to marry me, Keturah."

But he would. I laughed. "You can't tell me you mean to go against our families' wishes."

"Is that all it would be for you? Obedience?"

I stopped walking and leaned my back against a tree. Taking my water skin from my belt, I said, "Zeke, of course not."

He stopped and turned to face me. He looked at me as if he didn't recognize me but felt like he should.

I drank and then returned the water skin to my belt and offered him a smile. "How could you even think it?"

He raised a brow, but not unkindly, and moved closer.

"So what have you been thinking about?" I asked him.

He smiled. "It's none of your—"

"Yes it is! I told you what I was thinking!" And I reached out and pinched him.

He pinched me back so quickly, so instinctively, that I laughed out loud. Had I forgotten how he could tease? How his eyes could be bright with humor? He laughed too, and it felt good to be laughing with him. I had missed it so much, and I turned away from him for a moment so he wouldn't see the tears that stung my eyes.

If tears fell from my eyes, this would end. Even if they were tears of happiness.

This was exactly the way it had been before, but it wasn't until later when I was alone in my tent that I would realize how very sad that was. It had been three years since the stripling warriors had left for the war. Zeke and I had grown, learned, been tried, and progressed in many ways, maybe every way possible except one—our relationship had not progressed.

Later when I was alone in my tent, I would tell myself a strong relationship would have been able to withstand all that had happened.

And what had happened? All Zeke had ever done was love me.

"Just tell me," I laughed, trying desperately to hide the deep ache that filled my chest. Lately, God had filled me with such peace and light that this feeling scared me.

"I was thinking of how you've changed," he said slowly, as if he thought he might make me mad, as if he were bracing himself for my angry outburst.

And the fact that there was no outburst coming was evidence that I had changed.

I eased my hand into his, and still the ache in my heart did not calm. The familiar clasp of our hands kept the tears stinging at my eyes, but I blinked them back.

I swallowed hard. "It seems God can even change the

heart of a brat like me," I said. I tried to keep it light. It even sounded light, I thought. I may have fooled Zeke, but I did not fool myself. God had touched my heart, and I could not deny it.

"I never thought you were a brat," he said sincerely. He touched my hair. "Honestly, I never meant to make you feel that way."

"I know," I said. "It was the way I felt about myself—that someone as good and sincere as you could never truly love someone as undeserving as me. I'm impulsive and too headstrong. I talk when I should be silent. I thought you had convinced yourself you loved me because of duty to your family. And when you did not support me—"

"But I did support you!" he cut in. "I asked Helaman to intercede with your Mother. I counseled with Lib and Seth, Micah, your mother, Kalem and my father. All to ease your way, to make your dream possible! Don't stand there and tell me I didn't support you."

I was not the only one with tears that threatened to fall.

I took a breath. "When I *thought* you didn't support me, didn't understand me."

"Not like Gid?"

I instantly gripped his hand tight so he wouldn't let go of me. My mind raced for the perfect thing to say. But I wasn't perfect, and I couldn't find it.

"That is in the past," I finally said. "We cannot stay the same as we were. You think I have changed, but you have too. Sometimes, I feel we are strangers. I hate it."

I held tight to his hand. He couldn't go anywhere without me. I wouldn't let him. I reached up with my other hand and fingered the crinkles at the corners of his eyes and the hard angles of his jaw, hoping somehow that my touch said what my words could not.

"Say you understand me," I said as I let myself rediscover the small changes in his handsome features.

"It's not possible," he said, the hint of a sad smile

touching his lips.

I searched his eyes. Familiar. Warm. Beloved. "Then say you still love me."

His answer was a kiss, warm in the cool air of the forest and filled with all that was right between us.

Then he murmured, "Duty," against my lips, as if the very idea that he kissed me out of duty was ridiculous. He eased me back against the tree and showed me that it was.

"I could not stop loving you if I tried," he said when he pulled away. "And believe me, I've tried."

Chapter 5

Helaman planned to take Manti without a battle.

"If possible," he said, "we will enact a decoy similar to what we did at Antiparah. But this time, we will send men back to take the city in the army's absence."

After Shem had conducted the captains' meeting and most of the captains had departed, Helaman laid out the particulars of his stratagem to the members of the council and detailed the parts each of us would play in it.

I would be among the men who took the city. Micah and Zeke would be part of the decoy—the bait for our trap. Darius and Jarom would be out with Kenai, acting as scouts for the first time.

"I don't understand," I said to Gideon as we left the large stone building with Seth and Eli. "You and Teomner are to march out unseen by the enemy? How is it to be done?"

"Maybe Kenai can give us some pointers."

Gideon had to work with Kenai frequently, but I knew they weren't on very friendly terms. Kenai was Zeke's best friend, but since the day I had walked into Antiparah as a spy, Kenai had all but given me over to Gideon's care. He had accepted what none of the rest of us had—what none of us could.

"I'll take Seth and Enos and their hundreds. Teomner will lead two hundred of the Nephites."

"Do you plan to take Manti with only four hundred men?"

"And one pretty girl."

I blushed and pushed him playfully away.

Seth cleared his throat in an obvious attempt to put a stop to any flirting. "We can take Manti," he said confidently.

Not if their entire army doesn't leave, I thought wryly. But that wasn't how I truly felt. I knew—because I could feel it—that God was with us. I knew that He would preserve us and make our arms strong. I knew that he could speak to His children through their hearts.

I wanted to tell Seth and Gideon, two of the men I admired most, that I was going home after the campaign for Manti. I wanted to try out the words, but I hesitated and after I had hesitated too long, the moment passed.

"How long will it take to get to Manti?" I asked instead.

"Weren't you listening?" asked Seth.

Gideon laughed. "She only listens to things that are none of her business."

"When she thinks no one will notice," Seth added with a grin.

Eli, as usual, did not say anything, but he laughed with the others.

I would miss these men so much when I went home.

That wasn't the first time I considered never seeing Gideon again after I went home, but it hit me hard that night. It didn't make me feel better to realize his good mood that evening was because of the prospect of improving his military career. If the campaign against Manti was successful, his rank would rise again.

Gideon did not like to shed blood. I had come to know

that he abhorred it. But he wanted liberty and the freedom to live safely and worship as one chose. He wanted to protect those freedoms for others, because he could—because God had made him strong where others were weak. It was a calling he felt in his soul and one he did not put off lightly.

Men like Zeke and Micah, Seth, Lib and all the others would go home and become fathers and protect their families. Men like Gideon would give their all to protecting the nation.

I slept little that night, and by the third watch I crawled out of my tent intending to sit with whoever guarded my door.

To my great surprise, Jarom sat quietly scanning the grounds.

Nearing sixteen, Zeke's younger brother looked exactly like Zeke had at that age—tall and muscular in stature, with long dark hair, a prominent, hooked nose, and deep, soulful brown eyes.

Just then he wore one of Zeke's expressions as he sensed my movements in the moonlight and let his eyes follow me while he stayed still as stone.

"I thought you were Zeke for a moment," I said softly so as not to wake anyone.

He snorted. "Disappointed?" He scooted a little so I could sit near him on the log at his small fire, which was little more than coals.

"Of course not," I said.

I liked Jarom a lot. In fact, the more time went on and the older he got, the more I liked him. Jarom was good-natured. He teased, but he was never annoying in it. He always knew when enough was enough. He was smart, intuitive, and compassionate. He was capable. Anything he didn't know and had a need to know, he just learned. He was also very in tune with people and their feelings, though I would never have thought to describe him as sensitive.

"Quiet night?" I asked when I had been sitting near him for a few moments.

"Yeah."

"I didn't know you were part of this ridiculous watch on me," I said, though I didn't feel it was ridiculous anymore, not since the nightly raids during the siege on Cumeni.

"You're my sister," he said simply, surprising me because, though we had grown up practically as siblings, I was not his sister. "Which is unfortunate for me," he went on. "I wish Zeke didn't have a claim on you."

I looked over sharply, catching his rueful gaze into the fire. Jarom could tease, yes, but this didn't sound like teasing.

"Jarom?"

For long moments he didn't reply, just stared into the coals trying to control his breathing. "I shouldn't have said that," he said at last.

"Did you mean it?" I asked, tentatively stepping into a topic I knew could be quite delicate and also volatile if not handled with great care.

He took a deep breath. "Yes, I meant it." He leaned forward and rested his elbows on his knees, clasped his hands between them. He looked back at me over his shoulder, which had become broad and strong. "You've no idea what effect you have on people, Ket—your laughter, your healing hands." He shook his head and looked down at his own hands. "You don't just heal physical wounds. You make every boy in this army feel like he's important, like someone loves him and cares if he dies in this rotten war."

"Jarom."

"You do."

"I can't help the way others see me."

He sat up. "So it's just an act?"

"Of course not. I do love the warriors. All of them."

"Do you love me?"

I didn't know whether to laugh or smack him upside the head. "You know I do."

"But not the way you love Zeke," he insisted.

Scooting closer to him, I said gently, "I could not love anyone the way I love Zeke."

"You can tell yourself that, Ket." He leaned closer to murmur, "But I don't believe you."

His breath was warm on my neck, and even though the coals were barely lit, my face flamed. I was suddenly aware how alone we were and how close we were sitting to each other in the darkness, and how, despite what he had said when I sat down, he was not my brother.

I slid away from him. "I'm sorry Zeke is first in everything," I said. "I never thought what it must mean to be a second son."

But I thought of how Hemni, their father, had spoken with such admiration of Jarom's skill at the hunt. I thought of how Mother loved him like her own son and how highly I esteemed him and his acuity. I thought of how Darius depended on his friendship, hardly able even to communicate if Jarom wasn't completing his sentences for him, and I thought perhaps Jarom had very little idea of the effect he himself had on people.

"Have you thought to talk to Kenai? I bet if anyone would understand, Kenai would."

He shook his head. "Kenai is Zeke's best friend."

"He is also Micah's younger brother," I pointed out, and I wondered what Kenai might feel toward Micah if the kingdom still existed, if Micah had become a ruler over our people.

Jarom shrugged.

"Darius said Kenai has been training your unit to spy. Is it like hunting?"

I thought only to remind him that he was a better hunter than his older brother, but a darkness slid over his eyes and his breaths became deliberate.

"Sometimes," he said, "it is very much like hunting."

"Jar—"

"Zeke doesn't deserve you." He interrupted me. "He's not even nice to you."

"That's because I cause him so much worry. I'm a great trial to his patience."

"The person you love should not be a trial. She should not be someone you have to tolerate."

He was right.

"That's not love, Keturah." He turned to look at me with a lidded gaze. "If I were in Zeke's place, I would not treat you so callously. I would not raise my voice to you or ever cause you heartache."

He sounded so much like Zeke had back in the village, when he had first decided we should become betrothed, so ardent and sincere, and he looked so much like him. I nearly laughed, but there was nothing funny in Jarom's feelings or his conviction, and the similarities stopped at his expressions. He really wasn't very much like Zeke at all.

"I know you wouldn't," I said, making sure my sincerity sounded in my voice. "You are too much like your father."

"I wish I was older than Zeke." His words vibrated with emotion, and he sounded almost angry.

Generally, when speaking of betrothals and marriage, a family would arrange a marriage for their eldest son first, and when that had been successfully done, they would seek marriages for the remaining children in descending order. Zeke's marriage would come first, and if he chose me, Jarom would never have the chance to. But he was forgetting that I could refuse either one or both of them.

"Maybe Zeke won't choose me," I suggested, not that it would help. "Maybe he will find me too great of a trial and choose Eve of Judea instead."

I could see my mistake because he seemed even more determined than before. "Refuse Zeke and wait for me," he said softly. "I would always let you do what you want. My brother won't."

Maybe he was right, but choosing Jarom over Zeke would create problems of its own.

"I know you would, Jarom."

I also knew that he did not love me enough to insist upon the rules that I now knew I must abide by. He would let me recklessly destroy myself.

At first I had resented Zeke's worry for me. I had fought against all his fears for me. But over the years I had come to see that his fears were not unfounded, and he had foreseen so many things that I had not.

Lib's constant guard had helped me recognize this. At first I had felt imprisoned by it, but gradually I had realized that the only real freedom I had was inside the circle of his protection because the snares outside of it were so much worse.

"Wait for me," Jarom said. "Until I get older."

I wondered if he realized he was actually asking me to marry him. I searched his face. He was sincere. He thought he loved me. But this was new, it had to be. I wondered what had happened, what had changed.

Nothing had changed for me. I still thought of him as a brother, though it was different from what I felt for Darius. I shouldn't encourage his feelings, but there was no need to hurt him, either.

"I am not currently considering any offers of marriage," I said, looking him in the eye. "That's what you're offering, right?"

He stared at me and his jaw tightened, and for some reason, that worked like a nod.

"When the time comes, I will consider your offer then," I told him.

He had the same way of showing relief while still schooling the look on his face as Zeke did. He leaned toward me, and he looked as though he might seal our agreement with an unwise kiss.

I stopped him gently with a hand to his chest. "Only think what the next moment will mean if I choose your brother."

I thought the hand on his chest would discourage him, but he covered it with one of his own and leaned in to place a soft kiss on my lips. His boldness startled me as much as his sweet kiss did. This was Jarom!

I expected awkwardness to follow. Jarom didn't seem to feel it, but he should have. He should have felt the utter wrongness of it, like I did. There were no circumstances under which I could return his feelings.

"Does Darius know?" I asked him. "About this?"

"No one can know."

I nodded slowly as I returned my gaze to the fire. Did he think we would marry in secret?

"If you'll get this fire going, I'll start the morning meal," I said with a glance to the east where the sky was beginning to lighten.

Obediently, he knelt and blew softly on the glowing coals to coax a fire from them, and when the embers were swirling, he looked up at me.

I blushed as deep red as the coals and hurried away to wake Joshua so he could go with me to get the rations. But I wasn't quick enough to miss Jarom's smug, knowing smile.

We left Cumeni that morning. Having disassembled our entire camp, we each carried our own gear and divided between us the camp's supplies.

As we marched through the city, I thought about the Lamanites we had half-starved there. I thought of the wives of the men I had killed on the Cumeni crossroad, the children I had deprived of a relationship with their father.

But for most of the morning, I thought of Jarom.

At times the terrain was very rocky and the hills were difficult to traverse. That was just through the morning. It got more difficult after midday when the road we traveled dwindled until it was barely discernible from the undergrowth. By mid-afternoon the column no longer existed and we traveled in pairs through an unbroken wilderness. Lib and I hiked together at the rear of our unit.

I marveled that Kenai and his men had run from Manti

on the day of the battle at Cumeni, and I was sure they couldn't have taken this route.

The sun was hot, so I braided my hair and twisted it up, securing it with a slender stick I broke from a tree as I trudged along beside Lib. We had long since stopped conversing when I tripped over a large root that stuck out in my path.

Lib caught my arm before I fell to the ground, but I knew immediately that my ankle was hurt badly. Lib scooped me up like a child and carried me a short distance to the side so the others could pass us.

He knelt before me and frowned as he examined the ankle I extended.

"I heard it snap," he said grimly. "Is it broken?"

I wanted to say no, but I honestly wasn't sure. "I don't know," I said. Tears pricked the backs of my eyes, not from the pain, though it was painful, but from fatigue and frustration. I wouldn't be able to walk on it, and I knew we wouldn't camp until nearly nightfall. The whole of the army could not stop for me.

Lib had done no more than give a deep thoughtful sigh when Zeke came up, followed a few moments later by Micah and three of his men.

After Lib explained how I had twisted my ankle, Zeke went to his heels next to me. "It could have happened to anyone."

Most of Helaman's command had passed us, and down the trail I could see Teomner's men. Hundreds more soldiers would see me sitting idly on the side of the path before the day was out. I sighed and glared at the offending root.

Micah took charge. "Lib, you take her pack. Zeke, grab the rest of her gear." Then he turned to me and put his hands on his hips. "There are a few ways we can carry you, but the simplest is for you to climb onto my back."

"What? No! That's so unladylike."

All three of them burst out laughing. Even Micah's men chuckled.

Micah was already taking off his own pack. He passed it

to one of his men who willingly took it and began to distribute some of the bigger items between the two other men.

"You're no heavier than my pack."

And I probably wasn't. I looked around at the other men and sighed in resignation. There was no real choice. We had to continue on. I didn't protest when Micah hauled me to my feet, hefted me onto his back, and began to walk.

Micah carried me for an hour or so and then passed me over to Lib. By the time Zeke was taking his turn, it was late afternoon.

We had fallen back a little behind Micah and Lib, and I took advantage of the privacy to ask something that had been on my mind all day.

"Zeke, how long has Jarom been taking the watch outside my tent?"

"I didn't know he was," he replied. "Though I think he sometimes sits up with Darius."

"He took the third watch alone last night."

"That doesn't surprise me. He thinks of you as a sister."

Like you think of me as a sister, I thought. I bit my lip and didn't say any more about Jarom. I had to figure out what to do first.

The stripling army stopped to make camp near the headwaters of the Sidon River. Zeke told Lib to set up my tent, and as he carried me toward the river to soak my throbbing ankle, I wondered if he gave Lib instructions a lot. I wondered if they had established a hierarchy among themselves of who was more in charge of me than the others. Though I loved them all and had grown accustomed to their constant guard, the thought made my skin prickle with heat.

The sounds of the forest were familiar and the light was beginning to soften. The area around the river was green with lush vegetation. Zeke let me slip off his back, and then he lifted me into his arms the way Lib had and set me gently near the bank of the river.

"I can't believe this happened," I said as I slid my foot into the water. I hoped it would provide instant relief, but it didn't.

As we sat quietly, letting the water slowly numb my foot, I thought again of water being like God's love. Would there ever be a time, could there ever be a time, when God's love did not instantly balm the wounded heart? When the pain was so intense that the cooling relief could not soothe it immediately?

My mind went to Kalem. He had sought the balm of the love of God for years. He had suffered grief and pain so deeply that it took time for the love to seep to all the hurt places.

I looked at Zeke who knelt near me rummaging through his satchel, the only gear he had left which Lib was not carrying for him, searching for a bandage with which to wrap my ankle. Would God heal his heart? Would Zeke let love seep to all the parts of him I had hurt, or would he shun it? Because, even though he sat by me now, even though he had carried me and sought to serve me, I knew that he did not trust me with his heart. And I knew that since the day Zeke had shaken the moonflower from my hand, he had tried with everything in him to extinguish any love he felt for me.

He made a satisfied sound and pulled out a folded length of bandage. "This should do. Let me see your foot."

I pulled my foot from the water, but held it away from him.

"Try to find some algae," I said indicating the water before us.

He eyed me curiously as he passed me the bandage to hold.

"One of Mother's tricks," I assured him. "I've seen it work miracles."

Chapter 6

When my ankle was wrapped tight, Zeke helped me to my feet.

"Steady?" he asked with his hands at my waist.

I nodded as I balanced on one leg and the toes of my injured foot.

He bent and swept me effortlessly into his arms. He was stronger than I remembered, and his leg had healed well. The silence between us as he walked saddened my heart.

When we were nearly to camp, he cleared his throat. "I should talk to Lib about increasing your rations. You don't weigh anything."

I didn't tell him I had been cutting my own rations and mixing them in with the food for the rest of my unit. I didn't say anything at all, just rested my head on his shoulder and let him carry me, and I pretended everything was good between us.

My unit treated me like a queen when Zeke set me down near our cook fire. They had already set up my tent and prepared a meal for me. They wouldn't let me get up for anything, though

Zachariah brought me a walking stick he found for me among the trees.

"I can see you're in good hands," said Zeke who stood with his arms folded over his chest and looked around at all the men in my unit. I had to give him credit for not letting his eyes pause on Gideon.

"Thanks," I said. "For the ride."

He nodded, picked up the gear Lib had carried for him, and left.

Gideon watched him go and then met my eye. He took a deep breath and looked away.

That night we had fish from the headwaters of the Sidon River courtesy of our fishermen, Corban, Cyrus, and Mathoni. The simple meal was hearty and satisfying. Helaman had given us permission to forage what we could from the forest and hunt during the march, and my unit had tremendous luck. In addition to the fish, we ate sweet berries, wild roots, and fresh rabbit.

In the past, I had eaten rabbit so much that it had become quite mundane, but that night it was so delicious it made my mouth water.

After Lib and Ethanim brought me back from the forest, Gideon approached Lib and rested a hand on his shoulder. A look passed between them, as if perhaps they had already spoken. Lib gave a slight nod and left me alone with Gideon.

Since the battle at Cumeni, Gideon had been making himself scarce around camp. I didn't think it had much to do with me and how he had seen me cry for Zeke, but at times, when he wouldn't meet my eyes, it felt that way.

Helaman called on him more and more and had begun to rely on Gideon's gut instincts about the enemy. He had a head for matters of war and for stratagem. It all made sense to Gideon. He could see the big picture in his mind, and his skills did not go unnoticed by our great commander.

"Did Lib make you schedule an appointment to talk to me?"

He shook his head, not even smiling at my private joke. "I wish I'd known about your ankle today."

"Micah took care of me," I said.

"And Zeke."

I closed my eyes. I'd already had this conversation once with Zeke, and I didn't have the energy to do it again, notwithstanding the excellent meal.

"And Zeke and Lib and three of Micah's men," I pointed out irritably.

"Can you walk?" he asked.

"No one has let me try."

He stepped to the cook fire and retrieved my walking stick. It was really more of a crutch, and I was able to walk if I leaned heavily on it.

"Come on, I'll walk you down to soak your ankle in the cold water again," he offered.

"I don't know why we had to travel that rocky road anyway," I mumbled as I hobbled along beside him and envied his strong, easy stride.

He looked down at me. "It was part of the plan," he said.

"I don't believe you."

"It's true. Helaman will lead his men into the wilderness on a small road that winds through it, hopefully luring the bulk of the Lamanite army away. The first chance he gets, probably after nightfall, he will lead the column back to Manti over part of this trail. We travelled it today so the men would become familiar with it. They will probably have to do it in the dark next time. You're lucky you got to do it in the light of day."

I stopped walking and stared at him.

"There was a road?" I exclaimed.

He laughed.

"It's not funny! *This* is not funny!" I said, holding my injured foot out.

"No, it's not," he agreed. "But you are. And it's not often little rabbits are so easy to snare!" He bent, swept me up, and threw me over his shoulder.

"Gideon!" I cried as my crutch clattered to the ground and he took off through the trees toward the river.

I stopped struggling when I realized he was not going to put me down until we reached the river.

"You plan to carry me off as the Lamanites do?"

"Maybe."

I scoffed.

"Maybe I'll take you to Zarahemla and keep you locked in the fortress there."

I scoffed again. "It would be more difficult to convince the Nephites to imprison a woman there than it was to convince them to let one into their army."

"Probably," he admitted.

He took a few more steps before he pulled me around and cradled me against his chest in his arms.

I resisted as long as I could, but he held me so close it was impossible not to slip my arms around him in return, which was probably his aim.

"I want to go home," I said into his neck. I hadn't planned to tell anyone yet, but it felt good to say it to Gideon. "It's time."

He didn't answer right away. Did I imagine his arms tighten? I waited, but he kept moving toward the river, and he did not answer me at all. I wondered briefly if he had heard me, but I knew he had.

I could hear the water before I could see it. As we approached, Gideon surveyed the area and set his course for a place that swirled into a small pool. He settled me on my feet and pushed a flat stone up to the edge of the water for me to sit on.

I unwound the bandage Zeke and I had placed over the wound and inspected the damage I had done.

"It's not that bad," Gideon said after inspecting it himself.

I glanced up at him. "No," I agreed. "And the throbbing has stopped."

He shifted and knelt next to me. "Does this hurt?" he

asked as he fingered my ankle and moved it into different positions.

"No," I said with each movement, though the movements were tender. "I'll be able to walk on it by tomorrow."

"Nah. We can carry you tomorrow. Rest it another day so it will be strong for the battle."

I didn't want to be carried for another entire day, but I focused instead on the stratagem. "So there will be a battle? I thought the whole idea was to avoid one."

"There will be fighting. Any guards left at Manti are not going to give up the city without a fight, especially when they see our small number. But yes, Helaman's men should be able to avoid a battle if they march quickly. I do not think the Lamanite army, even with its vast numbers, will come against us once we control the stronghold."

"I'd rather fight than walk over that trail again."

"You've roamed the forest all your life. I know you love it. What made that trail so difficult?"

I shrugged as I idly dipped my heel in and out of the water.

"Did you have your mind on something else?"

How like Gideon to see things the way they were. I was having a hard time keeping my mind on the war, focusing on what I must do to vanquish the enemy. That was one of the reasons I was planning to go home. It was time for me to focus on other things.

"Maybe," I conceded.

Gideon went to his heels next to me. He sat perfectly still, staring across the water.

I wanted to reach over and touch the scar at his brow. I wanted to ask him if he ever thought about those nights above Antiparah. Instead, I asked, "How would you react if your brother fell in love with me?"

He raised both eyebrows. "Jashon or Lamech?"

I had only been thinking of Lamech. "Does it matter?"

"Well, if Jashon fell in love with you, I would yield to him."

"But not if Lamech did?"

"Why? Has Lamech said something?" he asked as he tossed a stone into the water.

"No, Lamech doesn't even like me, so I think you're safe on that front. But if he did, you wouldn't consider his feelings?"

He thought for long moments with a slight frown on his lips. The breeze ruffled our hair, and when several long strands broke free of my braid and moved across my neck, I shivered. It reminded me of the day I had met Gideon.

"Well?" I asked after a while.

"Of course I would consider his feelings, but they wouldn't be my main concern. There would be many things to consider."

"What would be your main consideration?" I pressed.

"My feelings. Keturah, why are you asking this if Lamech has said nothing to provoke it?"

I shrugged. "Why would you yield to Jashon and not to Lamech?"

"Jashon is my elder brother, and I respect him. If he had not yet taken a wife, the choice would be his. I would not dishonor my brother, even for love."

"You would not feel he had dishonored you? If he knew of your feelings, that is."

That was a hard question, and I didn't blame him when he didn't answer.

This talk about his brothers and his reaction was all hypothetical anyway, since Gideon would be going to Zarahemla without me, despite his threats to take me there and lock me up.

I threw a pebble into the water and changed the subject. "How will leading the column on that back trail do any good? It leads to Cumeni."

He gave me a strange look. "Not only weren't you watching the ground, you weren't watching the sky. That path circles around and meets the road. There are all kinds of intersecting trails up on that mountain, and the Lamanites will never suspect that we've attempted to take an entire column over them. Where were your thoughts today?"

I frowned. "I guess I really wasn't paying attention." My foot had been numb for a while, so I withdrew it from the cool water and set it on a rock to dry.

As I got a bandage from my satchel, Gideon said, "Our unit will carry you tomorrow. Zeke can stay with his fifty."

I did not miss the emphasis he put on Zeke's name. "I can walk," I said, though I wasn't sure I could walk the entire distance that remained to Manti, especially if the terrain didn't even out. I took a breath. "And if you will not speak for me, Gideon, you can have no decision on who does."

I saw his eyes flash with temper, something he nearly always kept in check. Gideon did not let his emotions rule him.

But his voice was a hard growl when he said, "Keturah, do you not think my logic tells me to stay with you? To speak for you and claim you as my own beautiful, vivacious wife? Everything in me screams for me to do so!"

My eyes shot to his at the sudden fierceness in his words.

He sighed. Taking my hand in his, he gentled his voice. "Everything except for one still, small voice. The one voice I cannot ignore."

I had no breath. I did not want to have this conversation. Not with Gideon. Not then. Not ever.

He got to his feet and paced away. "Just because you are not mine does not mean I enjoy the thought of you with another man," he ground out. "Loving him and living your life with him."

I tried to make my voice strong when I spoke, but I didn't succeed. "You can't have it both ways."

"Neither can you," he shot back, but then he said, "Oh, Kanina," and he put both hands into his hair. "I just want to keep you with me for as long as possible. I'm jealous and selfish, and I'm sorry."

I didn't say anything for several minutes, though I knew what must be said. Finally I took in a shallow, shaky breath and stood. He came to me, and I went into his arms.

"I won't keep you from your duty," I said. My voice was muffled in his chest and my tears wet his tunic.

"I know," he sighed. "That is the thing I love most about you. I could never love a girl who did not have your fierce warrior spirit."

I didn't have a response to his beautiful confession.

"You know, it's funny," he said after a time. "I'd rather you married Lamech than Zeke."

I drew back and looked up into his face.

"It's your love for Zeke that pains me. I saw the way you looked at him, on the battlefield, when he was wounded."

"You don't want me to be with someone I love?"

He smiled ruefully and shook his head. "It's hard to explain."

But I understood, except it wasn't the thought of Gideon falling in love with another girl that I dreaded. He would simply not allow it of himself. It was the thought of Zeke falling in love with another girl that kept me awake nights. Despite his loyalty to me, he was smart and self-preserving, and I feared he would realize at last how different I was from what he truly wanted and give up on me entirely.

I couldn't change who I was, not even for Zeke. Perhaps God could change me, a small voice whispered in my heart, but another voice whispered that I shouldn't have to change.

When my ankle was wrapped, Gideon carried me back toward camp. Halfway back I pointed to my walking stick where it had clattered to the ground, and he lowered me so I could pick it up, but he continued to carry me. When we reached camp he knelt and placed me inside my tent. He looked at me plaintively for a moment and then cast a glance at the other boys in camp. They seemed to be ignoring us, so he crawled into the tent after me. I moved to make room for him.

Tender moments did not come easily for Gideon, but when we were inside the tent, the tenor of his voice changed, as if perhaps he had rehearsed the words many times inside his head. Maybe I had known there was something he wanted to say and hadn't yet said. Maybe I had known it at the river. Maybe that was why I had turned our conversation to his brothers.

"You don't know how many times I've wished I had not tracked you that first day. If I hadn't, you wouldn't be in this situation with Zeke. It has caused you much heartache." He took a breath. "I have caused you much heartache."

I hated that he thought so and that he felt guilt for it.

"My situation with Zeke is not your fault," I said as I pulled the strap of my satchel over my head. I set the satchel aside. "And if it wasn't you, it would be someone else."

He studied me, his brows knit together. Then he said with sudden realization, "It's not Lamech. It's Jarom."

I shrugged.

"Keturah." His voice bore sympathy. "I think that might be worse on Zeke than if you loved me."

The way he said it was almost a question. Was it possible he did not know how I felt about him?

"If I felt the way about Jarom I feel about you, maybe."

But he was right—it was bad. I wanted to hurt Jarom about as much as I wanted to hurt Zeke, and that was about as much as I wanted to chop off my hand with my axe.

He nodded slowly.

The sun was setting outside. The light inside the tent was soft and beautiful but getting dimmer.

"What are you going to do?" he asked.

I sighed and rubbed at my tired eyes. "Hurt someone."

"Kanina." Apology filled his tone. "I will not be the one to ask that of you—to ask you to go against something that was as good as done long ago."

Was it as good as done? Did I have a choice? Micah had said he would accept Gideon. But Gideon was too noble, too honorable. He was stepping down. Yielding.

Or he was simply freeing himself so he could become Chief Captain of the Nephite armies.

"I'm not the right man, Kanina." He turned to look at me with the deepest regret in his black eyes. "Zeke is the one."

I closed my eyes and turned my face away. "That is not your choice to make."

His voice was resolute when he said, "I have made my choice." He took ahold of my chin and turned my face back to his. He held my chin until I opened my eyes. Then he looked into my face and didn't flinch from the pain he saw there. "Helaman has offered me a place in his personal guard after the wars are done, and I have accepted it."

I held his gaze, but I had never felt such a knot in my throat. "Then I accept it too."

I leaned up on my knees and kissed him lightly but with a growing desperation that embarrassed me and a finality that broke my heart. I lingered over his lips longer than I should have, my hands on his biceps, my thoughts going wild. I could not be without him. But he would not stay with me.

In a sudden wash of heat, a balm soothed the rent between the pieces of my heart. A sweet feeling of love emanated from us and filled my tent. Was it telling me that what Gideon said was true, that he was not the right choice for me?

Or was it telling me what my heart told me, that Gideon was the only choice for me? That loving him like this was a good thing?

I thought of Gideon's face the moment before Kenai and his men, sweaty from their long sprint, had reported the attack on Cumeni. He had just taken a bite of my warm corn cake. He had been grinning and telling me how grand Zarahemla was. He wanted to go there. The morning sun shone on his hair. I thought of the next moments, how the prisoners had thrown themselves upon the swords of their guards.

At the time, I had thought how dishonorable it was for us

to lose the prisoners we had charge of, to allow their escape. But Gideon had thought only how it freed us to go back to Cumeni and save our countrymen.

Gideon was freeing me to go back and save my countryman, to do what had to be done, and he was essentially throwing himself upon the sword to do it.

Gideon set me away from him and moved to leave the tent.

I clutched his arm. "You would yield to your older brother?" I asked him quickly before he left.

He didn't turn to look at me again, but he answered, "Yes. And I will yield to Zeke."

Chapter 7

The next afternoon was overcast. We entered the land of Manti, and as we neared the city, we stayed close to the wilderness, circled, and prepared to set up camp in the trees.

Seth and Enos and their hundreds fell out, and we camped in the rear near Teomner's men.

"Well," said Reb surveying the city in the distance as he dropped his gear in the grass. "Don't pound the stakes in tight."

What he meant was that our camping there was only for show. Our orders were simply to rest, but waiting for the Lamanites' reaction to our presence would make resting difficult.

Still, we had all learned to sleep under difficult circumstances—soaking wet, cold, hungry, hot, dehydrated, frightened. We were prepared. We were prepared to lay siege, we were prepared to retreat if it would lure the enemy out of the gates, and we were prepared to give battle.

No one knew how far Helaman's men would have to

retreat if the Lamanites came out to battle or how hard Gideon's and Teomner's men would have to fight.

We set up the tents anyway and prepared a simple evening meal.

I had truly spent the day being hauled like a sack of provisions on the backs of the men in my unit. When Corban set me down I gingerly tried my ankle, and it felt just fine—a little weak, but not painful. The healing tissue of my javelin wound hurt more than the ankle.

"It's hardly fair," I told him. "Nobody carried you when I hurt your ankle."

He laughed. "If you only knew how long every guy in this unit has been dying to get his arms around you."

"Really?" I asked, the heat of embarrassment stealing over my cheeks.

"Well, yeah. I mean, we all know about Zeke and Gid, but Ket, you're the best thing about this war."

I grinned at him. What else could I do?

"And besides, did you think we didn't know what you were doing with your rations? We would carry you to the moon if we could."

My grin faded. I thought they hadn't known.

Corban scratched his ear. "I don't know if the small amount of food made a difference, but the fact that you did it..." He gave his head a hard shake and didn't finish.

I felt myself flush again and stooped to enter the tent Lib and Ethanim had just finished putting up for me.

Kenai and his men would be moving still, getting a view of the inside of the city. They would need to glean a lot of information from what they could see, and I knew from my spy mission into Antiparah that they weren't getting their information from a distance. I knew Darius and Jarom would be with Kenai, scouting around the city, and I prayed they would be safe. I also prayed they could bring Captain Helaman the information he needed.

The men at Cumeni had not come out to battle, and the men at Manti might not either. Waiting for them to decide could take days or even longer. We were only camped a half an hour's walk away from the city. Their scouts would report our numbers, and they would know we were easily conquerable.

I thought I would not be able to rest with the enemy so near, but after the long march, sleep was both necessary and inevitable. Knowing that Kenai and his men had eyes on our enemy put me at ease, enough to close my eyes.

Before I had even opened them to the dark pre-dawn, I heard Lib at the door of my tent.

"Get up, Ket. We're moving out."

The Lamanites were already moving. Our scouts had done their job. If we were to have a chance at taking the city, we had to be gone before dawn in order to set the snare.

We dropped the tents but left them behind when we slipped swiftly and silently into the wilderness behind Gideon and Teomner. Teomner's scouts had already been out, probably weeks ago, to find the perfect place to hide four hundred men. The whole stratagem depended on it.

We traveled north for an hour or so. Teomner and his men fell away to the west into a shallow gully covered with thick vegetation. We watched from the road as they hid themselves until Gideon was certain the passing armies would not see them.

Gideon led us a little farther north, stopping at a place where the east side of the road fell away into a deep ravine.

He spoke to Seth. "Tell your men to slide to the bottom." Then he jogged to the rear, presumably to tell Enos the same.

Most of the men had no trouble sliding down the steep hill, but we all had to shake the dirt out of our sandals at the bottom. The vegetation was scarce, but the ravine itself provided excellent cover as the bank was deep and very steep. We would be hidden from the road as long as no one happened to go to the edge and look straight down.

We caught our breath as the sun rose, but when nothing

happened on the road above us, we simply waited. We talked quietly, some men even played ball, while we waited on word from the spies.

Before midday Darius and Jarom came sliding down the steep hill. Noticing them immediately, Gideon stepped forward, and glancing around, they located him quickly.

Seth caught my eye. "Go on. Do what you do best."

I laughed and nudged him along with me. We would eavesdrop together.

"Where is Teomner's band of men?" Darius was asking Gideon. "Kenai said we would see them before we reached you."

Gideon grinned. "It's a well-hidden army when even our own men can't see them. What news have you?"

The news spilled out of them quickly. The two boys had spent most of their waking hours together since birth, so they slipped easily back and forth between listening and interjecting, filling silences, and finishing each other's sentences.

"The army of the Lamanites appears to be making preparations to come out to battle," said Darius.

"And we've forced them out of so many cities, they are numerous and angry," said Jarom. "It's obvious they've been prepared to come against us for a while."

"They will be out of the gates today for sure," said Darius, and then with a glance at the gray sky he said, "They have probably marched out already."

"And Helaman still plans to retreat?" asked Gideon.

"Yes," they both said.

"Estimated time of intersection? When will they pass us?"

They looked at each other. "No later than midday."

Gideon gave a single nod. "Did you run here?"

"Yeah," said Jarom, and I caught a surreptitious glance from him.

"Helaman ordered us to stay with you once we've delivered the information."

Gideon gave another curt nod and laid a firm hand on each of their shoulders. "Drink, and stand ready. March with Lib's men." Then he turned to Reb who stood nearby and spoke to him in a low voice, dispatching him to relay the message to Teomner. Reb started up the steep ravine.

Seth left me and went to meet with Gideon and Enos a short distance away. They turned their backs to the men. It was all the privacy they could find here.

I went to talk to Darius and Jarom, and I could feel the watchful eye of both Lib and Ethanim as I moved among the men.

"Hey, Ket," Darius greeted me as he replaced his water skin at his belt.

"Hi, guys," I said, and my eyes flicked to Jarom to include him in the greeting.

"How long have you been waiting here?" Darius asked.

"Since a little after dawn. Do you really think the Lamanites will march out?"

"The men were lined up inside the walls," said Jarom.

I didn't want to know how they knew that.

"They were hefting the gates open even as we ran to report the lines to Helaman," added Darius.

Jarom crossed his arms over his chest and scuffed his toe in the dirt. "I wish we could have given them more warning."

I shook my head. "Helaman was prepared to go against them. He hoped for it, planned for it," I said. "How vast are their numbers?"

"Vast."

I grimaced. "There's a small creek over there if you need to fill your water skins," I informed them, and gestured toward the east.

Darius offered to take them both and left after Jarom handed his over.

When I was standing alone with Jarom amid the two hundred men that surrounded us, he looked down at me as if we were alone. When had he gotten taller than me?

"Zeke told me you hurt your foot. Are you okay now?" He leaned out to get a look at the bandage on my ankle.

"It's fine," I said, sending up a silent prayer of thanks that it was.

"I'm glad," he said and then began to describe all they had seen within the walls of Manti.

"It sounds similar to the layout of Antiparah. Where was the army camped?"

"When were you in Antiparah?"

I bit the side of my cheek as I looked up at him. His dark, interested eyes showed only curiosity where I expected disapproval. Maybe the things he had said by the fire were true.

"Kenai," was the only answer I needed to give. "How long has he been training you?"

"A while."

"Kenai's the best at what he does." I wanted to add that not even Micah was better at spying than Kenai, but I didn't want to bring up such a sore subject again. That wasn't the time for it anyway.

I could feel Jarom's dark eyes on my face, searching, memorizing the lines of it like I was a girl he was free to look at. But I wasn't.

"Have you heard from your family lately?" I asked, uncomfortable under his scrutiny.

He gave me another searching look. "Yes."

"Is there news then?" I asked, brightening a little, hoping for word from Cana.

"Didn't Zeke tell you? Or Micah?"

I bit my lip and shook my head. Did Micah know the news then?

He looked at me for so long I became uncomfortable.

"Jarom?"

Before he could answer, Reb slid back down into the ravine near us in a shower of dirt and rocks. He looked around for Gideon. I caught his eye and pointed to where Gideon stood with Seth and Enos at the edge of the men. I wanted to go there and hear his report, but I stood still and watched closely from a distance.

After a moment, I saw Darius returning. I smiled when he slowed his pace as he passed the chief captains and perked his ears.

He hurried back over to us and tossed a water skin to Jarom, who caught it easily.

"Teomner's spies have seen the armies. Helaman and the men are retreating in this direction as planned, and they are moving rapidly."

Gideon called his men to attention.

"Fall in as close to the west wall of the ravine as possible. The armies are approaching quickly and will be upon us within minutes."

"Come with me," I said to Darius and Jarom, and I led them to stand beside me in the small column next to Lib and Ethanim.

I expected a little bit of confusion, but all the men fell quickly into rank facing south. Gideon came down the lines and divided each unit into two shorter rows and urged them closer to the wall.

Building anticipation rolled through the ranks as we waited, and I stared up at the edge of the ravine wondering if it would fall down on us when thousands of men marched along it.

"Nervous?" Jarom's voice was low in my ear.

I craned around to look at him over my shoulder. "Not really," I said honestly. "Are you?"

He grinned. Obviously not.

"I'm more nervous about the ravine wall raining down on us than about Ammoron's armies," I admitted.

"Are you worried about Zeke?"

"I'm not going to talk to you about Zeke," I told him. It was a strategy I should make and stick to.

"So he's still mad at you?"

"I didn't say that."

"You didn't have to. I know how it is."

How, how do you know? I wanted to demand, but it was too dumb of a conversation to be having right then. Instead, I curled my lip and glared at him. Then I rammed my elbow back into his gut.

I got a good hit, but he just laughed.

"Zeke is your brother. Doesn't that evoke some loyalty from you?"

His words were hot on my cheek. "Not when it comes to you."

Darius looked over at us. "What are you talking about? Is something wrong with Zeke?"

"Besides his attitude, his personality, and his ugly face?" Jarom asked. "No."

Darius didn't respond, just rolled his eyes, and in the silence I noticed a deep rumble in the ground.

"What's that sound?" I asked, turning anxious eyes to Darius.

They both fell silent and listened.

"What is it?" asked Lib, leaning around Jarom to see me. "What's wrong?"

"Don't you hear that?" I asked.

"It's them." Jarom said. "Helaman."

He turned to tell the men behind us, but it wasn't necessary. Everyone could hear it now. The noise had increased quickly from a thrum to the sound of footsteps on the path above us. We all ceased talking and shifted nearer to the ravine wall, though this first army was supposed to be our own.

I knew that Gideon would be waiting up on the road for any additional commands from Helaman and any changes that might have been made to the plan.

The ground shook and flakes of dirt rained down on our heads. I looked up, trying to see the army as they passed, but I had to look down to protect my eyes. I thought of Zeke and Micah still with Helaman's men, and since my head was already bowed, I prayed that God would make them swift. Even if the Lamanites overtook them, our orders would not change. We were not to go to their aid. We were to go and take the city.

It didn't take long for the entire army to pass. Then all was silent and still except for a few remaining leaves and flakes of dirt that drifted down into the ravine and fell around us.

For long moments nothing happened. As the dust settled, talking resumed quietly. I looked at the men around me and took a breath. Darius gave me an encouraging smile, and Jarom raised his brows, excited that the plan was going forward.

I craned around to find Gideon and saw him sliding down into the ravine at the far north end.

I chanced a look up again. The gray clouds had blown away, though they had been replaced by white ones that drifted peacefully past us. I watched one pass over the ravine completely before I felt the rumble of the second army. Ammoron's army.

Though no one gave a command, we all ducked down into the brushwood as much as was possible. I didn't even know if I should, I just did it without knowing why. We needed to be as close to the inside wall of the ravine as we could to avoid being seen. It was a large ravine, but there were two hundred sweaty men in it.

As we huddled together, listening to the army above us, Jarom wrapped his arm around me and pulled me closer to him.

I was debating whether to tell him to stop his nonsense or just punch him in the neck when Darius put his arm around me too, making the situation much less perplexing, and the three of us huddled together, waiting for the way above to be clear.

The Lamanite army took much longer to pass by than our own army had—not because they moved more slowly, but because their numbers were so much greater.

My heart gave a stab of worry for Zeke, who was leading the enemy away. I hoped that God would not require Zeke's effort to become a sacrifice, but I silently vowed that I would not let his effort be in vain, and I turned my mind to what I must do.

When the sound of the army had faded and enough time had passed in silence, Seth gave the command and we began climbing up the ravine. All our experience in the trenches while building the embankments around Judea served us well, and we were able to efficiently dig out steps that aided in getting everyone up and out of the ravine quickly.

Gideon waited for us on the road, and up ahead I saw Teomner's men. Together our forty lines of ten didn't look big enough to take a city. I hoped that the seeming greatness of the second army meant they had not left many men in Manti to guard it.

Gideon did not waste time, and we were moving out within moments, running toward the city behind Teomner and his men.

When we had been moving for a quarter of an hour, I thought I saw movement from the corner of my eye. It wasn't the normal movement of nature, of an animal or the trees moving in the breeze.

"Did you see that man?" I asked Ethanim who ran next to me on the outside of the column.

He looked around. "Where?"

I didn't answer him, but broke out of rank to catch up to Gideon.

When he looked down at me, I said, "Captain, I saw a man over there." I pointed. "Is he with us?"

He looked over his shoulder toward where I pointed, but there was nothing to see now. That didn't matter to Gideon.

"Take Lib, Reb, and the two scouts that came in and go find out."

Darius and Jarom had likely been scouting this area for several weeks. They were the perfect choice, even though it crossed my mind that Gideon might have been perpetuating the problem with Jarom and Zeke on purpose. Gideon was not vindictive, but he had shown he could be jealous.

"If they're not our men?"

"Capture if possible. Death if not."

I nodded and fell back.

"Oh, and Ket?"

"Yeah?"

"You don't have to call me Captain, just because...you know."

Oh, but I did. It reminded me that he was no longer my Gideon, but my captain. He was still my friend, maybe my best friend at that time, but that was even more reason to remind myself who he was and what he was not and never would be.

I didn't answer him, just turned, gathered my men, and ran into the trees, knowing they would follow me.

The forest wasn't as dense as it had been near Cumeni, and the places to hide were not as plentiful. When we were away from the column, I turned to consult the others who fell in around me.

"I saw a man," I informed them hastily and indicated the area he had disappeared into. "He was headed south."

"Was he alone?" asked Lib.

"I don't know. I only caught a glimpse of one man in the trees." I turned to Jarom and Darius. "Where could he have gone?"

"There's a trail up this way that leads back to Manti," said Jarom, and he and Darius were already moving in that direction.

Lib, Reb, and I followed without another word.

Chapter 8

I didn't like the idea of being on one of the back trails again, but thankfully this one was carpeted with moist, soft earth and fallen leaves instead of jutting rocks and roots.

We ran swiftly and silently with our eyes watchful and our senses attuned. My brother and Zeke's brother, just twelve years old when we had left Melek, ran through the wilderness now with the ease of seasoned scouts, knowing the way and leading us down it. I thought as I ran that I could resent this. I could choose not to trust them because of their youth and their imperfections. Others of the world would say it was foolish to let them lead me. And I might have thought so too if not for the warm feeling inside me that told me they would not lead me astray nor into danger, for God would not let them.

Suddenly I saw three men moving through the trees and undergrowth. Definitely Lamanite.

I wanted to be sure the others had seen them without alerting the enemy to our presence. I sounded the shrill call of the margay and when Darius and Jarom slowed and looked back at me, I pointed and held up three fingers.

If this trail led to Manti, then the men, probably spies, were headed there. I knew they had seen our small column of men. They were moving swiftly, hoping to give their men at Manti as much warning as possible. I thought they would have been moving much faster if they supposed our force to be a great threat. That didn't bode well for us when it came time to take the city from the Lamanite army, but it did provide us with the opportunity to overtake these three.

They were swift, but we were fast and light. God was with us—and we all knew it.

God made our footfalls silent as we approached the spies from behind.

We didn't have a plan, but one fact was obvious. We outnumbered them. Jarom, in the lead, leapt through the air and landed on their slowest man, taking him easily to the ground. Darius was only a second behind him, pinning down the next man, and Reb was on top of the third just as he turned to see what had caused his companions to cry out.

Lib helped strip the spies of their weapons, though they did not put up much of a fight, and I stood with my bowstring taut and my arrow trained on them. Jarom, Darius, and Reb tied the prisoners' hands together at the wrists and forearms.

The boys yanked their prisoners up and we continued on toward Manti. We would meet our column there.

It wasn't long before we could see the city below us. We had arrived before Teomner and Gideon so we waited for them under cover near the trail.

When they came into view on the road below us, I reached for the blade on my arm—I kept it shiny for just this purpose—and I signaled Gideon of our position. His return signal came a moment later.

"Gid says to wait here," I told the others. "He's coming to us."

In a few moments I saw Gideon jogging up through the

trails toward us. I heard the call of the margay and Darius returned it before I could.

The prisoners glanced at each other. They remembered hearing it.

Gideon hid his pleasure well when he saw that we had cut off the spies and taken them prisoner, preventing them from reporting our troops to the men at Manti. But I could see it in his eyes and in his posture.

He came forward and spoke to the men in a completely foreign tongue. The spies' eyes widened and they looked at each other as one of them hesitantly answered Gideon.

Gideon nodded. He seemed to adjust the way he spoke when he replied to the man, adding more guttural sounds to the words.

After a short conversation Gideon turned back to us. "They said the greater part of the army marched out. There remains only a heavy guard of approximately two hundred men and they are young. They have yet to experience a battle."

"And you believe them?" asked Jarom, throwing a mistrusting sneer toward the prisoners.

"I offered them their freedom in exchange for the truth. If we find this to be true, we will let them go, and they will make an oath to come against the Nephites no more."

Did he have the authority to do this? We all stared at him, and I was still waiting for Reb to say something funny to break the silence when Gideon went on.

"Stay with them here. Bring them to the gates when the battle is over. I'll signal you."

He waited for Lib, who was of the highest rank among us, to nod his assent, accepting the command, before he turned on his heel and jogged away.

"Is it just me, or did Gid just kick us out of the battle?" asked Reb as I watched Gideon disappear into the forest.

"He kicked us out," Lib affirmed, already resigned to it.

All four of them turned to look at me.

"It's not because of me," I said. Gideon knew I was having trouble keeping my mind on the enemy, but he had faith in my fighting skills.

"Yes, it is," Reb said.

"No, it isn't. Gid is led by the Spirit."

Reb glanced at the others. "Gid is led by his heart."

I shook my head and took a step back. Hadn't he just sent me headlong into the wilderness after the spies, not knowing what danger lay beyond the trees? Hadn't he trusted in my word even though he hadn't seen the man himself?

People saw what they wanted to see, what they expected to see. Reb and the others had been observing the relationship between Gideon and me for over three years by then. They didn't know that Gideon had made his decision to leave it behind—to leave me behind.

And now I could see why he had to. No soldier would ever take his commands seriously if he thought Gideon's motivations were compromised.

Still, Gideon could have wanted us out of the battle for any number of reasons, not the least of which being that someone had to guard these prisoners.

Finally, I said to them, "Every good man is led by his heart. Can the Spirit guide him in any other way?"

They all looked uncomfortable, but they considered what I said. Darius frowned in confusion, and Jarom looked into the distance at the place where Gideon had disappeared.

"Can I be any less than honored if he protects me out of love? Can you? Do you not think Gid loves those he commands? Perhaps he saves us for one of your sakes. And do I dishonor my country to guard these men until the battle is won?"

Nobody had anything to say to that.

My own words echoed through my mind. I had actually said that one did not need to be on the front line of the battle to be a necessary part of it, and I believed it with all my heart.

We stood with our prisoners and watched from our

vantage point in the hills as Teomner and Gideon led their troops against Manti.

The watchmen in the towers must have been feeling comfortable in the absence of Helaman's army, because Teomner was upon the gate before the Lamanites even tried to close it against him. Their complacency was so great the gate had been standing wide open!

It was a futile attempt and the four hundred Nephite troops poured through the gates without even breaking their column. But instantly upon clearing the gates they fanned out in every direction. Every man seemed to know where to go and who to subdue. There was resistance, there was fighting, but it was over very quickly.

Our three prisoners talked quietly among themselves, and it surprised me that they did not sound angry or resentful. I recognized their word for home several times and wondered if they were planning to go home once Gideon released them.

I thought of Zerahemnah, how Darius had loved that story. When Darius next caught my eye, I smiled at him and he placed his arm over my shoulders. It was tanned and heavy, though I knew he didn't rest the whole weight of it on me, and it was well-muscled, something I still had not achieved. My arms were strong but ever willowy and slender.

"They are going home," I said. "As soon as Gideon sets them free."

We waited there together and kept our eyes on the city of Manti until after perhaps an hour we saw Gideon's signal flash.

They were in, and they had taken control.

The men whooped like boys, but I turned into Darius and hugged him tight. I felt his other arm come around me. My little brother was so tall now, and he smelled like such a boy—like leather and camp smoke and sweat.

"Come on," said Reb. "Don't want to keep the captain waiting."

We marched our prisoners to Manti with our swords

drawn, but it wasn't necessary. They went willingly enough. The gates, now manned by a unit of Seth's men, were shut tight, but when we hailed them, they hefted them open and waved us through.

"Where's Gid?" Lib called out.

"The main square securing the prisoners," called a guard.

The people of the city had been instructed to stay in their homes, and the invading Nephite army was busy to a man preparing to defend the city. Men raided the stores of supplies and redistributed the weapons they had taken from the prisoners in the square. They manned the guard towers and lined the tops of the walls with their bows at the ready.

We made our way to the main square where we found Gideon speaking to the Lamanite prisoners. They were indeed all young, as the spy had said, and I thought that perhaps Gideon was offering them their freedom as well.

I marveled at his gift with languages as I listened to him speak. It sounded like yet another dialect he spoke to these young men, no older than us really. I knew it was a dishonor that they had been left behind and not allowed to go out to battle. Perhaps that was why they listened so closely to Gideon and looked on him not as though he were their conqueror, but their own commander. The kindness Gideon appeared to be showing them, speaking to them in their language and offering them a chance to know their God, had destroyed their fighting spirit—if it had ever existed. Perhaps Ammoron had compelled these men to invade our country with the lying and deceit he and his brother, Amalakiah, were so famous for.

No wonder Gideon showed compassion for them.

When Gideon was done, he turned and strode toward us. He spoke in the more guttural dialect to the three prisoners that stood with us, and they went to join their young brethren.

One of them turned back as he went and spoke to Gideon with a smile.

Gideon nodded and waved him on.

"What did he say?" asked Jarom, glancing with suspicion at the prisoners' retreating figures.

"He said to thank you for your decency."

We all looked at each other.

"But we captured them and took their weapons," Reb said.

Darius glanced over his shoulder at the prisoners. "We tied them practically up to their elbows."

"And we made them watch while we took their city," Lib added.

Gideon grunted and folded his arms. "That's apparently better treatment than they were expecting."

The capture had gone rather easily, and I wondered if the Lamanite spies had possibly wished it that way. I wondered if perhaps they were as tired of this fighting as we were.

"There are many tasks yet to complete before the army arrives," Gideon said.

I prayed the army that arrived first would be ours.

Gideon spoke briskly, with authority, and he was very unlike the boy who had camped and eaten with the rest of us for the past years. Leading men. Planning attacks. This was what he was good at, what he was meant to do.

"The city is well-fortified, better than we imagined. She should be easy to defend." He was walking us toward the outer city. "I've got men guarding the prisoners, securing the weapons, scouring the army tents for soldiers, seizing the government buildings, and manning the fortifications."

"And what are your orders for us?" asked Lib.

"Rest up. You'll man the gates tonight."

With those words, he left us so he could see to his other duties.

We looked around at the warriors running through the streets to fulfill Gideon's orders. I could see striplings on the tops of the walls and in the guard towers. Resting didn't seem like the right thing to do.

Darius stepped toward me. "Gid says Jarom and I can return to the outer terrain to scout for the incoming armies. We will bring in the advance notice he needs," he informed me as he checked to be sure all his gear was tied on tight.

I nodded and let my eyes rest on Jarom. He had been staring curiously at me for much of the afternoon. It was all that talk of Gideon following his heart. He didn't know what to make of it.

It took him a moment to realize I was watching him, but when he did, he gave me a slow smile.

"Be careful," I told them both.

Darius was already moving away, but Jarom stepped close to me and held out his closed palm.

"Here," he said. "It's from one of the swords we took at Antiparah."

I stretched my hand out, and he dropped a small shard of obsidian into it. It was rough and shot through with white, very unlike the obsidian from our swords.

"It was chipped off a sword during battle. I picked it up as a kind of souvenir I guess."

I inspected it more closely. It was flaked and broken and sharp and surely had come from the battle. It was a good gift, and a meaningful one because it held meaning for him.

"Thanks," I said.

Our custom said I must return his gift with one of my own. It was a common custom and meant little more than a hand clasp of greeting or parting. But it was like a hand clasp each person could take with them. And while it was a common practice among all ages, it could take on a different meaning during the courting years.

I reached into the leather bag at my belt and withdrew a smooth, rounded stone and held it out. It was kind of a pretty stone, if a stone could be pretty, and its smoothness was in complete contrast to the shard he had given me. It was a river stone, made smooth by water and time.

I was aware that Reb and Lib waited for me a distance away now. Darius waited for Jarom in the other direction, and all three of them watched us exchange these small gifts.

Jarom took the stone and ran his thumb over its smooth surface, clearly pleased with it.

"Bye, Keturah," he said and when he might have turned to go, he lingered and stared into my eyes with that lazy smile playing at his lips. Then he slowly began to walk backward, holding my gaze.

"That stone is in no way a promise," I said.

"I didn't think it was," he replied and finally did turn to catch up with my brother.

"What do you think it is then?" I called quickly, for I did not know when I would see him again.

"A stone waiting to be slung!" he called back over his shoulder.

Then what was this stone I felt sharp in my hand? This broken stone that he had picked up in the aftermath of a fight and saved.

I stared after him for as long as I dared. He walked next to Darius with confident, easy strides. I turned my eyes to Lib and Reb, both waiting, both wearing speculative looks.

"You can wipe those dumb looks off your faces," I said as I approached them.

"But what would we replace them with?" Reb asked.

"That does present a problem," I laughed.

We walked together in the direction Gideon had directed us. As we passed through the camps of the Lamanite army, I couldn't help staring at all the tents. Their army was huge, and I knew that if they overtook Helaman, the striplings could not stand against them.

Joshua and Zachariah made the evening meal out of spoils we took from among the Lamanite provisions and then, as our captain had commanded us, we settled down to sleep. I slept deeply, despite all the unknown scenarios that had been racing through my mind, until the first watch when Lib called from outside my tent.

"Are we on all night?" I asked him as we walked through the city.

"The first and second watches."

We waited and watched half the night in a weighty kind of silence, but our army did not arrive. No spies came through the gates, either.

"You worried?" Corban asked me.

I spit out the nail I had been gnawing off. We were next to each other, leaning back against the wall of the city.

"I don't mind being outside the gates," I said. "It doesn't bother me."

"I meant about your brothers and, you know, Zeke."

"Yes," I said simply, and we left it at that. They were out there running from a large and angry army, and I had no way of knowing yet if they would return to the city safely or go to their eternal glory. I couldn't think about them, but not thinking of them on that cool, dark night seemed like a dishonor.

The watch passed uneventfully, and when our replacements came, we made our way back toward our tents inside the city. Teomner and Gideon had established guards to enforce the curfew for the residents of the city, and we waved to the guards as we passed. There were also soldiers manning all the towers and watch posts. At least half our army was awake, but all was quiet as we walked through the city.

We approached a fire at the head of our army's camp and saw that Gideon sat with Teomner. Their heads were bent together, but as we neared, I could see they were in fact bowed, and the two men were in prayer.

Gideon joined us as we passed. All the boys hailed him a greeting, but he fell in next to me. I didn't know how he wanted it to be between us now, but I was tired and scared for the others and grateful for his concern.

"What are you doing?" I yawned as he dragged his bedroll

from the other side of the fire to the door of my tent.

"It's the third watch."

He meant to guard my tent while I slept.

"Gid, you can't," I said. "You need your sleep. One of the others will do it."

"Stop calling me that." He sighed. "Now is not the time for me to be disobedient to the commands of the Holy Spirit. Get some rest, Kanina."

I got into my tent, putting my head near the door, and as the others were settling into their tents and bedrolls, I said, "I'm afraid for them."

He peered in at me. "I know." Reaching in, he took my hand in his. I shouldn't have, but I reached toward him to accommodate his gesture. "Your fear will not help them, but your faith will." He squeezed my hand. "They are worthy of the highest blessings of protection, and so are you."

I fell asleep with his hand in mine and his words of comfort filling my heart.

When I woke, my hand had been returned to my side, and Gideon was not in camp. Ethanim was on a knee in the center of our tents and bedrolls building a fire.

"Is there food?" I asked him, rubbing the sleep from my eyes.

He pointed to a sack of what was probably grain and grinned.

It had to be corn flour.

Cumeni hadn't had much in the way of stores when we had taken it, and even though I was hungry and grateful for the food, I did not feel victorious taking spoils from the enemy.

That day Gideon commanded us to walk the perimeter of the city to look for weaknesses in the walls. We found none, but it took us much of the morning and afternoon. Then we tried to sleep because we were assigned to the gates again that night.

When twilight was falling, Lib woke us, and we began to make our way together toward our post.

"Gideon stopped by earlier," Lib said to us. "The spies came in this afternoon. Helaman has been spotted on the back trail."

"The treacherous one?" I asked, but my heart lifted.

Lib sent me a commiserating smile. "I don't know, but they are coming."

They arrived just after full dark. Reb ran to inform Teomner and Gideon. I searched the ranks as the others in my unit heaved open the heavy gates.

The striplings had been marching since I had heard them pass by the ravine two mornings before. They must have been exhausted, but the noise they were making made it clear that adrenaline was still running high.

I wanted to run through the ranks to locate Micah and Zeke, to see if Kenai had returned with the army. Darius and Jarom had likely arrived that afternoon, but if I knew Kenai, he would still be out keeping a studious watch on the enemy.

I watched the troops for a few moments as they marched through the gates, and finally I thought I saw Micah in the moonlight.

"Micah!" I called softly.

He turned toward my voice, and I saw it was him.

"Ket!" he said. "You're safe! You look well."

I nodded. "I am fine. The takeover went peacefully."

"Good. That is what I've heard."

"And you?" I asked. "Did you have to engage the enemy?" I knew they hadn't. The Lamanite army was so large there was no way Helaman could have fought long enough to defeat them and return.

"No. We led them on a chase halfway to Zarahemla. When the first evening fell, we made like we would camp for the night. And when darkness fell, we took the back trails to return to Manti by moonlight. By morning, we had a good lead on them. Some of it was slow going in the darkness, but we made it."

"Where is the enemy army camped?" I asked. Most of the

men had passed by us now, and we stood alone in relative quiet.

"They are a full day's march away. We'll have time to sleep and rest before they arrive here, and we'll fight them if we have to."

"Gid says they won't attack us," I said. "He says the city is well-fortified."

"They probably won't then. But their numbers are many. Their leaders may yet feel they have enough of an advantage to take the city back. They know we are but few."

I bit my lip. "Where's Zeke?"

Micah put a hand on my shoulder and smiled. "He's making camp. Wait until morning."

I nodded slowly.

Micah squeezed my shoulder and bid me goodnight.

I went back to leaning against the wall as the boys closed the gates behind Micah. I could hear the guards on the other side slide the bars home.

I looked at the moon, obscured by the heavy clouds, and let the relief wash over me.

Chapter 9

The next afternoon, the other men were not in camp when Lib walked me back from the forest. Gideon was the only one who remained, and he seemed to be waiting for us.

"You're to tend to the needs of the women and children here," Gideon told us as he headed off in the direction of the government building. "You will find the men working their way through the city, stopping at each home."

"Isn't the language a barrier?" Lib asked.

Gideon threw a look at me and took a brief moment to smile. "Go and see for yourselves."

We found our unit halfway down the third street we passed. They had divided into small groups and were doing exactly as Gideon had said they would be. They were knocking on doors and conversing with the people.

"What are we to tell them?" I asked Lib.

"Ask them if they need anything, and make sure they receive it," Lib instructed, and then he loped to the end of the street to talk to Ethanim.

I didn't know who to join, so I just went alone. I slogged past Joshua and Zachariah on the muddy road, giving them a little wave, and knocked on the next doorframe.

After a few moments the thick mat over the doorway eased slowly aside. In the dim interior I could see a very old man lying on a pallet. But the person who had swept back the mat was a very young woman, just about my age. She was taller than me, slender, curvaceous, and beautiful with black hair and skin like mahogany. She wore a wary look on her face.

"Shalal," I greeted her. That was one Lamanite word I knew, and Gideon had said it was at least recognizable in most of the dialects.

"Hello," she replied, glancing at the other members of my unit on the street. She had probably been peering out at them for a while. I would have been.

Not knowing whether she spoke my language or the Spirit was interpreting for us, I spoke as I would have to anyone of my acquaintance.

"I am a soldier with the Nephite army, which has taken control of this city. I am here to ask after the health and wellness of the members of this household and to offer you any assistance I may be able to provide."

Her eyebrows rose. "You are a soldier?"

"Yes," I said simply.

"And you conquer here but you wish to see if we need anything?"

"Yes," I said again.

She eyed me with her lips twisting insolently. I thought she might be chewing on the inside of her lip in worry rather than insolence, but she hid it well.

"I don't need anything from you or your people," she said boldly after a moment. "But my grandfather suffers with dysentery. Many in the city suffer with it." A sardonic smile touched her lips. "I think you may not be so glad you conquered here."

I reached into my satchel, and she tensed visibly but relaxed when all I pulled out of it was my little herb book. I turned the pages until I came to the picture of the hyptis plant. I turned it to her.

"Does this grow here?" I asked.

She studied the picture, taking the book into her own hands so she could get a good look at it.

"It might," she said. "There is an area they preserve for plants. I have only just moved here. Actually, I am only passing through in search of my father. My mother died and I—" She cut herself off and snapped her mouth closed, pursing her lips.

I touched her arm gently. "I understand," I said. "My father died when I was young."

She met my eye. I could see she tried for an expression of defiance, but she was not quite achieving it. The sorrow in her eyes belied it.

"If you will show me where this plant grows, I can show you how to prepare a tea from it that will bring your grandfather a measure of comfort."

She glanced up the street. "Is it safe to come out?"

"You will be safe with me," I assured her.

I turned and called for Lib and Ethanim, who had just been turned away from a home across the way. When they approached, I told them about the man inside the hut. "We are going to find the herbs he needs. Will you see that he is made comfortable and minister to him?"

They both nodded and ducked through the doorway.

"Lead the way," I told the girl. "I'll follow you."

She nodded, but quickly slipped back inside to speak to her grandfather. When she came out again, she sent a nervous look in both directions, but she bravely led me away.

After we had walked to the end of the streets and come to a wooded area inside the city walls, the girl asked me, "What did you mean when you asked those men to minister to my grandfather?"

"Oh," I said. It had not occurred to me she wouldn't know the meaning of the word. We had been conversing quite easily. "I just meant that they should see to his needs, physical and emotional, and bless him if he was willing to be blessed."

"Bless him?"

"Yes," I said. "We believe that God has given his power to worthy men, and they may bless and heal the sick with it."

She considered this but did not comment on it. "What's your name?" she asked after a moment.

"Keturah," I said. "Most of the men call me Ket."

She smiled for the first time. "There are some handsome ones, like the one with the hair of sunshine." This comment was accompanied by pretty spots of color on her cheeks.

"Lib? Yes, he's very handsome."

"I am Melia." She gave me a sideways glance as she turned down a path. Hyptis did indeed line both sides of it, and sage and many other useful plants. "I think," she continued, "I prefer still the dark hair of my people, but I have never seen anything quite as happy as this...Lib's hair."

I laughed. "It does make you want to smile, doesn't it?"

She blushed again. "Here," she said and indicated a hyptis plant. "Is this the plant of your book?"

I nodded. "Yes. Have you used it before?"

"No. I do not know how to use the plants of the forest."

Many people knew enough of the common medicinal plants to prepare simple remedies, but most people had not been taught as I had. I showed Melia how to strip off the useful parts of the plant, and as we walked back to her hut, I explained how to make the tea and picked several other plants that might ease her grandfather's pain and reduce his fever.

"You have been very kind," Melia said. "If only all the armies were made up of women."

I shook my head. "All the men of my army are very kind." I thought of the time Reb had nearly pushed me into the latrine, and I couldn't help a smile.

She looked at me doubtfully and changed the subject. “I’m afraid my grandfather will not be long for this world. He is very old, and he is not strong enough to fight the dysentery. That is why we must find my father.”

It was a frustrating truth of our society, but she needed a man’s protection and support. Even Mother, who had raised us alone, had accepted help from Hemni and Kalem. She couldn’t have taken care of the fields without Hemni’s help, not while she was taking care of us. And as much as I had resented Kalem’s gifts of food, I knew at times she wouldn’t have been able to feed us without them. Of course, Melia did not have children as Mother did, but she also did not have the skills to keep herself safe as she traveled. There were ways for a woman to make it alone, to trade cloth or pottery or baskets if she could make them, but it was not common, and it was difficult.

“Will you leave him when you continue to search for your father?”

“No,” she said. “I won’t leave him, and he can’t travel anymore.”

“I’m sorry,” I said quietly and let it stand between us for a few moments before I asked, “Is your father a soldier with the Lamanite army then? I’m surprised you did not find him here. The army is so large. Most of the Lamanite warriors in this quarter of the land have been forced from the cities and have congregated here.”

“No. My father is with the Nephite army, so I am glad you have taken over here.” She turned hopeful eyes on me. “Maybe he is here in the city even now.”

“I don’t think so,” I said regretfully. “All the men of my army are very young. The oldest are not much older than you.” Though it was possible her father was among Teomner’s men, it wasn’t likely. Not likely enough to get her hopes up.

“Oh,” she said, clearly disappointed.

I took her hand and squeezed it tight. “You will find him.” Then I added more tentatively, “If you do not, come to Melek.

You can stay with my family."

She didn't answer, and I knew her initial reaction was negative. But she might someday change her mind. She might have to.

We spent the rest of the afternoon working on our assignment. We had not made contact with every resident of the city, but we had been able to help many of them and assure them this was not to be a hostile takeover. We assured them they were not prisoners and would be allowed to leave when full control of the city was in Helaman's hands.

The Lamanite army did not attack the city. Instead they fled the entire southwest quarter of our lands, and Kenai followed them until they had gone nearly to the land of Nephi to be sure.

With the possession of Manti and some smaller holdings around it, we had gained back every city the Lamanites had taken.

Years ago, the people in this quarter of the land had been fighting amongst themselves and had thus become weak, allowing the enemy forces to conquer their cities. Before the striplings had come to strengthen Antipus at Judea, Captain Moroni, Chief Captain over all the Nephite armies, had been trying to preserve the strongholds we still had left. He had called the people to repentance and stopped the advance of the Lamanites.

It had taken those efforts of Moroni, and then it had taken us nearly an additional four years, to regain what had been lost during that time of rebellion and unrighteous intrigues among our own people.

After the takeover, many of the residents of Manti stayed in the city, though many that had traveled there with the Lamanite army left and went in pursuit of their men. Gideon explained to everyone who left with their belongings that the army had traveled south toward the land of Nephi, and Helaman ordered Kenai's scouts to guide anyone through the mountains who needed guidance.

Others who had once lived in Manti returned. I saw many families reunited while I was stationed at Manti. I felt pride and honor and gratitude.

That was why I had come, why I fought in the army. Not because I liked bloodshed or even because I thought I could do the work of a man better than he could. I thanked God for letting me be his instrument and see the fruits of what I had helped accomplish.

The days went on and life returned to the way it had been in Judea and Cumeni. The work and training were sometimes tedious, but I tried not to complain. The work was tedious because I was good at it, because I was practiced, and that was a blessing for all. I knew that from practice and work and preparation would come rewards when I needed them most.

I went to Melia's each day when I could and we became great friends very quickly. I hadn't had a female friend since leaving Cana and Leda in Melek, and it was very nice to have someone to laugh with and talk to about the things I couldn't talk to the boys about—namely themselves.

"Tell me again about your Zeke," she said while we were tending to her grandfather.

"I told you. He is the boy I am to marry."

"But you say this with a frown!" she laughed.

Did I?

"It is so far in the future. It hardly seems real." I shrugged as I folded the clean bedding and placed it on a crude shelf in the corner.

"He must be ugly."

At that, I laughed and shook my head. I could feel myself blushing.

"An ugly boy will do just as well as a handsome one," Zeram said.

"Oh, Grandfather!" exclaimed Melia. "An ugly boy will never do."

He tried to convince us we should both marry ugly boys because they would treat us better, but he was in a good humor, and I saw the gleam of mischief in his eye.

"The boy I marry will be worthy in every way, and that includes being handsome," Melia informed her grandfather.

His eyes became sad. "I wish I could meet him," he said. Then his eyes got a faraway look, and soon he had fallen into sleep.

We finished folding the linens in silence, and then Melia walked me out into the street.

I turned to bid her goodbye and saw Gideon leaning against the hut.

"Hey, Rabbit." He came off the wall. "Ready to go?"

It wasn't unusual for Lib to send someone to walk me back, even after all these years and even within the walls of the city. I had long since stopped being annoyed by it. By preparation and diligence and habits long-formed, I would have a guard in the time when I did need it.

Gideon wasn't smiling, but his eyes were, and when I saw him, I broke into a welcoming grin.

"I thought you were at the government building today."

"Noontime. You hungry?"

I nodded and smiled down at the ground. Since the day at the Sidon, I had become unsure of how to act around Gideon. I thought our friendship might be over, but he deliberately sought me out each day, showing clearly that he meant to keep our friendship intact. I looked up when he greeted Melia.

"Melia, this is Gid. My captain."

Melia was very curious about the soldiers of my army, and I had told her much about them—especially Zeke and Gideon—and how I managed to live among them. She was astute enough to understand that Gideon meant something different to me than the others did.

Melia widened her eyes, looked Gideon over from head to toe, and then turned to me and mouthed, "Oh my."

She was astute. But she was not subtle.

Gideon and I were both blushing when we left the street and turned toward the city.

"You like her?" he asked.

"A lot. I miss having a girl to talk to. I didn't know I was missing Cana so much."

"Zeke's sister."

"Mm-hmm. My best friend." It seemed so long ago. Would things be the same when I returned?

"Is she as ugly as he is?"

"Eavesdropper!"

He held up his hands. "I learned from the best."

He bought me food in the market and we went to the steps of the government building to eat it.

"Helaman's thinking of disbanding the army. Sending the striplings home," he said as we ate.

We had been gone over three years. I wasn't surprised. And I wasn't surprised that Helaman had talked to Gideon about it, either.

"When?"

He shrugged. "Not terribly soon. There is still work to be done. They need a governor here. We have to reestablish Nephite rule." He gestured to the square. "Even that market was under Lamanite rule. And the Church of God needs to be rebuilt."

Many of the leaders and teachers of the church had been killed during the war. The people were scattered, and though belief in God had increased because of the people's need for Him, the Church needed its structure restored.

"Are you still planning on going home?"

His words sounded casual, but I knew they were not.

"Yes. I am even more determined now."

"I think you should."

Gideon did not very often tell me what he thought I should or should not do. He just helped me do what I wanted to do. I was pleased that he had thought about it but disappointed that he wanted me to leave.

"Have you requested it?"

I shook my head and swallowed. "Of whom should I request it?"

He was done eating and leaned back on the steps. "I can tell Seth if you want."

I thought on it for a moment. I was close enough friends with Seth that it would be insulting if he heard it from Gideon. "No." I shook my head again. "I should tell him."

Gideon waited for me to finish my food and then held a hand out to help me to my feet. Our eyes caught for a moment, but then he looked away.

"Thanks for the meal," I said.

He watched me dust myself off, but looked away again, jerkily, as if he had to remind himself to do it.

"You've fed me plenty of times," he said quietly.

I wasn't sure what he meant. He had taken his turn at fixing the meals for our unit as often as I or any of the others had.

"You should smile more," I said as I started to walk away. "It makes your ugly face more bearable to look at."

Gideon grabbed my arm and spun me into him, even as he threw back his head and actually laughed.

I pushed away from him and scampered down the stairs again. I turned to see Gideon taking the stairs two at a time after me, but as I turned, I saw Micah on the main portico above us. He was leaning against a pillar, his arms were folded, and there was no question he had been watching us for a while.

Had Gideon known Micah was there today? He had to have known. The government building was not large, and they worked together frequently as two of Helaman's advisors. They had probably been strategizing together with Helaman that morning.

I looked at the ground before me as we walked back to camp.

What kind of stratagem was Gideon enacting? Had Seth

been right about his motives?

I glanced back over my shoulder.

Or were Gideon and Micah enacting some stratagem together?

Chapter 10

When at last Mother arrived in Manti, I took her to meet my new friend and her ailing grandfather. Melia told us of other families she knew that needed assistance from the healers, and together Mother and I made many visits to these families over the weeks.

One day, Zeram was feeling especially weak, and Melia was feeling especially weary of caring for him. So Mother stayed with Zeram while I walked with Melia to the market.

We walked through the square, stopping at the tables and shops, and Melia haggled with the merchants for the things she needed. I had determined that her Nephite was quite good, and she was very skilled at talking the prices down.

The Standard of Liberty hung from the highest tower of the government building. Melia asked me about it, and I told her what it said and explained its meaning.

"You hold these things dear," she said. "Your family. Your freedom."

"Yes."

"I admire that you have joined yourself with the army to protect them. I could never do that."

"You can do it in other ways," I replied.

She rolled her pretty eyes. "Like what?"

I thought for a moment, thinking of the best way to word what was running through my mind.

"When my brothers and I were little, my Mother explained to us that faith in God is like a seed," I began.

Melia did not know God. She had only a vague idea of some unknown Great Spirit. We had talked of plants and healing, weaving, cooking, laundering, travel, our far away homes, and of course, the boys in my army, but we had not talked much of religion.

She looked at me dubiously. "And this is how I shall protect my family's freedom? With a seed?"

"Mother said that if the thing we had faith in was good, our faith would grow just as if we had planted a seed in the earth. Only this seed was in our hearts."

She nodded, but I wasn't sure she understood.

"You see," I told her, "Mother taught us that if we did not doubt God's power, if we had faith in it, He would protect us. This is how we developed our faith in God."

She looked at me quizzically.

"Mother taught us," I said simply at last.

"You are saying I can protect my family by teaching them to protect themselves?"

"Yes," I said. "You don't have to be on the front lines of a battle with a sword in hand to defend freedom."

"But you do, defend it with the sword."

I laughed. "I fear I am not as nurturing as my mother. All my skill seems to be with the blade."

Melia picked out a blue sarong from the table we browsed at and held it up against me, admiring it. "Have you no faith that your God can yet give you the qualities of this protector of the home?"

I smiled gently at my friend. "He is your God too," I told her softly.

She looked away from me, but she wasn't angry. I had made her uncomfortable with my talk about God, but I wasn't ashamed to tell her about Him. I didn't blame her for being uncomfortable. I would let her mull over these ideas for now, and I would do the same.

Something across the square caught her attention.

"There is a handsome warrior," Melia murmured, and I followed her gaze to see Zeke approaching us.

"Yes," I said, my eyes locked on Zeke's.

When Melia saw that he approached, she clutched my arm. When he stopped in front of us and stared at me, she looked between us.

"This must be your Ezekiel," she said with a sly smile, understanding dawning in her bright, laughing eyes.

I felt myself flush, but I nodded and said, "Zeke, this is my friend, Melia. Melia, this is Zeke."

His eyes left mine for a moment as he turned them to her. Laying a brief hand on her shoulder, he said a polite, "Hello."

"Hello," she replied. Then she turned to me. "I have been away from home for too long." Her tone was conspiratorial. "Your mother must be weary of my grandfather by now. I will go and check on them. See you tomorrow," she said, and she left quickly.

We both looked after her, and I had to smile. She was a very good friend indeed.

I turned to Zeke.

"Walk with me?" he asked.

We began walking toward the edge of the city. I let Zeke lead the way, though I knew where he intended to go. The trail Melia had shown me where the hyptis grew led into an area of forest that had been left untouched by the building up of the city. Paths ran through it and plants and flowers grew up over small mounds and rocks. It was a perfect place to find herbs, and I thought it had perhaps been preserved for that purpose. It was a place of healing. It was the perfect place to walk with Zeke.

"Melia seems nice," he said after a while.

"She is. It's nice to have another girl to talk to."

"And just what have you girls been talking about?" he said with a teasing grin, and he pinched me lightly in my side.

I swatted his hand away.

"*Your* Ezekiel?"

It didn't matter that I had known Zeke for my whole life and had shared many embarrassing moments with him. For some reason, just then, I couldn't look at him and I didn't know how to respond to his teasing—not about this.

I swept my hair over one shoulder. "Don't tease me," I said.

"What?"

"It embarrasses me."

"It embarrasses you that Melia repeated your words about me?"

I didn't say anything.

"You mean to say you actually used the words, 'Oh look, Melia, there is my Ezekiel?'"

Amusement replaced most of my embarrassment, and I laughed despite myself at his imitation of my voice and the batting of his eyes.

"Do you think she's pretty?" I asked.

"Yes."

I smacked him in the chest.

"You asked."

That was true, and I wasn't sure why I had asked. I didn't want to think of him noticing other girls. But that was an unfair thought, and I knew it.

"She is Lamanite," he observed after a moment.

"Yes," I said. "But she searches for her father who is in the Nephite army."

"She won't find him here."

"I told her that already, but her grandfather is too ill to travel anymore. She plans to stay here until, well, I guess until he dies." It was very sad to say it that way, to think of it that way.

Our walks weren't as silent as they had been in Cumeni when we were healing from our wounds, but we fell silent as we walked through what I had come to regard as a wild garden. I touched the plants as I walked, giving them some of my energy and feeling theirs in return. I needed strength to do what I was about to do.

"Ket," Zeke said quietly, but he didn't follow it with anything.

"Will you hold my hand?" I asked him.

He hesitated for a moment—because he was afraid, because he didn't want to, or because he had promised himself he wouldn't, I didn't know why—but after a moment, he took my hand in his and held it firmly.

"Can I tell you something?" I asked him.

"You know you can tell me anything," he said, but I could almost feel him retreat.

I told him anyway. "I want to go home."

He stopped walking and pulled me to a stop as well.

"To Melek?" he asked.

"Yes."

He frowned. "I like having you here."

"I like it too."

"And yet you go?"

"The Spirit whispers it into my heart."

Frowning more deeply, he let go of my hand and backed away from me, but I could see it was only to pace and think.

"Don't say you told me so," he said after a few agonizing minutes.

"Never," I said.

Before leaving Melek, before joining the army, Zeke had insisted I stay home where it was relatively safe instead of marching out to the battlefield where it most assuredly was not.

"How would I have gone these years without seeing you?" he asked.

We had been at odds with each other for much of that time—about the danger, about my choices, my living arrangements, and about Gideon.

He turned back to me and smiled ruefully, maybe a little sheepishly.

"It hasn't always been easy, has it?" He took both of my hands in his and stared down at them while we both considered his words.

"And it has all been my fault." I could not get those words out above a whisper.

Zeke shook his head. "No. Never think that. Half the blame is mine. There have been so many times I was not the friend you needed me to be, the friend I thought I was."

It was kind of him to offer to shoulder the blame, some of the burden, but I couldn't let him.

"You are not responsible for my actions," I insisted.

"Then I am at least responsible for my own. If I had foregone jealousy for understanding, you would have had no need to seek love and friendship elsewhere."

I had never thought of it that way, but I had not been looking for love or friendship when I had met Gideon. Still, it did not absolve me of blame.

I looked up into Zeke's face and smiled. "Let us not fight over who gets to shoulder the blame."

"Let us share it equally," he said.

I started to shake my head, but he took my chin in his large, firm hand to stop it.

"Let us share it equally," he repeated.

I looked away and nodded.

"Now," he said, waiting until I looked back into his eyes. "There is something I want to tell you, too."

My heart started to pound in the moment he took to form in his mind what he wanted to say.

"I know that Gid has accepted an assignment in Zarahemla," he began.

I didn't respond—I hoped I didn't in any way, hoped I didn't flinch at the sound of his name, hoped my eyes did not betray the pain I felt about that. I didn't know whether to stop Zeke, to correct him and ease his misgivings, or wait and let him say it all. I braced myself and waited for him to finish.

"Until just now, when you said you wanted to go home, I thought the two of you might be making plans to go together, or meet there after some time. See, Ket—Keturah, I—" He ran a hand over his hair and gripped the back of his neck. He looked up at the sky, then down at his feet as he started to speak and stopped himself several times.

"Zeke," I finally broke in, causing him to look back at me. "Until this moment, I thought you could not love me again."

He swallowed hard and slowly shook his head.

I stepped closer to him. "Gid has not asked me to betroth myself to him." I made sure I had Zeke's eye firmly before I went on, because this was the most important part. "And I would not do so if he did ask it."

Please understand, I thought, *that you are not my second choice.*

He nodded as if he had heard my silent thought, but he gave no other indication that he heard what I said, no sign that it pleased him.

"There is one more thing you must know," I told him, fighting down my disappointment in his reaction. "I want to keep your brother's confidence, but I fear keeping this a secret from you will only cause heartache. Then again, telling you will likely cause just as much."

"Jarom?" His eyes narrowed. "What has he got to do with us?"

I couldn't say the words, not to Zeke, though I had said them to Melia. She had advised me to tell Zeke of his brother's feelings. If I had no romantic feelings for Jarom, she had said, then the problem was between the brothers. In order to deal with the problem, Zeke had to know about it. And since Jarom was unlikely to tell Zeke of his feelings, which went much beyond his professed interest in me, until they had become volatile, it fell to me to see that Zeke had the information he needed to handle the situation.

"It is Zeke's situation to handle," Melia had said. "You take too much on yourself. You honor Zeke in trusting him with this burden. Give it to him and let him bear it, for he will if he is as kind and good as you say he is."

"Ket? What are you talking about?"

"Jarom does not think of me as a sister."

"What do you mean?"

He couldn't possibly mistake my meaning, so I didn't offer an answer, just held his eye and waited for his mind to process it.

"When...how do you know this?" It clearly upset him.

"Jarom told me before we marched on Manti."

He looked at me with the slightest bit of mistrust in his eyes. I recognized it because I had seen it a lot in the past four years.

"He wasn't just joking around? You know Jarom."

I did know Jarom, and he was serious in his affections. I wondered if Zeke knew him.

But Zeke had not seen that look in Jarom's eyes when he had blown the coals into flames.

Thank goodness.

"I don't believe he was joking." I shook my head and added more firmly, "He wasn't joking, but Zeke, I really think this is about his feeling toward you, not me. He believes he loves me, but it is only jealousy of you."

Zeke nodded slowly. "He said all this?"

"He did."

Zeke stared off into the distance for a moment as he thought on this information, processed its potential impact, and considered his own relationship with his brother.

"I cannot think through this situation. I do not want to hurt him, but under the circumstances, I cannot return his feelings."

"And under different circumstances?"

"Jarom will be a very good man, and I love him. Like any girl, I would be foolish not to consider his offer."

That was a mistake. I winced when Zeke's nostrils flared and his face filled with color as he realized what kind of offer his brother had made to me. After a moment he took a deep breath and looked back at me, his face softening. He slid my hair back from my face with a long finger and kissed me above my brow where the hair had been.

"Don't worry," he said.

"But it is a problem that needs to be worried over," I protested.

"And I will worry over it. You just be your normal, caring, considerate self with Jarom."

I nodded. He was generous to say I was considerate, given all I had put him through.

"Besides, I can't say that I blame him. You're so pretty." He sounded exactly as Jarom had, and his gaze was equally as intense.

I was so often sweaty and grimy like the men. I didn't often feel pretty. I turned flattered eyes back to the path and began to walk again. After a moment he caught up.

"I'm amazed at how well you have healed," I told him as we passed through an area of low-hanging ponderosa bows. I could smell the needles, spicy in the warm woods, and I knew I would never forget this moment walking through them with Zeke. "You don't even have a limp of any degree."

"I'm amazed as well. The healers said they thought to take the leg, but you wouldn't let them. 'That vehement little girl,' they said." He chuckled. "I think you scared them."

I smiled, remembering.

"Lamech said you stayed by my side until Seth ordered you to bathe."

"That's true," I admitted with a fond laugh. "And Lamech told me you treat him well, better than the others, he thought, though he was a little embarrassed to admit it."

"You asked me to."

I hadn't. I had asked him to be sure he wasn't inadvertently harsh on Gideon's younger brother.

"That's probably why he took such dedicated care of you and your leg. He bore the brunt of your care after I left."

His brows lifted. He hadn't known that.

"I heard that I also owe much to the ministering of your unit."

He stepped into the brush at the side of the path to pick me a pink flower. I brought it to my nose when he passed it to me. "Yes," I said. "Gid gave you a beautiful blessing on the battlefield while I wept on your chest."

Silence fell between us, but it was replaced by birdsong from the trees, crickets chirping from the underbrush, and the buzz of bees around the blooms.

"I think that is when he knew," I said softly into the sounds of the wild garden.

"Knew what?"

I was nineteen years old. I had been through many battles, through a war. I had been wounded a number of times. I had known soldiers—healed many of them, loved many of them. Fallen in love with two of them. I had learned to value love and faith and loyalty as I valued safety and peace.

All this, and I still did not know how to tell Zeke I loved him.

"That was when he knew my love was given elsewhere," I said. "It was strange. I saw myself through his eyes, watched myself sprawled across your chest sobbing. You were so pale. You wouldn't wake up. I was..." I paused, searching for the word. "Inconsolable. I can imagine how he must have felt watching that. But even then I knew it could not compare to the anguish I felt when I thought you would die."

"He knew it too?"

I nodded.

"Have you...talked to him of this?"

"We have made our peace. He is happy for us."

"Though he nurses a broken heart?"

"Don't sound so smug," I said even though he didn't. "I break a lot of hearts."

"And is your heart broken, Keturah?" His voice had a huskiness that came from deep within his chest.

"Yes," I told him truthfully, my eyes clear and steadily trained on his. "Help me mend it?"

He squeezed my hand tighter and walked me back to my unit's camp.

Chapter 11

"Lib," I said. "I need to talk to you."

He looked up from the scroll he was reading. His eyes took a moment to focus on me. "What is it?"

I bit my lip. "I need Seth to be here too. Can you take me to find him?"

He rolled up his scroll and set it aside. "Sure."

Seth was busy talking to two of his men near his tent, so Lib and I waited at the cook fire until he was done. While we waited, Onah walked past and I waved to him.

"Is he from your village?" Lib sat next to me, and my shoulder brushed his arm.

"No. He came to our village once seeking the midwife."

He looked down at me with a question in his eyes.

"My mother."

"Ah. I didn't know Leah was a midwife."

"She hasn't been doing a lot of midwifing with the army."

But she had been doing some. Her skills and knowledge had been put to good use since we had left Melek, and she always seemed to be in the right place to help those who needed it. The people in the cities we conquered and camped in called upon her services, as did many of the army wives.

Lib gave me a grin, and then we fell silent. It was the first uncomfortable silence we had shared in a long time. We talked about many things, but we had never had occasion to talk about midwifing or childbirth. I was glad when Seth told his soldiers goodbye and came toward us.

Lib stood quickly. "Keturah needs to talk to you."

I stood too and pushed Lib playfully aside. I could speak for myself.

"I need to talk to you," I told Seth with a sideways smirk at Lib.

Seth looked at the sky and then looked at us. He glanced toward the other boys in camp and asked, "Do you want to walk?"

"Sure," I replied and looked to Lib, who shrugged his agreement. It was only right to allow him to speak for himself too.

They fell in on either side of me as we walked out of the camps. When we neared the woods, I took a silent breath and addressed Seth.

"Captain—"

"Whoa, Ket," Seth cut me off. "Is it to be like that with me, too?"

I frowned. "What do you mean?"

Seth and Lib exchanged a glance.

"Oh, you mean because of Gid."

"We've all noticed you've been addressing him, uh, more formally."

I pursed my lips together. "Well," I said. I didn't want to discuss Gideon with these two, or why I had chosen to address him as Captain from now on. "Today my business with you is formal." I took another breath. "I want to formally request a discharge from the army."

They both stopped walking. I took a few more steps and turned to face them. I could see I had surprised them.

"You want to go home?" asked Seth.

I nodded. "I do."

"Why?" they asked in unison.

I smiled at them and shrugged a little. "Look at me," I said. "I'm not that little girl anymore."

They exchanged another look, sheepish smiles. They both shifted their weight. Lib put his hands on his hips. Seth rubbed the side of his nose and took a step back, smiling into the dirt at his feet.

"The Lord has other work for me to do." I bit my lip on a nervous smile of my own. "Someone else for me to fight with."

"Are you taking volunteers for that position?" Seth asked.

I laughed and shook my head.

Turning, I started again along the path that wound through the garden, and again Lib and Seth each fell in beside me. I closed my eyes. I would miss them at my side when this was over.

Seth cleared his throat. "You know you can go home any time you want. I'll speak to Isaiah." Isaiah was the chief captain over our thousand. He was directly under Helaman. "We'll get it arranged. When do you want to leave?"

"Never," I said on a sigh. "And before the harvest moon."

The harvest moon was about three weeks away. My own unit was assigned to escort me home. I didn't think I needed their protection, but since Mother and Kalem were returning home with me, I welcomed the extra protection for them.

One day about a week later when I was getting off of a guard duty in the towers with Noah, Zeke was waiting to walk me to my camp.

I waved to Noah as he discreetly veered away to take another path back to camp.

"I'm coming with your unit to Melek," Zeke said, glancing at me from the corner of his eye as he walked next to me.

My first impulse was to object, because I would be safe enough with my unit. My second impulse was to protest, because I thought it might be hard for his family to see him and then let him go again. And my final impulse was to utterly refuse, because I didn't want him there when I said my final goodbye to Gideon.

Instead of protesting, I said, "I would like that, if you can get permission." I let my eyes sparkle up at him because a part of me did want him to come. Melek was not home without him. A part of me wanted him to protect me, but it was a part of me that had existed in the past, and I didn't know if just being home in the familiar forest would be enough to bring it all back.

"Micah's coming too," he said, clearly surprised when I did not refuse his company. I was glad I hadn't. "He wants to make the betrothal official."

I lost my breath. Was he talking about us? It was what I wanted, essentially the reason I was going home, to prepare, but nobody—not Zeke, not Micah, not Mother—had discussed it with me. For a moment I felt betrayed and helpless.

Zeke went on. "He'll come back for a year to finish in the militia while Cana prepares to start their home."

Their home.

"Whose home?" I slowed, staring unfocused at the ground as I tried to figure out what he meant.

"Micah didn't tell you yet." His question fell flat when he realized Micah had not told me anything.

"Tell me what? No. What's going on? Whose betrothal is becoming official?"

He didn't answer.

"Zeke?"

"Micah and Cana," he admitted. "I thought someone would have told you by now."

By now? How long had it been? Micah and Cana? But it was Kenai who loved Cana. And Cana loved him. At least, that was what I had always thought.

But there was an apology in Zeke's voice. Was it because he knew this was wrong? Or simply because he felt guilty that no one had told me about our families' plans?

It made my heart ache to think of Cana loving Kenai and betrothing herself to Micah just because he had offered.

"When did this happen?" I asked, but I didn't wait for an answer. "And Zeke, why? What about Kenai? Why did Cana agree to this? How can she do it?"

"Ket—"

"What was Micah thinking?" I burst out. I wanted to let Zeke talk, let him answer my questions, but question after question tumbled from my mouth. When had Micah gone home? Who allowed this? Did our parents know? Did Kenai know? Where would they live? Where would Kenai live? Because he certainly couldn't live near them.

When I finally ran out of questions, Zeke sighed and said, "Kenai is fine with the arrangement."

I shot him a dubious look I knew I had picked up from Melia, who had been disappointed so many times and lost so much.

Was I disappointed? Cana would be my sister. That was what I had always wanted. And Kenai was fine with it. Maybe I had misjudged their feelings.

No, I wasn't disappointed.

I was inexplicably heartbroken.

I turned my face suddenly away from Zeke and, to my dismay, I began to cry. I tried to cry silently, but I knew I hadn't succeeded by the tone in Zeke's voice when he said, "Keturah?"

I just shook my head.

He took hold of my elbow and led me to a large stone a short distance off the path.

"Sit down," he said firmly.

I did, dodging the nettles that grew around the stone, and I kept my eyes on the ground while I waited for him to pick a fight with me.

He knelt in front of me. "Does it bother you that much?"

Couldn't he see that it did? I nodded, though I didn't think it was necessary.

"Why? What is it that really bothers you? Is it about Jarom? I told you I would deal with that." He paused. "Is it about Gid?"

My eyes shot to his. They were brimming over with concern. His words were so gentle, but they cut into me like an axe.

"I just, I thought Cana loved Kenai. That's all. It's a surprise. A shock." I stood and scrubbed my tears quickly away. They were embarrassing. No one else in the army cried.

Zeke did not get up. Before I could step away, he took hold of my fingers and gently pulled me back down. "Sit," he said and when I did, letting my knees bend slowly until I met the stone, he searched my eyes.

"I'm trying to understand what about the betrothal upsets you so." His voice was calm, and I was starting to realize he wasn't going to say something mean or defensive.

"Then ask yourself why no one told me about it for all this time, why you yourself hesitated to tell me just now."

"I think they didn't tell you because it is not official yet. How often do you really see Micah anyway? How many opportunities have there been?"

I bit my lip.

"I did not tell you because I thought you knew. And I hesitated just now because I could see it hurt you." He took a breath. "And I can see that the pain goes deeper. It is caused by more than Micah's neglect to inform you. I don't know why. I'm not even sure you do. But you can talk to me, Ket, even if you think it will hurt me."

Still unsure what he meant, but recognizing his genuine concern, I leaned into him and rested my head on his shoulder.

In the end, Zeke did get permission to go to Melek. So did Micah. They both had capable men to take their commands while they were gone.

I said many of my goodbyes over the few days leading up to our departure.

"Melia, promise me you will come to Melek if you don't find your father in Nephihah," I said.

That was where she intended to look after Zeram passed on, which Mother said would not be long now.

We squeezed each other's hands, and she said, "I promise."

Then I sought out Onah, and we played a game of ball while we talked.

"I'm glad you were here," he admitted when I said goodbye and started to leave. "You know, when I got here. It was nice to know someone."

We hadn't actually known each other. We had only met briefly the one time. But there was something about Onah I liked, and I had been glad to see him, too, standing here in the cause of righteousness.

"I'm glad I was here, too," I said. "Be safe."

I also made a special effort to see both Eli and Seth before I left.

Eli was Darius and Jarom's chief captain, and I had learned he was Seth's best friend, though neither one of them had ever said so. Over the years, Eli had been a kind of quiet presence in my life. He had taught me many skills, including the correct way to slip a blade through an enemy's ribs to inflict immediate death, a skill which had saved many Nephite lives and minimized suffering.

Eli was excruciatingly handsome. He was also excruciatingly shy, and his shyness was compounded when he was around women. It had taken me a long time to realize he was shy, since every time I got near him he walked in the other direction. At first, I had thought he was disdainful and proud, but after getting to know him, I found him to be one of the most caring and humble men I knew. And having lived among

Helaman's stripling warriors, as they had come to be called, I had met many humble men.

I found him alone spearing fish down at the stream, up to his knees in water. Other men fished, but not close by. I approached and sat quietly, watching Eli until he had a half dozen fish tossed into the grass on the bank. I was sure he sensed me there, but he never turned to look at me.

"You should hold your spear closer to the water while you wait for the fish," I said.

He tossed the last fish onto the bank pointedly and finally turned to look at me. "Did you come here to tell me how to fish?"

"I came here to tell you goodbye."

He gave a slight nod, then stepped out of the water. "I heard you were leaving."

"Yeah. I guess it's getting around."

I watched him wipe his spear down with a cloth from his satchel. I knew I was making him uncomfortable. He was probably wishing I would leave.

"What is Eli short for?"

While he decided whether or not to tell me, I got up, moved to the stream, and began gutting and cleaning his fish.

"You don't have to do that," he said after watching me for a moment.

"It's the least I can do after all you've done for me."

He made a questioning sound, and I was sure his expression would have matched it if I had turned to see it.

"You taught me a lot of combat skills," I reminded him. "You watched out for my younger brother. You didn't insist on discovering me that day at the training ground."

I did look up at him then and was rewarded with the first full blown grin I had ever seen him break into.

"When I saw you fight Gid, it only took a moment to figure it had been you in the trees that day. You have a quick-thinking and protective brother."

I grinned too. "Do you still think I look like a boy?"

His eyes locked on mine, but after a moment he looked away, embarrassed. "No."

Our conversation fell off, but the silence was not awkward. He went to one knee next to me and finished the last two fish.

Then it was time to go, and I hadn't told him anything I had wanted to. But Eli wasn't the kind of man to whom you could come right out and say *I admire you. You have meant something to me.*

I knelt back on my heels, preparing to stand and leave.

"Elijah," he said with a sideways glance.

I smiled a little and felt the tears prick at my eyes. "I wish you the best in everything, Elijah," I said.

Seth was next.

I waited for him outside the training ground when training was done for the day.

"Make sure he walks you back," said Lib as he walked away with the others.

I rolled my eyes. It was hard to believe sometimes that he was still so concerned about my safety, even inside the city walls. His vigilance was both endearing and annoying.

"You busy?" I asked Seth as I fell in beside him.

"No."

"Good. Do you want to take your weapons back to camp?"

"Do I need to? What's going on?"

"I just...wanted to talk."

"About?"

"You know I'm leaving in a few days."

He glanced around at all the other boys leaving the training field. "Did you have someplace in mind?"

"No."

He hesitated. "I know a place. Come on." He offered me a smile, but more noticeable than the black tattoo that lined them, was the measure of sadness in his eyes.

At first I thought he would lead me toward the large herb

garden with the walking path through it, but he skirted it and led me toward the north wall of the city. We soon came to a grove of trees that hid us from the guard towers. Within the grove we found an area that had been set with several upended logs for stools around a pit for a fire.

"I think they have church meetings here sometimes in the summer," Seth said as I looked around.

"It's pretty."

"That's what I thought. I come here a lot to be alone."

"I wish I'd known about it all these months," I said. "Then I wouldn't have been alone."

Our eyes caught.

He broke the contact by looking down. Positioning a stool near a tree, he sat and leaned back against it. It was probably the place he sat when he was alone, the place he felt comfortable.

I positioned a stool so I sat near him. I held my hands in front of me and just looked at him.

The tattoo on his leg was half-covered by his long moccasin boot. The one on his neck was half-covered by his tunic. But the lining around his eyes was as striking as ever. I remembered the first moment I had noticed the lining.

"From the day I met you, when Micah introduced us, I knew you were the right captain for me. Even though you looked really scary, I always had a peaceful feeling around you."

"I scared you?" he asked on a laugh.

"No," I said, a little defensively. "You just looked kind of mean." I let my eyes find his. "Until you smiled."

He couldn't hide his smile then, but looked down at the ground in an effort to.

"Seth," I said. "During these years, you have been my captain, my friend, even my confidant at times. Your advice has been irreplaceable, your conduct exemplary. Your kindness and understanding immeasurable."

He was quiet for a moment. "That sounds rehearsed."

"It was. You could tell?"

He nodded slowly. "Tell me something you haven't rehearsed."

Suddenly, under the intensity of his gaze, my heart began to pound. I recognized that the Spirit could speak to me this way, confirming an action I was about to take. I looked at his dark, lined eyes, his crossed arms, his skeptical smirk. This couldn't be right, but I did it anyway.

Leaning slowly toward him, I placed a light kiss on Seth's lips.

"I'm sorry there could not be more between us." There was more to say, but that covered it well enough.

He swallowed and nodded.

"I hope that didn't make it more difficult to say goodbye," I said as Seth walked me back into camp.

He huffed out a laugh. "It didn't make it easier."

The hardest of these goodbyes to say was the one to Enos.

I had spent a lot of time with Enos at council meetings, on hunts, and during downtime. After a year or so, we became friends and he began volunteering to take a watch outside my tent at night.

He and Gideon were as close as brothers. I had known that since the day he gave us the spears on the training ground. I thought Gideon was closer to Enos than he was to Lamech. I knew Gideon loved him. But what really bonded Enos and me was that Enos loved Gideon too.

"Thank you, Ket, for letting him go. It is, *really is*, what he was meant to do, and I know he considered giving it up."

I got a painful knot in my throat.

"For you," he continued when I didn't reply, as if I didn't know what he meant.

It was never really any contest, but that Gideon considered making a life with me at all was an honor I couldn't fully fathom.

When I still did not reply, just held my arms around myself wishing I could say something light to change the subject,

Enos said quietly, "You must love him a great deal."

I shook my head, not to deny that I loved him, only to deny that it had been all my decision. It hadn't. I had made my own decision, but so had Gideon.

"No. He chose to go."

"You didn't ask him to stay."

He said this so positively, but he couldn't know. I couldn't imagine Gideon talking about our conversations or relationship, even to Enos.

"You don't know that," I said.

He laughed a little. "He wouldn't be going to Zarahemla if you had. That's what I know."

I didn't want him to tell me these things. I only wanted to say goodbye. My mind searched for anything else I had in common with Enos.

"You know, after I leave, you might actually be the best wielder of the javelin around here. But don't let it go to your head."

He laughed again, and to my surprise, he pulled me into a kind of hug. "I can see how you bewitch a man."

I pushed hard against his chest.

He stepped back smiling, making it easy to push him away. He held my gaze with eyes that looked so much like his cousin's. "Goodbye, Ket."

We set out early on the morning of the harvest moon. Men darted around us through the camps, everyone in a hurry it seemed to get on with the business of the day.

The dew was still on the soft green grasses. I imagined the smell of the ponderosa pines in the garden, wanted to go there one more time, but everyone was geared up and ready to move out.

We went to collect Kalem and Mother from their camps and circled back around toward the gates of the city. But as we approached the gates, I saw that the road was filled with people—mostly the striplings, but also some older Nephite soldiers and people from the city that I recognized.

The soldiers fell quiet as we passed through a narrow path they made for us. Soon the only sound was the rustle of fabric as all the soldiers knelt to one knee.

I cast my eyes over the large crowd. "What is this?" I asked Lib in wonder, but he didn't answer until we reached the gates, and then his answer was to kneel, along with the rest of my unit.

I stood alone in the square. Was this for me? I put my fingers to my throat, took one last sweeping look around the city and turned quickly to leave before I shed tears in front of the entire Nephite army stationed at Manti.

"Keturah." I heard the deep voice behind me. It was unmistakable. I had heard it often enough at the council meetings.

Captain Helaman.

I turned to see him striding toward me. When he neared, he held out his arm. I reached for it, and he grasped my arm in his large warm hand. I did the same, grasping his powerful forearm with my small hand.

"Well done, my little daughter," he said. Then he looked out over the warriors, still kneeling before us. "I once had a welcome like this. Is it not humbling?"

"Very," I laughed.

"There is much honor in it. But there is honor, too, in raising up God's warriors. The battle for good will ever be fought." His eyes were warm and kind as he counseled me. "On whatever battlegrounds you find yourself, Keturah, never doubt your worth in the cause of righteousness. In all things," he said. "And in all places."

I swallowed hard and nodded.

Then he very deliberately released my arm and rested his hand on my shoulder. "Let the Spirit guide you, follow its direction with exactness as you have followed the commands of your captains, and you will find happiness." He took his hand from my shoulder and started to turn away. Almost as an afterthought he said, "The Lord does not want your heart to be in turmoil."

"Thank you," I began, "for allowing me to join—"

He actually cut me off, waving away my comment. "If only there were more youth with your faith," he said.

My unit stood then and prepared to leave. Zeke came to stand beside me.

When he clasped Helaman's arm, Helaman said, "Bring this girl to my home in Zarahemla, Ezekiel, when the wars are over." Then he turned and winked at me. "And bring her marvelous sword."

Chapter 12

Kenai met up with us on the West Road and continued with us to Judea where we planned to spend the first night. He waved to me and greeted Mother as was polite, but Micah was walking with her and Kalem. It wasn't long before he joined Gideon, who had been alone at the head of our group.

"What is Kenai doing here?" I asked Zeke.

"He looks to be consorting with the enemy."

I tried a laugh. "I mean, is he coming home with us?"

He shrugged. "I haven't talked to him in weeks."

When we approached Judea, I was filled with memories of the city and of the boys around me. Hardly boys now. They had grown into young men. They were strong and courageous and humble. They made me laugh. They brought me comfort when I was sad. They strengthened my faith in times when my own faltered.

I couldn't help but inspect the fortifications as we drew near. The trench was deep, and the wall was tall and sturdy. Guards peered at us from the towers. The heavy gates were closed, but when Micah spoke to the guards, one gate slid back enough to let us enter two at a time.

"I miss this place," I said as we walked through the streets toward the army camps.

Zeke looked around. "Why?" he asked. But before I could form an answer, he let out a breath. "Oh, no."

I looked around, too, in time to see the beautiful Eve coming toward us. Her eyes were bright and intent on Zeke. When she saw he had noticed her, she skipped a step, started to run, and flung herself into his arms.

The entire traveling party stopped to see what was happening. Mother looked confused. Micah barely gave them a glance before he urged Mother on, bending to say something into her ear. There were some catcalls from the other boys, and Kenai was among the ones making them. Gideon watched the display with surprised interest, and his eyebrow rose when his gaze flicked to mine.

I turned back to Zeke. He was surprised, hopefully reluctant, but his arms came around her for a moment before he set her down.

"Enjoy your reunion," I said under my breath and moved away from them. I stepped between Ethanim and Lib. "Please keep moving," I begged quietly, and they did, escorting me quickly away from the embarrassing scene behind me.

At the evening meal, Zeke joined me while I was passing around food.

"Did you kiss her?" I asked.

He laughed. He had always been able to see through me. "If I did?"

"You could use the practice."

Reb spit water from his nose, and Noah choked on his first bite of food. Joshua had to pound on his back. I smiled smugly up at Zeke.

"You know that was nothing," he said as we moved on.

"No I don't." I wasn't ready to let him off the hook yet.

"Yes, you do. Ket, I told you before—"

"You embarrassed me in front of everyone!"

He leaned close to my ear. "How does it feel?"

I looked up sharply at the scathing words, but he leaned back and pasted the carefree smile back on his face.

"I couldn't stop it."

"Yes you could," I shot back and added an elbow jab to his gut. But the teasing had lost its playfulness, and I felt as if we were putting on a show for the others.

When everyone had food, I sat next to Kenai, and Zeke sat on his other side. Kenai cast me a curious glance, and I was sure he cast Zeke one as well, but we ate in silence.

As I was finishing up, I said, "I can't believe I am going home without you guys."

Kenai swallowed and turned to Zeke. "Keturah says she can't believe she is going home."

I smiled at my brother's antics. How many times in our youth had he been our mediator? How many times had Zeke mediated between brother and sister?

But Zeke said contritely, "Tell her I am sorry I embarrassed her."

Kenai turned to me needlessly. "Zeke says he's sorry."

I leaned around Kenai. "Forgiven. It wasn't your fault. I'm sorry I made a big deal out of it. I am only surprised every girl in this city didn't jump into your arms."

"You didn't," Kenai said at the same time Zeke said, "Don't be dramatic."

I wanted to punch Kenai, but he was so right. I peered around at Zeke. Did he want the kind of girl who would jump uninvited into his arms?

"I'm going to the river," I told them as I gathered their dishes. They both nodded a goodbye, but it wasn't long before Kenai joined me. He didn't say anything, and neither did I. We walked in silence toward the pool in the river I had used for bathing when the army had been stationed in Judea. It lacked the rush of water I loved about the waterfall at home, but it was my place here and the only place I knew to be alone for a while.

I sat beside it. After a moment, Kenai sat too. I picked a flower and began to twirl it between my fingers.

"Are you traveling to Melek with us?" I asked him.

"No. I just wanted to say goodbye."

Why did he sound so sad? It wasn't going to be forever. According to what Gideon had told me, Kenai would probably be home within the year.

"You're going back to Manti in the morning?"

"Not to Manti, exactly, but back to my work, yes."

"Will you see Darius?" I began plucking the petals from my flower and tossing them into the water one by one. They fluttered down and floated on top of it.

"You should be more direct and just ask me what you want to know."

I sighed. Of all the things he had forgotten about me during these years, this was what he remembered of me.

"Jarom needs to talk to you."

He stretched his legs out in front of him. "I already talked to him. It was so obvious."

"His problem with Zeke?"

"He's got a problem with Zeke?"

I frowned. "What did you talk to him about?"

He cast me a sideways glance. "His crush on you."

"Oh, that. I kind of thought that was secondary."

"To what? Is something wrong with Zeke?" His gaze shifted back toward camp where the others were.

Besides his personality, his attitude and his ugly face? I nearly laughed.

"Jarom is jealous of him. Extremely so."

Kenai waved the idea away.

"He thinks Zeke gets first pick of everything."

"It's his right. He's older." He paused. "But he meant you, didn't he?"

"He thinks he loves me. I believed him when he said that."

Kenai sat up straight. "He said it? Outright?"

I threw away the stem of the flower and flopped my hands down into my lap. "It is just a passing fancy."

He looked down at his own hands for a moment and then his gaze drifted again toward camp. His jaw worked until he said, "It has to be."

As I looked at him, I noticed he bore a new scar. This one ran down the outside of his left arm, as if he had used it as a shield. It had healed well, and I could see Mother's touch in the healing.

"Why won't you tell me about your scars?" I asked him.

He folded his arms. "They are my burden to bear. Did you at least tell Jarom goodbye?"

I knew he wouldn't tell me. He hoarded the scars like prizes that were his alone.

"Not privately. Zeke said to act normal with Jarom."

"You told Zeke?"

"Melia said I should."

"Zeke says, Melia says. What does Keturah say?"

I sighed wearily. "I say it's time to go home and be a wife to the man I love."

Neither of us knew what to say to that.

"How much longer do you think the war will last?" I asked when I couldn't stand the silence anymore.

This had been the main topic of speculation in the camps since we had taken Manti, but I had yet to hear Kenai's opinion, and I valued Kenai's opinion above almost all others.

He squinted into the distance above the tree line. "I think the war is all but over in this quarter of the land. The enemy armies have completely retreated except for some rogue bands, but they are friendly to neither side. They are the reason you have this fine escort home." He placed a hand to his chest with a flourish, and I wondered what exactly the work was that he was returning to in the morning. Scouting this trip from a distance? "Now our work will just be restoring things to the way they were here. I don't know how long that will take. I don't know if Helaman will retain all of the striplings here to do it. You and Mother may not be alone for very long."

"Well, Micah will not be coming home to stay." I was going to say how Micah would build his own hut for Cana and himself, but the pain in Kenai's eyes stopped me. It was fleeting, but it had definitely been there.

"Ket, it's okay," he said before I could ask, before I could demand he tell me the truth. "Cana and I never even spoke of it." He took a deep breath. "It wasn't like with you and Zeke."

"What Zeke and I had has not given us any guarantees, either," I said. It was stupid. It was not helpful.

"She doesn't matter to me," Kenai said flatly. That was even more stupid, and it was a lie.

I studied his face. "Let's go." I couldn't stand one more second watching him try to convince himself this was okay.

He helped me to my feet, and we walked back to camp in silence.

We left at dawn and climbed up and down through the hilly terrain. I looked around for Kenai and his men in the trees. I couldn't see them, but I definitely felt their presence. Were there so many rogue bands of men that we needed the double guard?

The trek home would be long and boring. I took the opportunity to walk for an hour or so with each of the men in my unit. I wanted to thank them, to tell them goodbye, but it all seemed much too inadequate for the years we had spent together, the battles we had been through.

By the time we had reached the southern border of the land of Melek, I had talked to almost all of them.

At the sight of the yellow fields below, I slowed my pace and sidled up beside Gideon.

"I was wondering when you'd get to me."

"Well, it's not now." As if I could say my last goodbye here, like this. Did he think he was the same to me as the others were? Did he think I had kissed them all in the guard tower? "I was just wondering if you were going to stop to see your parents." I gestured to the fields we were passing.

"Not this trip," he said. "If we went there now, my father would make everyone help with the harvest."

"The other men would help. They're strong. They would be willing. Perhaps it's fortunate that you're here during the harvest."

"There is nothing fortunate about this trip," he said quietly.

"Well, I don't suppose we can change our minds now." I recognized an unauthorized note of wistfulness in my voice and hoped Gideon hadn't noticed it.

But he had. His eyes shot to mine.

I looked away from him. I couldn't help but think of the things Enos had told me. Was Gideon not so very firm in his decision?

I changed the subject quickly. "Gideon, how come you don't like your parents?"

I had met his father several times when he had come to bring provisions for the striplings. I had eaten barley he had harvested with his own hands. He was a very nice man and very much like Gideon.

Gideon looked at me with surprise. "I love them."

"But you resent them."

He lowered his voice a little. "It's difficult for me to accept their decisions. I can't always be there to protect them."

"I understand that, Gideon, I do. I still wonder if my father's death was necessary, if it could have been prevented, if he could have shown his commitment in some other way. And I think of that time with Mother in the meadow. I can't stand to think of what might have happened if I hadn't been there or I hadn't been able to protect her."

Gideon looked down at me. "I forget sometimes that every man in this army struggles with the same feelings."

"You just called me a man." I feigned offense.

"And you, Kanina, just called me Gideon."

I had been avoiding that. I had been trying to call him Gid or Captain like the other men did. But to myself, I thought of him as Gideon. I always would. Gid was my commander. Gideon, my friend.

I wore a bracelet with gold discs my mother had given to me. She said it had been my father's. I loved it, but glancing ahead to see that no one was watching us, I slipped it off.

"I want you to have this," I said to Gideon. I hadn't planned it, but I suddenly loved the idea of him having it.

He stared down at the bracelet in my hand. "I can't accept that."

The reluctance in his voice stung, but I could see his hand was halfway poised to take it, so I quickly pressed the bracelet into his hand.

I thought of that moment he had eased my hand away from his scar. Had nothing changed within his heart? Was I the only one of us who fallen in love?

"Ket, I can't take it." But he clutched it in his hand. "I couldn't wear it. Everyone knows it's yours."

That's the point! I wanted to cry, and *I don't care what everyone thinks*. But I did care. "I want to talk to Lib before we get there." Without waiting for him to give the bracelet back, I jogged forward to catch up to Lib where he walked with Ethanim at the head of the party.

When Lib noticed me at his elbow, his posture changed, and he gave me a sad smile.

"So this is to be goodbye," he said.

"It had to come sometime, Lib. We cannot stay at war forever."

I had already spoken to Ethanim early on, but he kept pace with us. I thought he would discreetly fall back, but he didn't, even when I made my eyes wide and nodded to the rear in a gesture that told him to disappear.

Ethanim grinned. "Lib was hoping for a more private goodbye."

I understood immediately, and I could see by Lib's embarrassment that he hadn't wanted Ethanim to blurt it out like that. "Okay," I agreed quickly. "I'd prefer that myself. In Melek then."

When I fell back to walk next to Zeke, he smiled at me. "Did you get everyone?"

I hadn't discussed it with Zeke, but everyone could see what I was doing, trying to have a last conversation with each of the men I now loved so much. My heart was breaking a little more with each goodbye, but through the sadness I could feel the excitement of returning home.

"Almost."

"What were you and Gid talking about?"

Had he seen me pass over the bracelet? "His parents. I asked if he would stop to see them before he goes back to Manti."

He quirked a brow.

I laughed. "Did you think we were planning to run away together?"

"If I did?"

"You have so little faith in me?"

"I guess I never thought of you two as being friends."

I knew what he thought, and it was true. But it couldn't matter, not anymore.

When we arrived in the village it didn't take long for the word to spread that a band of striplings had marched in.

The curious and welcoming faces of the people greeted us as we walked in a group down the main road of the village. When we neared Zeke's home, Dinah came rushing out to greet us on the street.

She flew into Zeke's arms first, hugging him tightly and then stepping back to hold him at arm's length and look at him.

Then she glanced around.

"Your brother is not here?"

Zeke shook his head. "No. And I am not here to stay. We are escorting Leah and Keturah home. They will be staying."

She was disappointed at his words, but she continued hugging everyone—Micah next, Mother after that, and they hugged and giggled like girls.

As I watched this, I noticed Cana and two of her little sisters come forward. Cana hugged Zeke, but the other girls were too shy—they barely knew him.

The rest of my unit stopped in the road and watched the happy reunion, perhaps wondering what their own reunions with their loved ones might be like.

Dinah finished greeting both Mother and Kalem and stepped toward me.

"Where is Hemni? I asked as she enfolded me in her arms.

"He's out at the tannery. He's got Isabel with him."

When she released me, Cana stood at her elbow waiting to embrace me.

"I can't believe you're really here," she said and then lowered her voice to a whisper. "Did you hear about the betrothal?"

"I can't believe it either. And yes, I heard." I wanted to ask her so many questions about it, about how it had come to be—all the things I couldn't ask Micah.

All Micah had told me when I finally asked him about it was that he had taken some extra time during one of his embassies to Zarahemla to travel here and discuss it with Hemni. That wasn't nearly enough information for me.

"Good. Then we may speak openly about it."

I stepped back and searched her face. Her eyes were bright, but her mouth was slightly pinched. She was happy with the arrangement, but nervous. I caught a shy glance she sent toward Micah, and I was convinced it was what she wanted.

"Here, let me introduce you to everyone." I led her around the crowd of men, my unit, who had no family here to greet, and I introduced her. Each one in turn laid an appropriate hand on her shoulder and said hello. The way they looked at her though, I wanted to announce she was spoken for. I sent my own glance to Micah where he was conversing with some of the men from the village, and I wondered if perhaps he should be standing here next to us.

"And this is Gideon—Gid," I said.

Gideon gave me an all too knowing glance before he greeted Cana.

Cana sent me a glance of her own. She knew about Gideon. She had been my only confidant before I had left the village. But that had been four years and a thousand experiences ago.

"Keturah and I are to be sisters," Cana said brightly, rising up slightly on her toes in her excitement.

Gideon stilled but gave her an uncomfortable nod. I could see he fought to keep the smile on his face, and the glance he sent me then was much darker than before.

"Cana is—"

"Zeke's sister," he finished. "I'm familiar with the way it works."

I had been going to say Cana was to be betrothed to my brother, but I didn't get the chance because Dinah was herding us all to her home so she could feed us. Other women were already bringing more food.

"Gideon," I began again.

"It's Captain," he said.

Both amused and exasperated, I said, "You're no longer my captain."

"Then it's Gid."

"Alright," I said, trying not to show how it hurt me. "You misunderstand."

"What is there to misunderstand? You've wasted no time

in betrothing yourself to him."

And before I could respond or refute this, an accusation the way he said it, he stalked away.

"I'm going to wash up in the stream," I told Cana quietly.

She hesitated, her attention shifting toward the busy yard. "I should help my mother serve the food."

"So should I," I said, recognizing that here in the village my role would be different. "But I need a few minutes alone."

She had heard the whole exchange and sent me away with a sympathetic look.

"There will be time to talk later," she said.

I nodded and hurried away. How wonderful it was to talk with Cana again. I would be bidding farewell to many friends, but I was returning to friends, too.

I sat on the edge of the stream, not washing up at all.

"Is it true?"

I hadn't even heard his footstep behind me, but of course he had come.

"No, it's not true. Well, yes, Cana is to be my sister, but because she is going to marry my brother."

He sat beside me and put a comforting arm around me.

"Why does it have to be so confusing?" I asked him and dropped my head onto his shoulder.

"If you are still conflicted, perhaps you have made the wrong choice."

I sighed. "You're not exactly in a position to give me advice about men. You're completely biased."

I felt him smile. "I am the only one to give you advice, because I love you. I would never lead you astray."

"Lib, that is not helping," I whined pathetically.

"Your happiness. That's all I want. You can trust me."

"What do you think I've been doing for the past four years?"

"Fighting me, complaining, disagreeing, sneaking away unprotected..."

I laughed and looked up into his worried eyes.

"I don't like leaving you here," he said, his eyes roaming over the forest I loved. "With no walls, no guard towers, no embattlements."

The village was vulnerable. His worry was not unfounded, but this was my home. "If there is danger, we can run to the walls of Melek. I will be fine here."

He was quiet for a moment. "You're not fine, Ket."

I sighed. He wasn't talking about my home any longer.

"So, Gid thinks you're already betrothed to Zeke," he said. "Why does it matter?"

There was a sudden tightness in my throat. "I don't know."

But of course I knew. I had hurt him. It was exactly the thing he had tried to prevent that day at the Sidon when he said he would yield to Zeke. That had nothing to do with Zeke. He meant to spare me from having to hurt one of them.

And I had done nothing but hurt all three of us over and over.

"You have chosen between them?"

I nodded.

"Zeke?"

I nodded again.

"And the Spirit has confirmed this?"

I looked up at him and knew my anguish and confusion showed on my face. "I think so."

He searched my face until I turned away and rested my head on his shoulder again. He stayed silent and strong beside me while I thought glumly about things. I had grown to find comfort in Lib's presence, but I knew I had to stop relying on him.

"Ket," he said quietly. "If you plan to betroth yourself to Zeke soon, what difference does it make if Gid believes it's true now? It is doubtless better anyway. It will help him move on."

I nodded slowly. I hated the idea of Gideon moving on.

"It's just, I thought Zeke would speak to Micah, make the arrangements while he was here," I confided quietly. "I thought that was why he came. But as far as I know, he hasn't said a word to Micah. I don't..." I swallowed hard. "I don't think he wants me."

Zeke and I had rebuilt our friendship, but I knew I was still very different from the kind of woman he wanted for a wife. I wasn't the kind of woman who could prepare a meal. I was the kind of woman who could prepare a meal with one hand and slit a throat with the other.

"Perhaps he doesn't want to encroach upon Micah's own happy betrothal."

So the news of it had been announced in my absence. Everyone knew. Of course he didn't want to infringe upon his sister's happiness. I hadn't thought of that.

"Perhaps he'd like a chance to speak to his parents about it, or spend some time with his family before he takes on other obligations, a consideration Micah did not have to make before taking a wife."

I hadn't thought of that either.

"Or perhaps he waits for you to know your own heart."

"What do you mean?"

"I wouldn't want you to marry me because you thought you had to. I doubt Zeke wants that either."

I didn't say anything to that, and we sat in silence until someone spoke from behind us.

"You two look very cozy."

I felt Lib turn. I didn't have to.

Zeke.

Chapter 13

"Just talking," Lib said easily with none of the panic in his voice that I felt.

I turned to look at Zeke from within the curve of Lib's arm. He leaned against a tree a short distance away with his arms crossed over his chest. He stood close enough to have heard our conversation, but I had no idea how long he had been standing there. His expression was unreadable.

"Keturah's telling me goodbye." Lib sat firm and didn't remove his arm from around me. He even pulled me closer in a hug. If he felt any guilt in our closeness he didn't show it to Zeke. I wasn't sure if that was admirable or very unwise. "But I think she's about done with me." He looked back at me. "At least, I've heard everything I need to hear."

"Oh, Lib." My eyes fell to my lap. I knew what he was saying.

He removed his arm from my shoulders and stood.

"Bye, Ket," he said, and I already felt the hollowness of his absence. I knew it was hard for him, too, from the terseness of his words and the way he turned on his heal and left me. He stopped in front of Zeke, but after a few words spoken in tones so low I couldn't hear them, he was gone.

I hadn't even thanked him for all he had done. I had only thought of myself. I drew my knees up to my chest and hung my head.

"My mother has the food prepared," Zeke said to my back.

I didn't want to face a group of people, but I reluctantly got to my feet and slowly turned to face Zeke.

I didn't know what I expected, anger maybe, but I was unprepared for the warm embrace he offered. He moved with care, urging me into his arms. I hesitated—why was I resisting?—and I knew he sensed it. He sighed and nearly let me go, but I took a step forward and relaxed into him, grateful for his affection. I had been relying on my unit for years, but I had to learn to rely on Zeke now.

"It must be torture saying goodbye to all your friends at once. Your unit. They're more than friends, more than brothers. I know mine are."

I nodded.

I felt his chest rise and fall as he took a deep breath. "I wanted you to be free during this journey to say goodbye to them without feelings of guilt. You have developed a closeness with them—all of them—that you can't just ignore. I know that when you commit to something, Keturah, to a betrothal for instance, your loyalty will be boundless and unbreakable, and to betray it would give you unbearable guilt."

That meant he had heard most of my conversation with Lib. He knew I had been expecting the arrangement of our betrothal to be made final.

I eased away from him so I could look into his face, but he looked down at where he absently stroked my shoulder with his thumb, avoiding my eyes.

"I thought my presence could give you strength, but all it

has done is cause you confusion." His eyes found mine then and he said earnestly, "Keturah, there is time. Take it."

How could I ever, ever deserve Zeke?

"I overheard what happened. I'll speak to Gid and tell him you are not betrothed to me."

I couldn't. I couldn't ever deserve him.

"No, Zeke. You don't have to. Lib's right. It doesn't matter." I couldn't even imagine that conversation.

He didn't reply, but I felt his resolve when he kissed me, a kiss that fell flat for both of us.

"Once, my friend gave me this." He drew away, and I saw he held the beaded tie I had made for his dark hair. It draped over his long fingers. "He told me..." He paused for a moment and considered the tie. "He told me the truth. He removed the clouds of my emotion and gave me the chance to make my decisions fairly."

I fingered the tie. "You never wear it." Not since the battle of Cumeni.

He pressed the tie into my hand. "It holds a promise you are not ready to give. Come on." He jerked his head toward the village. "I'm dying for one of my mother's meals."

I led out, and he followed me through the forest.

Micah and Zeke stayed in the village with Mother and me, but the other men departed to deliver letters from the militia to their families in the nearby villages. Mother and Dinah offered to mend and launder their extra tunics while they were gone, and I was glad when they left them because it meant they would come back before they left the Land of Melek to return to Manti.

Mother and I cleaned our home and made it habitable again. Zeke helped me clear the kitchen garden and prepare it for planting the winter vegetables. Micah helped us too, but he spent a lot of time helping Cana with her chores and making her giggle. He was gaining the affection of the younger girls even faster than Zeke was. Seeing them together that way eased my mind about the arrangement.

On the third afternoon, I carefully wrapped my weapons in cloth, determined to put them away because the time of war was past, and I was placing them beneath my hammock when Mother came into the hut and said, "Keturah, there is someone here to see you."

Zeke was standing in the yard when I slipped through the mat at the door. I recognized what I had not on those evening walks here in the village so long ago, that since he had sought first permission from my mother, this visit was part of a formal courtship.

"Walk with me," he invited.

I smiled at him and walked out through the gate. "Would you like to go to the waterfall?" I glanced at the sky. We had plenty of time to get there and back.

"If you don't mind, I'd rather not," he said.

I understood why immediately and was sorry for even thinking of it. The waterfall had once been our childhood place of play, but now it was a place I shared many memories with Gideon.

"Why don't we go see the old training ground?" he suggested instead.

"I would like that." It was a better idea.

We walked through the field, careful not to trample any of the plants growing there. They were large and lush, and it was nearly time to harvest them. I led him to a small rise at the edge of the field and we climbed to the top of it.

"I used to hide here to watch the striplings," I confessed.

The sun was hours from setting, but it had crossed the midpoint and was falling in the sky.

"Kenai told me." I could tell that wasn't what he wanted to speak of, so I just waited silently for him to pull his thoughts together.

He clasped his hands behind his back and squinted into the horizon. "I spoke to Gid," he said. "Before he left."

I folded my arms over my chest.

"He loves you."

I shut my eyes, but I didn't say anything, and for a long time neither did he.

Finally he cleared the emotion from his throat. "I've been thinking of that morning in Cumeni."

I knew the one he meant.

"When Gid took command of the prisoners to Zarahemla. You were mad at him."

"I was."

"He gave you a flower."

"He did."

He cleared his throat again, but unsuccessfully. "Your eyes were closed—like they are now."

I remembered the moment vividly.

"But I saw his face when he offered you the flower." He put his arm around my waist and pulled me to his side, and I allowed it. "You really get to him."

"Please stop," I said.

He was trying to say I had made a mistake and done it willfully. He was trying to say I was a distraction and a nuisance to the men and they were worse for knowing me.

"Keturah, you are what every man wants to fight for."

I turned by degrees to look at him.

His deep brown eyes were gentle and full of compassion. "It is okay to mourn him," he said.

I slid into his waiting embrace. His arms were protective and comforting and hard as stone. I finally understood what he wanted to be for me, and feeling miserable, I finally admitted I needed it. He stood there and stroked my hair, and this time when I mourned for the loss of Gideon, he did not storm away in bitter jealousy.

Slowly, in His time, God was teaching us both what it meant to love another person.

"Do you remember," Zeke murmured into my hair, "that time we came across the wounded buck in the forest?"

"Of course I do," I mumbled into his shoulder. It had been mangled, broken, left for dead.

"I told you to turn away from its suffering."

"You didn't want me to see it."

"But you pushed past me and knelt by it. You stroked its ears, talked to it, and then mercifully slit its throat."

I watched it in my mind as Zeke spoke.

"That's when I fell in love with you."

He couldn't have been more than fourteen when that happened. Had I ever known? Had I seen it in his eyes?

As we started back toward the village, I thought of the wounded buck, of Gideon, and of marching out of the training field, this field, with Helaman's army.

Later that evening, my unit returned to the village. They carried bundles and gifts and provisions to be taken back to the militia. I knew they would leave at dawn the next morning, so I worked quickly to help the women of the village prepare a large meal and pack food for their journey.

It was the last time I would cook for them, and my heart felt heavy even as we talked and laughed in the yard of our little hut. Gideon stayed on the far side of the fire, and I might have thought he was still upset, but he couldn't keep his eyes from tracking to mine.

Don't say it. You'll wish you had never said it to me.

But oh, how I wanted to hear the words from his lips just once, the ones he was so clearly saying with his eyes.

You can't take the words back.

He wanted the army. Not me. I looked at the stars, into the fire, into the dark woods, but he was in every place my eyes went to. Finally, I just closed them and rested my head on my knees. I wouldn't make it harder for him. I would make it quick and brutal. That was who I was.

When the men finally unrolled their bedrolls and let the fire die down, I got up and went to the hut.

"Keturah."

My name was soft in the night, but I turned to see its owner in the shadows at the corner of the hut.

"Are you just going to leave it like that?"

"Zach, I have to."

He moved suddenly toward me, took me by the arm, and pulled me to the far side of the hut where no firelight glowed and no one could see us.

"You're killing him."

I shook my head. This was the better way. We couldn't have a long and forbidden farewell in the woods. That would kill us both.

"He wants the army, and the armies need him."

Zach scoffed. "He wants you. If you don't know it by now, you're blind."

"It doesn't matter what either one of us wants."

He drew in a breath and looked at me in the darkness. I thought I had made it clear.

"You are a fine warrior, Keturah," he said slowly, deliberately. "But you are not the woman I thought you were."

Did he intend for that to sting? Did he think it was a surprise to me? I had always been a better warrior than a woman.

"That's why I joined myself with the army," I said as I turned and walked to the door of the hut.

I had pulled back the mat when he called quietly, "Do you love him?"

I pretended I didn't hear and ducked through the mat. It was easy not to tell him. He wasn't the one who needed to know it.

The morning broke calm and clear. It would be a perfect day for travel, and I tried not to wish I was leaving with my unit. I kept busy as the men prepared to leave, and when they were ready and lined up on the road to say goodbye, I approached them with a smile I had to muster from deep within my saddened heart. When would I see them again? How had I come to love them all so much?

I reached back ten times and gave them each an arrow from my quiver with tremulous fingers, which they all returned with gifts of their own.

I accepted three bracelets made of pure white sea-shells from the fishermen, Corban, Cyrus, and Mathoni. Cyrus and Mathoni each handed me one and then Corban stepped forward and handed me his. "Stay faithful," he said.

Josh produced a necklace of red gemstones from his satchel. "Don't waste time on people who don't like you for who you are."

Reb tied a belt he had woven from yellow fibers around my waist. I expected him to say something funny, to make me laugh one last time, but he didn't say anything—just sniffed and stepped back, red rimming his eyes.

I ran my hands over the belt. It was unique and beautiful. "Thanks, Reb," I said, pretending not to notice he was fighting tears as I fought back my own.

Zach stepped forward and handed over a piece of jewelry made from green jade and fashioned into the shape of a leaf. I thought of the knowledge we shared of plants and their various uses and all the power that gave to us. He didn't say anything, which was not unusual for him, and it was as though the previous night had not happened.

Noah gave me a soft purple feather that I thought I might add to my dancing dress.

Ethanim placed several sets of orange beads into my hand and closed my fingers around them with his. "To adorn your axe," he said.

And Lib, with the sunshine hair and vigilant, watchful guard. He pulled an exquisitely soft blanket from his bedroll and passed it to me with a glance back over his shoulder at the other men. Red tinged his neck and was making its way up into his cheeks.

"Think of me sometimes," he said in a low voice. "When you pull it around you."

They each hugged me at the gate of our courtyard, and most of them pinched me in the side, pulled my hair, or slugged me in the arm.

"I've been dying to get my arms around you," Joshua joked as he squeezed me too tight.

I laughed as I pushed him away and looked at the last man in line.

Gideon.

He smiled at me. His smiles had always been rare, and I knew that I would treasure this one.

I tried not to think of all the people who watched us—all the boys, Mother, Zeke, Zeke's parents, Micah, half the village.

Gideon's embrace was too brief.

"There is so much I want to say," I told him quickly.

He shook his head. "You always did let your actions speak for you." He allowed himself a moment to look into my eyes. "Here," he said and pressed something into my hand.

I looked down at a ball, the kind we used when we all played together in the camps between work assignments. It was newly made of golden brown buckskin, but not a pretty adornment like the others had given me. Puzzled, I looked back up at him.

"You'll figure it out, Kanina," he said. His words were mild, but they were accompanied by a fire burning in his eyes that dared me to discern his meaning. Then, with boldness beyond comprehension, he kissed me—and not politely. He was insulting nearly every person there. He knew it, and still he kissed me. One of his hands slipped around my waist, his thumb brushing the ribs over my heart. His other hand slipped into my hair.

It was completely silent in the clearing. No one gasped or clucked her disapproval. No one cleared his throat when the kiss went on. No one scuffed a sandal in the dirt as he tried not to stare. No one laughed or coughed or even breathed.

Gideon.

He rested his forehead on mine for just a moment, not long enough, and then he let me go. I doubted he even saw the other men when he shouldered past them and left the village.

With wide, shocked eyes, the other men smothered grins and followed after him.

I gave Lib a last wave, and he gave me a look that I could not interpret. He motioned to something behind me, and when I looked, I noticed Zeke standing there staring after Gideon.

I touched his arm, and he looked down at me.

"I will see you in a few months," he said, completely avoiding mention, discussion, or even acknowledgment of what had just happened.

Because there was just nothing to say.

Chapter 14

I was glad when Micah walked out of the village without a word, because I knew he was angry.

I stood alone on the village street, feeling the soft ball in my hand, feeling Zeke's arms around me, feeling the weight of Micah's glare, feeling Gideon's lips on mine. I stood there feeling guilt and shame, love, hope, and confusion.

Then I felt the weight of so many eyes on me and Mother's hand sweeping my hair to the side and smoothing it down.

"Are you okay?" she asked.

I shook my head. "I'm going to the falls," I said, and I stayed there all day, returning only because I knew Mother would start to worry. But when I got back and saw her face as she sat at the fire with Dinah, I knew she had worried anyway.

It wasn't difficult to keep our little home in the village, so I started helping at Kalem's in the city. He needed me, and I felt like I owed him.

One day while I was hanging his laundered tunics behind

his home to dry, I asked him, "Why have you never remarried?"

He sat nearby cleaning a rabbit for the evening meal. "I don't remember telling you I was married."

"You once said you had a daughter my age. Did you have a wife?"

He was silent for long moments. I knew I was being intrusive, but it wasn't like he hadn't been intrusive in my life.

"I still have a wife."

I straightened up and looked at him. "Oh." I couldn't think of anything else to say to that.

After a few more moments, the rabbit was done and he stood to take it to the pot of stew I had boiling over his fire. He slipped the pieces in and returned to his seat to clean up.

"You know of the battle in which I slew your father," he said at last, his voice flat.

"Yes." It was our oldest family story, and I had finally begun to believe it was true.

"When I saw that the people offered no resistance, I was overcome with shock and then horror at what I had done. It may be the practice of some to attack and kill unarmed men, but it was not my practice." As he spoke, a shadow came over his face, a darkness in his eyes that I had not seen since before we had left for Judea. "Over the days that followed, I was filled with deep regret. I despaired. But finally I began to feel hope, what I now know was the Holy Ghost."

"And you went to the king and sought his forgiveness," I said, reciting what I had always been told of Kalem's conversion.

"Oh no. I had killed—" He cut himself off and cleared his throat. "The king was dead," he continued instead. "I went to his brother, Lamoni."

The old king, Anti-Nephi Lehi, had given his kingdom to one of his sons, purportedly my father, though Mother had never so much as mentioned this. Lamoni was his brother. Lamoni had never ascended to the high throne of the Lamanites, but had been a king over his own people for a time. After moving to

Jershon, he had yielded the title completely, and we were ruled by judges just as the people of Nephi were.

Having been in the army for years and knowing something of the way battles ran, I knew that Kalem himself must have been of the noble class to have had the honor of slaying the enemy's king. I always thought of this without much emotion. Since I had never known my father, these events were just a story to me, one that affected my entire life certainly, but not one I had even believed until a few years ago.

"Well," he went on. "When I went back home and told my wife what I had done, joined the Church of God, she was furious about it. Her family was quite prominent and it was a great embarrassment to her."

I could guess what happened and wasn't surprised when he told me how she had demanded he leave and never return.

"So I did. I did what she asked. I honored her wishes, and it has been one of my biggest regrets."

"Why don't you go back? Find your daughter. She is a woman grown now. She probably has a home of her own."

He snorted. "Do you think she would allow me into it? After I left her abandoned all these years?"

I grimaced. "No, I don't suppose she would. But you are always too hard on yourself. You never know what life has been for her. She may welcome you."

"And she may disdain and shun me."

"But of course you wouldn't let the fear of that happening stop you," I teased.

The wash was done, so I told him goodbye and went to the falls to look out over the valley and think.

Many days passed like that, turning into a month, then two. The boredom of my days wasn't much different from the boredom of my work with the army. It was the work itself that was different. I asked myself a thousand times why I hadn't just stayed with my unit, within the circle of their friendship and protection. But each time I began to doubt myself and my decision to come home, I was revisited by the Spirit that had planted the idea in my mind in the wild garden of Manti.

So I stayed in Melek, and I began acquiring and making items I would take with me when I married, just as if I had been betrothed, though I was not. I had scarcely been alone in four years. Now I was alone nearly all the time, and I had too much time to think.

I often thought of that day with Lib and Zeke by the stream while Dinah fed the striplings who had escorted me home. Lib had suggested that I didn't know my own heart, that I had made the wrong decision. Zeke had both agreed and understood, and he had left me the time and the freedom to be sure.

Sometimes I wondered about Zeke and how he really felt about me. He had to feel the pressure of expectations as much as I did. I was so much less than he deserved. I was a warrior whose idea of mercy was a quick death, not a woman who would bring him honor.

I thought of Zeke lying unconscious on the battlefield, of how hard I had fought to keep him alive and whole.

And always, my mind went back to Gideon, to his kiss in the village and his determination to spare me from having to choose between them.

I let myself think about these things, mulling them over slowly as the days went on, but it never helped. Sometimes I took out the leather ball or the beaded hair tie, but they offered no clarity, and I knew the best thing was to lose myself in work, service, and preparation.

Mother began to encourage me to practice her intricate patterns of weaving cloth, and as we both had spare time, we spent it developing this skill together. She taught me more of medicines and of cooking with the herbs of the forest. She told me of my grandfather, the healer, and of her sister, Hannah, and we had many good days together.

When the rains had come and gone, we sat in the small

yard with Mui, my old milk goat, and her daughter, Abigail, bleating softly to each other.

I broke a long silence when I said, "Mother, did you know Kalem was married?"

She glanced at me but returned her eyes to her work. "Yes, I've always known."

"I always wondered why he didn't marry you," I said.

Her cheeks turned rosy. "Me?"

"You cannot tell me you never considered the idea."

She didn't respond, but her rosy cheeks continued to speak for her.

I smiled to myself. "Then you know of his daughter?"

"Yes, Kanina. So sad for them."

I tried to ignore the pang when she called me by that name.

"I've been trying to convince Kalem that he should seek her out. Right the wrong he did when he left her."

"I believe his wife forced him to leave," Mother replied calmly. "Got her father involved."

"But his daughter didn't," I insisted.

"I don't know what would be best. I know it saddens him. It was a blessing when you began to accept him."

I looked up at her, but my eyes slipped past her to a man who was entering the village on the path that led from Melek. He wore a red tunic and a brown leather kilt. He came from the trees into the clearing and looked around curiously.

He looked familiar, but it couldn't be him.

I watched as he questioned Chemosh, a man who lived at the far end of the clearing and carried a large, limp pheasant slung over his shoulder toward his home. Chemosh pointed down the main road toward my end of the clearing. It reminded me of the time Onah had come looking for my mother.

But I had a strange feeling in the pit of my stomach that this man was not looking for the midwife.

Mother noticed the direction of my gaze and turned too.

"What is it?" she asked quietly with worry in her voice.

"Nothing's wrong," I quickly assured her, though I wasn't quite sure yet. "It's just, that man. I know him."

She studied the man as he approached us. "Oh?" She brightened. "Is he one of the striplings?"

"No."

The man neared us. Our eyes met. He smiled and kept a steady stride toward me, even quickened his pace as he became sure of his destination.

"He's very handsome," Mother observed, and I felt her study my profile.

"He is," I agreed.

He stood at our gate, bronzed skin and sparkling eyes, sheepish smile. Hunting weapons. Travel pack. Two unbroken, whole arms. Someone else might not have noticed the scar at first glance, but I was looking for it.

I got to my feet, unable to break eye contact with him. I felt Mother at my elbow.

"Shalal," he said, nodding to us both.

I cleared my throat. "Mother," I said. "Meet Muloki."

"Shalal, Muloki," my mother said graciously.

I had mentioned his name to her in Judea over a year ago but there was no real reason for her to remember it. And even if she did remember it, she could not know that Muloki was the enemy warrior who had struck Zeke the blow that had nearly killed him, because I had not told her. I had not told anyone.

"Muloki, this is my mother, Leah."

He gave me an odd look and said something I didn't understand.

I looked to my mother for translation.

She looked delighted to meet someone with whom she could speak her native language. But she was confused when she turned to me and said, "He wishes to know why you don't speak to him in his language."

"I don't know it," I told her, and waited while she related

my comment to Muloki.

He spoke again, but before she could relate it back to me, I quickly explained to her where I had met Muloki and how I had miraculously understood him there at the gate of Antiparah.

Mother nodded and explained it to him, or tried to. He still looked puzzled, but willingly followed Mother's invitation to take off his travel pack and sit down to rest. He declined food but did take the cup of nectar I brought out from inside the hut for him. And the whole time he and Mother talked to each other so quickly I couldn't make out any of the foreign words I knew, which were admittedly very few.

"Does he speak the language of Middoni?" I asked Mother when there was a lull in their conversation.

"Enough that we understand each other sufficiently," she said.

"Did you ask him what he's doing here?" I asked her.

"Yes, Kanina. He came to look for you."

"Me? But why?" I asked, though I could think of several pretty good reasons. I remembered how he had talked to me at the gate of Antiparah, interest in his eyes and a smile on his lips. I remembered locking eyes with him at Cumeni, lowering our weapons. I remembered the last look he had given me after Zeke had nearly sliced through his arm with one blow to protect me.

Mother's voice was almost scolding when she said, "Oh, Kanina. How can you live in a camp of men for four years and be still so naïve?"

"I wasn't being naïve," I protested. "I was being modest."

Mother burst out laughing, and at Muloki's question, explained my comments to him. He smiled too.

I went back to my loom, distractedly weaving the intricate patterns, making mistake after mistake while Mother and Muloki talked. Sometimes Mother would tell me what he said—information about the Land of Nephi or his home or his family—but mostly I just listened to the rise and fall of their voices in the foreign tongue and wondered why he would come all this way to find me.

I found myself glancing often at the scar on Muloki's forearm. It was straight but rough. The muscles under the skin had healed with a bulge and a narrowing, the effect of which was actually quite attractive. I was astonished that he had been able to keep the arm. I had seen the unnatural angle of it after Zeke had broken the bone completely and severed the flesh. Zeke had been bleeding his life out onto the ground. And they both had taken a stance to continue fighting.

"Kanina, why don't you walk with Muloki to ask Kalem to dinner? I will get it prepared."

I knew she had already proposed the idea to Muloki because he was getting to his feet.

"But we can't talk to each other," I said.

"Go," she persisted gently.

Muloki approached and held out a hand to help me to my feet. I took it and thanked him.

I was not unhappy to see him. I was intrigued and flattered that he had traveled such a great distance to find me. I wanted to ask him so many questions. He hadn't expected that we would be unable to converse. Still despite the questions and unexpected obstacle in communication, the reason he had come was clear.

I went ahead of him and led the way until the path widened as it neared Melek. After that we walked side by side. I stole secret glances at him, but he looked down at me openly, intending to catch my eye. I smiled but looked away each time. There was no reason for him not to be bold. Since he had already traveled many days from the Land of Nephi in search of me, boldly meeting my gaze was an understatement of his intentions.

A man with intentions. That was the last thing I needed.

When we arrived at Kalem's, he was standing in his little courtyard, hands on hips, staring down at his fire.

"Hi, Kalem," I called over the fence.

He turned as I came through the gate, already smiling.

I gestured Muloki through the gate. "Meet Muloki," I said to Kalem. Then I turned to Muloki and gestured toward Kalem. "Kalem," I informed him.

While they clasped arms, I said, "Muloki is a Lamanite soldier. I met him while we were stationed at Judea."

Kalem gave a nod but thankfully did not ask me any questions. He had spent his time in the army. He knew that when a soldier did not offer more information, it was not kind to ask. Likely, it would not be something you wanted to hear.

Kalem questioned Muloki in the language I did not understand and after both their glances landed on me and then returned to each other, I stepped over to Kalem's fire and examined the pot with nothing but tepid water in it. How had this man survived without me coming by to clean, grind maize, wash his clothes, and prepare his meals?

He had come to our home at Mother's invitation whenever possible, enduring my disdain for the taste of a good meal and a few welcoming smiles.

Sometimes I was so ashamed of myself.

I turned to look at Kalem and Muloki, and the sound of their conversation made me think of Gideon, the only person I had ever known who had the gift of tongues, with a pang of sudden and intense longing—and it was not for his interpreting abilities.

I broke rudely into their conversation. "We've come to invite you to dinner."

They both turned to stare at me.

"Mother's waiting," I said and moved toward the gate after pouring Kalem's pitiful attempt at dinner on his fire.

Kalem, startled for a moment, chuckled, gestured to Muloki, and they both followed me back into the forest.

We traveled without talking. I hummed the rabbit princess lullaby to myself to keep my mind off of things I shouldn't think about—the quiet guard tower on a gray day with a drizzle of rain in the corner, a copse of trees filled with moonflower blooms, a muddy training ground, the sound of one step before whirling to block the arc or a sword, a hand tilting my bow to adjust my aim, kneeling in the shade among shards of black obsidian, forest-filtered light on my hands.

I hummed louder.

Mother had dinner prepared, and despite not understanding anything that was said, I felt the Spirit in our home and my mood lifted. After eating, Kalem read to us from the words of Isaiah during which Muloki spotted my scabbard under my hammock in the corner and brushed my arm to get my attention, silently asking permission to retrieve it. I nodded and when he brought it to the table, Kalem said something, and Muloki unwrapped it from its leather sheathing.

"Kalem made it," I said. Mother translated and Muloki's transfixed gaze flicked to Kalem.

Modestly, Kalem began pointing out how he had weighted it and fit the grip to my hand. Muloki stepped back and cut it through the air and seemed so interested that I retrieved the rest of my weapons. Mother and Kalem kept their distance from them, but Muloki, much to my pleasure, devoured them with his eyes as he inspected them with his hands.

I watched him for a time, watched as his hands ran over the weapons, his fingers over the blades. Before I realized what I was doing, I inspected the rough scar on his arm with my hands, running my fingers over it, thinking that Mother and I could have done a much better job with healing this wound.

The silence in the room changed somehow, and I realized everyone was staring at me.

I knew Muloki remembered that moment on the battlefield, saw Zeke in his mind as I did, the fierce enemy warrior ready to fight him to the death to keep him from me.

We locked gazes.

And Mother suggested Muloki stay at Kalem's.

Chapter 15

Muloki stayed at Kalem's for a long time. Kalem said Muloki had no plans to go back to his homeland because he resented being made to fight for causes in which he did not believe. I didn't blame him. It was hard enough to fight for causes in which you did believe.

To earn his way, Muloki helped Kalem with his business, often accompanying him in his travel and trade. He seemed to enjoy the trade, but what he loved more was apprenticing as a weapon maker. Kalem truly was an artisan, and Muloki eagerly learned at his elbow, taking to it very quickly. Despite their difference in age, Kalem and Muloki became great friends, and it eased my mind that Kalem had company and was not so much alone.

When Muloki was not working for Kalem, he worked with Hemni in my family's fields. Once, he had tried to help at the tannery, but Isabel had resented the intrusion too much and run him away.

"What did you do to her?" I teased him.

"I took her father's attention to myself," he said haltingly, still unsure of his words.

He was very astute, and he was right. Isabel worked hard and thrived on her father's approval of her skills. And Hemni's approval was well-deserved. Isabel made a fine, soft buck-skin that was in high demand throughout Melek.

Muloki and I were working side by side digging furrows that the heavy rains had washed out. I had always disliked working the fields, but after the things I had experienced in the army, I found digging furrows preferable to digging trenches or graves.

"Yes, she does seem to crave her father's attention," I said.

"She is like you."

I straightened up to stretch my back, rested my shovel against my side, and ran the back of my arm across my forehead to wipe away the sweat. "What do you mean?"

Muloki didn't always have the words for what he meant, and over the months, I had become accustomed to asking him for more explanation.

He straightened too. "She is like you." He pointed upward. "She seeks much her father's attention."

"Oh." I smiled. "You mean prayer."

"Yes, prayer. To your father?"

"To my Heavenly Father."

"This is God."

"Yes. But Isabel seeks her earth father's attention."

Muloki smiled at me and reached out to brush at my cheek as if he were brushing away dirt. "But this is not so very different."

I thought for a moment and then shook my head. No, it wasn't so very different.

I looked down the long row. The air was warm, and it was humid there by the plants. I checked the position of the sun. It had scarcely moved since the last time I had checked it.

"I can finish," Muloki said, reading my expression. "You go home. Rest."

"No." I grasped my shovel, and I began again to clean out the furrow.

It was so much smaller than the trench at Judea. I thought of that first week in the trenches and of spilling dirt on Joshua's head again and again. How he must have hated me! But he had barely said one word, just brushed the dirt out of his hair and carried on with the taxing work.

Later I had apologized, but he had just shrugged it off.

"It's not as if the dirt could do anything to conceal your good looks," I had said, thinking a compliment might smooth things over between us.

His eyes narrowed and he gave me a hard look. "Don't say things like that."

"Like what?"

"You must know what it's like when people only like you for your looks."

"I didn't mean—"

He cut me off. "Nobody ever means it."

I had pondered much on his words, and I had never commented on his looks again.

"You tire to dig the furrow," Muloki said, breaking into my thoughts.

"Oh," I said, embarrassed as I realized I had stopped working entirely. "No, I was thinking of someone. Something that happened a long time ago."

"Thinking of a man." He nodded. "This man," he said and traced the scar on his arm with a dusty finger.

"Zeke? Oh, no." My embarrassment deepened. I took a step back and tucked an errant lock of hair behind my ear.

"Zeke," he repeated, trying out the new word. It sounded harsh from his mouth.

"His name is Ezekiel. Zeke. He is Hemni's oldest son."

His eyes widened slightly. "Zeke is this man?" He

indicated the scar again.

"Yes," I said quietly. I swallowed hard, and I couldn't take my eyes from the scar.

"Zeke is your man."

I nodded. Then I took a breath and looked up to meet his eye. He only looked curious. "Yes," I said, afraid of hurting him, but wanting him to know my heart was given elsewhere.

He searched my eyes as he stepped closer to me. "Zeke is not here."

I shook my head, all too aware that Zeke had not returned to the village and had yet made no plans to return. Dinah said his work was not done, but there were questions in her eyes I could not answer.

"I only am here." Muloki stepped even closer to me.

I laughed nervously, but I was not afraid of Muloki. I was afraid of myself. I was lonely and vulnerable, and I knew it.

"No." I took a step back, then another. "You are there." I pointed deliberately. "I only am here."

He laughed too, throwing me the same irresistible smile he had shown me outside the gate of Antiparah when his friends had teased him for detaining me so long with his flirting. He closed the distance between us before I could protest any more.

"We two are here," he said. His eyes widened innocently as if he were simply clarifying the definitions of here and there.

"Yes."

He cupped the side of my neck with his hand, and threw a nod back over his shoulder. "Zeke is there."

My eyes widened too, not in mock innocence but in confirmation of what I had long suspected. He had come to Melek in search of me, I had known that, but months had passed since his arrival, and he had not tried to be more than my friend. He had not put his fingers into my hair and looked at me the way he was looking at me then.

Could I drop my shovel and run? Could I hit him with it? A very disloyal part of me wanted to let it slip from my fingers and accept the invitation Muloki conveyed with so few words.

I considered the invitation for too long, I knew. Muloki patiently let me.

I handed him my shovel. "I think I will go rest," I said, and I turned to leave.

"Keturah, I am here," he said to my back, his voice gentle and quiet and promising.

I paused, nodded, and then continued out of the field. I didn't go home to rest. I went to the falls to think. But when I got there, I pulled out my slingshot. I had told myself I carried it only for hunting, but I picked a tree in the distance and slung rock after rock at it until the bark chipped away and I was gasping for breath.

I was so much better at being a warrior than a woman.

That evening Mother and I went to Hemni and Dinah's for the evening meal. Muloki sat in the yard playing a kind of game with Sarai and Chloe. Or rather, they were playing a game with him. I watched as they showed him different objects and asked him for the words. They clapped when he got it right and giggled when he got it wrong. There was so much giggling that I began to pay closer attention and realized he was getting the words wrong on purpose. After a while, Muloki held up the objects and asked the girls for the word in his language. There was much less giggling, and he had the girls enthralled with his strange language.

After dinner, Cana invited Muloki to join us on a walk through the woods. We showed him where the striplings had camped and trained before they got their orders. The field was planted now with squash and beans. It looked like nothing more than a farmer's field, and I felt silly taking him there to show off a place that was so plain.

Muloki surveyed it with his hands on his hips.

"It is very humble," he said.

"Well of course we didn't have a large training ground in Melek," I said defensively. More than one person had explained to him that the people of Ammon did not fight, did not kill others, and depended on the Nephites for defense. There had been no need to train an army, and hence no need for a training ground.

Cana shot me a look and said more kindly, "What do you mean, Muloki?"

He thought for a moment, walked out in front of us quietly, careful not to trample the plants. "It is...the Spirit is here. Your Holy Ghost." He turned back to us and placed his hand over his heart. "Humble, yes?"

"Yes," Cana confirmed.

Feeling stupid, I stepped toward him and said, "When Helaman arrived on the field for the first time, every knee bowed with respect for him. The Spirit compelled us to do so. It has always been here, from the first moment."

"I didn't know you were here for that," said Cana. "Jarom and Zeke described it to us so vividly."

I shrugged sheepishly. "Sometimes when I stepped from the woods onto the field it appeared as though legions of angels trained here. And when I looked again, I saw only stripling youths."

"Zeke trained with these angels?" asked Muloki.

I glanced at Cana. I could feel my cheeks burning when I said, "Yes. All the boys trained here."

"And Keturah, too. She had to fight her way in. She had to prove her abilities in front of everyone," added Cana.

Muloki's eyebrows rose. "I have much wondered how a rabbit got into your army of boys."

"A *girl*," Cana corrected. "A *girl* got into the army."

I smiled. "He's teasing me," I told her. "Because my mother calls me rabbit."

She giggled, understanding. "Yes, well, rabbits are very quick," she said.

Muloki caught my eye. "They can steal past many guards."

Cana looked to me for an explanation.

"That's how we met." I licked my lips. "I was completing a spy mission for Kenai. Muloki stood guard at the gate."

Cana lost a little of her color. "Kenai," she said. "Have you heard from him?"

"We've had a letter or two," I admitted.

"Oh," she said, her cheeks filling with color again. "Of course you have. And he is well?"

"He is fine," I said. "He is a great captain. He leads many men and many successful and essential missions. His work is important."

"Did he...did he ask about me?"

"No." I wished Muloki wasn't standing there with us, though he did not appear to be listening—he had turned to wander out through the field a little. He didn't know the language well, but he was bright and quick and had obviously caught the turn in our conversation. "He said he was fine with the arrangements. I asked."

"Fine?" she asked weakly.

I leaned toward her and lowered my voice. "Believe me, Cana. You don't want them fighting over you. Not brothers. And I thought..." I lowered my voice even more. "I thought you liked Kenai."

"I do," she whispered back. "I did. I liked them both."

I looked deeply into her eyes. She was telling me the truth. And why wouldn't she have liked Micah all this time? He was tall and handsome, smart, polite, and kind to her. She had grown up as close to him as she had to Kenai.

"You'll be happy with Micah," I said firmly, assuring us both. "It will all be well."

We left the training field and Cana led us toward the falls, but she had become melancholy and her heart was no longer in it.

"Would you mind very much if I went home?" she asked us.

"We'll come with you," I said. I hadn't been allowed to walk alone in the woods for four years. It felt wrong to let her go alone.

"No," she said quickly. She was already starting across the meadow. "I mean..." she hedged as she glanced between Muloki and me. "I'd like to be alone for a little while. I won't have a chance when I get home."

It was true. There were too many people at her home. I spent so much time alone, it was hard to imagine Cana not having any time to herself. Though I was starting to hate my time alone, I realized that sometimes a person needed to be alone with their own thoughts, to feel of the Spirit and to pray.

"Okay," I called. "Be safe."

She nodded and disappeared through the trees.

Muloki and I looked at each other.

He knew Cana and Micah were betrothed, and I tried to explain that it was Kenai who had loved her and Micah had never shown any interest in her.

"Do you have brothers?" I asked him as I led him to the log above the main waterfall.

"Dead," he said.

"In the war?"

"Yes. Soldiers all."

"How many?"

"Five."

"Oh, Muloki! I'm so sorry. All five were killed?"

"Yes. In the north. I went south with my friend by command."

"So you weren't there."

"No."

"But are you sure then? Perhaps the report was wrong."

He shook his head and reached under the neck of his tunic. He pulled out a large, animal tooth threaded onto a thin leather cord. It was intricately painted.

"This tooth mine. Five teeth, same, come to my hands."

I looked at the tooth for a long time turning it over in my fingers examining the painting. I thought it was a jaguar tooth or maybe a bear.

"I have luck," he continued. "Not all Lamanitish dead are accounted for."

"What about your parents?" I said after a while.

He shrugged. I didn't pry farther.

"Why did you come here? To Melek?" I asked him.

We sat together on the log, the water rushing swiftly under our bridge. It was cool where we sat, a nice respite from the warm day and the hard labor. The sun was beginning to set. It would be time to go before long. Mother would be worried. She would be alone.

Muloki looked at me, but then let his eyes fall away, following the path of the river to the distant sea as he spoke. "When I first saw you at the gate of Antiparah, it was as if you shone like the moon. A light so pretty and your moonbeam shone to me."

I rested my chin on my raised knees and listened closely.

"Even in the battle at Cumeni your light shone, and I could not swing my sword to you."

I remembered when he had begun to lower his sword. I gave a soft hum of acknowledgement and turned my head to look back at him, resting my cheek on my knees.

"And I healed here." He raised his arm. "But there was no life left in my home and no one to shine like the moon, so I came to feel the light, to heal more." He laid a hand over his heart as he had done earlier to indicate he felt the presence of the Holy Ghost. "Here."

"The Spirit," I said quietly.

"Yes. I know this now."

"I'm glad you're here," I said. "I'm glad you came."

"You are much alone."

"Yes," I said. I took off my sandals and tossed them over to the grass. Then I dropped my feet into the water.

"And you are not alone with me."

I laughed a little. "No," I agreed and added, "You are persistent."

"Persistent?"

I thought for a moment. "You keep trying. You won't stop."

He shook his head as if he didn't understand. I closed my eyes and tried to think of a different way to explain the word.

Suddenly a slap of cold water landed in my face. I gasped, lost my balance, and fell into the water beneath the log. The water wasn't so very deep, but it was swift, so I braced myself against the log and wiped the wet hair from my face.

Muloki stood near me up to his knees in the water, a huge grin on his face, and he splashed me again.

"Hey!" I protested.

I had no sooner wiped the water from my eyes than he splashed me again. And again.

"Muloki!"

"I am persistent, yes?"

"Yes," I laughed.

"Relentless?" His eyes were twinkling with amusement.

"Yes!"

"Giving no quarter?"

I shook my head against another splash, and then I bent and sent large handfuls of cold water toward him. He began to walk toward me, and I barely got the water as high as his chest.

"And you take no retreat."

"Never," I said and kept splashing until he was too close and it did no good. He grabbed my hands, and I slipped, taking him down with me. We came up laughing, and I braced my hands on his shoulders to push him down again.

We knelt in the water above the falls braced against the log, but strong as the current was, we did not go over the edge.

I heard a giggle from the bank. I froze. Then I looked back over my wet shoulder and saw Cana standing there with Micah in the green grasses on the solid ground.

"Micah!" I exclaimed. "You're back!"

"We just got in," he said with a long, obvious glower at Muloki.

I waded toward them. I could hear Muloki wading behind me. "All of you?" I asked hopefully.

"Only Darius and me. Jarom and Kenai have gone to join Moroni in the east."

Moroni?

"And Zeke?"

"He's still in Manti," Cana said, and threw a look toward Micah. "Right?"

"He has work to finish there," said Micah. It sounded like the same half-truth Dinah kept telling me.

"Captain Moroni?" Muloki asked as he came to my side near the bank and held out his hand to assist me up. He went to one knee in the water to form a step for me.

Micah took my other hand and hauled me onto the bank. Then he extended his hand to Muloki.

"Yes, the great Captain Moroni," Micah affirmed. "He is gathering an army to force your people from our lands for good. He raises the Standard of Liberty in all the cities he passes through, and the people flock to him. They tire of those who would usurp our freedoms."

I wrapped my arms around myself, shivering. "Muloki is not our enemy, Micah," I said softly.

He looked down at me, taking in my soaked and clinging clothing, my wet and stringy hair, the chills on my arms. "I can see you don't think so."

Surprising everyone, Cana hit Micah lightly on his chest and scolded him. "Micah, do not be rude to our guest. Or your sister."

I tried to hide my smile as he reluctantly apologized to Muloki, introduced himself, and clasped arms with him.

"We should start for home. It will be dark soon," Micah

said and turned to go, gathering us all with a look. But Cana touched his arm and caught his eye.

"And I am sorry to you, Keturah," he sighed. "It has been a long day."

"It has been a long four years," I said, recognizing the same weariness in his voice that I had felt when I had returned home.

He nodded and led us home.

Chapter 16

Darius was still eating when we arrived home. He was talking to Mother as fast as he ate. When we stepped into the courtyard he was telling her about the messengers that had come to recruit volunteers for Moroni's army.

"A reinforcement of six thousand fresh troops just arrived in the south," Darius said through a mouthful of Mother's corn cakes. "So Helaman was finally able to give leave to the striplings, and the messengers recruited a number of them to move to the campaign in the east instead of going home."

"And Kenai thought this would be acceptable to me?"

Darius swallowed and gave a laugh. "Kenai has kept himself alive for four years in a wilderness roamed freely by enemy warriors. Fighting with Moroni, in a band of thousands upon thousands, hardly seems dangerous. And besides, Kenai is twenty-one now, grown, and hardly needs your permission."

Mother didn't say anything to that, just pursed her lips, and I could see she was not pleased with the news.

"Darius!" I called out to break the tension between them.

He turned, gave me his familiar grin, and jumped to his feet.

"What happened?" he asked when he saw that I was soaked through.

"I got wet," I said.

Cana went inside for cloths to dry with and blankets.

"Are you all right?" Mother asked, giving me a stern look that she hid from Muloki and the others.

I held my chin high. "Muloki had a question about the meaning of a word," I said.

"Oh?" Teaching Muloki new words was an endeavor of which she approved and worked studiously at herself. "What word?"

"I am persistent," Muloki said, placing emphasis on the word. "I..."

"Splashed," I filled in for him.

He nodded. "I splashed Keturah." He made a motion with his hands. "Persistent."

I glanced at his wet tunic and kilt, remembered him kneeling in the water so I could step up onto the bank. I made my tone smug when I said, "I am persistent, too."

Cana came out with blankets then and handed one to Muloki. She wrapped the other tightly around my shoulders, pulled my wet hair from under it, and rubbed my arms up and down.

"I'll walk you home," Micah told her.

"It's only twenty paces," Darius teased Micah. Then he turned to us. "You should have seen how anxious he was to get home. We could have camped one more night at the south end of the Land of Melek, but Micah said we'd make it before dark if we kept moving."

"We did, didn't we?" Micah sounded casual, but I could see he was embarrassed as he hurried Cana out through the gate and into the gathering darkness beyond the fence. And I wondered that anything in this world could embarrass my older brother.

Muloki stayed for a while to dry a little near the fire, but when the sun began to dip below the horizon, he said he wanted to get back to Kalem's.

Darius waited until after he had gone and Micah had returned before he asked, "Who is Muloki?"

Mother and I exchanged a look. She knew about Antiparah. But nobody knew about Cumeni.

"Apparently, Kenai took your sister on one of his spy missions with the intent to send her into Antiparah."

Darius and Micah turned their attention to me.

"I was a sixteen year old girl and the only Nephite soldier who could get into the city in broad daylight. Kenai spent three days showing me how futile it was to watch from a distance. Then he presented his idea, what I learned had been his intent all along."

They both seemed to be without words. Micah was the first to speak. "Kenai let you walk into Antiparah when the Lamanites held it?"

"He ordered me to."

"I don't believe that," Micah said, shaking his head.

I shrugged. I didn't really matter what he believed. It had been three years ago and it was long over. Kenai and I understood one another and had made peace with the decision.

"Muloki was the guard at the gate that day. He let me pass. He felt the Spirit of God when he talked with me, and as soon as he could, he came to find me so he could find out what it was."

"How did you speak to one another?"

"If he didn't know what the Spirit was, why did he think you could tell him what he felt?"

They had many questions and I answered them the best I could. Mother helped me with all she knew of him.

"So he saw you, and he thought he was in love at first

sight?" Micah asked, a dark, frustrated look stealing over his features.

"Yes. Is that so hard to believe?"

"No, but I—"

"Sorry if that makes your obligation to me more difficult. I can see that you have your mind on your own happiness."

"Keturah!" Mother said in surprise.

"Well, frolicking in the river with Muloki didn't make it any easier," he shot back.

Micah had always put the rest of us first, before his own comfort, before his own happiness. What I had said was unfair, and I knew it.

But he was scowling at me, so I scowled right back.

"Just look at yourself," he went on. "Your sarong was sticking to you like skin. You're not a little...you're not a little girl anymore!"

"So stop treating me like I am!"

"Stop acting like it!"

"Micah! Keturah!" Mother exclaimed.

Darius looked between us with wide eyes.

We did not often disagree or fight in our family. But we had all been through so much, learned to take care of ourselves or lean on men who were not members of our family. None of us were used to explaining our actions. It wasn't like when we were young and we asked Mother's permission for everything. Perhaps this was the way it would be from now on.

And it was how it should be. We would just have to learn to allow each other our independence and agency. We all had to make our own mistakes and learn our own lessons.

I turned away, ready to let it go, but Micah persisted. His tone was lower, but just as angry. "I told Zeke you loved him, because you swore to me that you did."

My eyes shot back to him.

"Don't make me a liar."

His words hung in the air between us all. No one moved.

Finally, Micah turned and swept aside the mat at the door to leave.

I spoke to his back, telling myself not to say the words even as they came out of my mouth. "You know, what Kenai did to me was no worse than what you did to him."

A slight pause as he passed over the threshold was the only sign he gave that he heard me.

No one said anything as we prepared for bed, and the morning was uncomfortably quiet too. Micah hadn't come in for the night, but like us, he had been sleeping on the ground for years. No one was particularly worried about that, and I didn't feel guilty for driving him to it. He probably preferred it anyway. Though I hadn't wanted to hurt him, I didn't wish my words unsaid. It was how I felt. I thought it was how we all felt, and maybe it had needed to be said at least once.

Especially since Kenai wasn't there to say it for himself.

As the weeks went on, Kenai's absence in Melek was glaringly obvious, and there was little question that Micah's betrothal was a big part of the reason he hadn't come home. He had signed himself up for another battle, followed the moving front of the war. How much more blatantly could he say he didn't want to be at home?

"Hello, Mui," I said as I knelt near my old goat. I scrubbed at her scruffy ears and then began to milk her. I gave her an extra pat before I moved on to Abigail.

"Keturah?" I heard the shy voice from the other side of our fence and looked up to see Chloe.

"Hi!" I said cheerfully, grateful for the sweet face that interrupted my dark thoughts.

I remembered how she used to call me Ket-ah because she couldn't say my whole name. She had called me Ket-ah on the morning I had left with the stripling army. She had run and jumped into my arms, clung to me. I had many such memories of her, all very fond, but I knew any memories she had of me must be very vague now.

Chloe came through the gate. She was tentative, but I could tell her exuberant nature had not changed. Her eyes were bright, and her smile was contagious. Besides, I had seen her playing with Micah and Muloki.

"May I help?" she asked.

"Sure," I said, moving back from Abigail to let her near.

Chloe moved close and began to milk Abigail, talking to her, almost cooing her greeting.

I observed for a moment. "Chloe, was Abigail your goat?"

"Oh, no," she said. "She is Mui's baby. She is your family's goat."

"Little Kanina," I tried again, addressing this sweet seven year old girl with the endearment that meant the most to me. "Is Abigail your friend?"

She just looked at me, and then at the goat.

"She is, isn't she?"

Chloe nodded.

Of course she had bonded with this goat. It had probably been born in her yard. She had watched it grow.

"Why do you call me rabbit?" she asked.

"It's what my mother calls me. To me, it is a way of saying 'I love you.'"

"You love me?" she asked, wrinkling her nose in disbelief.

"Yes. We were good friends when you were little. You probably don't remember."

"I remember you," she said. "You are the girl that fights with Zeke."

I laughed a little and shifted my weight so my legs wouldn't go numb from kneeling on them so long. "I am the girl who fights with the army," I clarified.

She looked at me a moment in confusion. "No," she said slowly, her eyes focused on something in the past. "Zeke said, 'I swear that girl lives to fight with me.'"

I laughed again at how she boisterously mimicked his voice. "That sounds about right. When did he say that?"

She frowned. "All the time I think."

"Did he say it when he came for his visit last fall?"

She shook her head. "No. He said, 'Father, the time is not right.' And Father said, 'Micah fears you will lose her if you wait.'"

I looked down at the top of her dark head, trying to keep my curiosity in check.

"And *that*," she emphasized, "is when Zeke said, 'If that's what she wants, she can spend her life fighting with someone else.'"

I thought about this for a long time, much longer than it took us to finish milking the goats.

The men of the village built a new hut for Micah and his bride on a small side street of the village. Micah had chosen the location for its proximity to the stream, the large mahogany trees that grew around the little yard, and, I thought, so they would be far enough away that Kenai would not have to look at them together at all hours of the day if he ever came home.

They were married on a hot evening in sultry air. I expected Zeke to show up. I hoped he would.

While I stared at the food on my plate during the celebration that night, Dinah said, "Hemni sent word to Zeke of the date, but he was not able to leave his duties."

He was a chief captain over five hundred now, she had said with motherly pride, and thus he had many important responsibilities in re-establishing the economic prosperity and the Church of God in the southern Nephite holdings.

Personally I thought Zeke stayed away out of loyalty to Kenai, his best friend. Zeke was loyal like that.

Kenai had done the same thing after Zeke and Gideon had fought at the falls. He wouldn't be a part of my training anymore or a part of my blossoming relationship with Gideon, and he had stayed clear of it in silent support of his friend.

I knew Zeke loved Cana. He loved Micah too—looked up to and respected him, regarded him as a brother. But I felt deep in my heart that his absence was a deliberate show of support for Kenai.

And I feared it was also a deliberate avoidance of me.

The day that followed the wedding was just as hot. The market was crowded with people when Mother and I entered the square with our small baskets.

Mother no longer made any pretense that her main purpose in coming to the market was to see Kalem. Now that I knew Mother was aware of his marriage, I could detect little things she did to keep a boundary between them. It always made me sad when she circled the table so she wouldn't pass closely by Kalem or left the market before he'd had a chance to flatter her or give her something pretty. I knew they loved each other dearly, and I was finally okay with it.

When I had been younger, I had deeply resented Kalem's presence in my life—giving Mother food and teaching my brothers to hunt, fish, and farm. Things a father might have done. But he and I had bonded over the sword I had gotten from Joab at the training ground. Despite concern over hurting my mother, Kalem had made it into a beautiful piece of art. One that was covered with blood stains now—but that only spoke to the quality of the sword.

When we approached Kalem's tables, he stood with a ready smile and greeted us.

"Where is Muloki?" I asked him as I cast my eyes around the square.

Kalem smiled teasingly. He was not as bent on my marrying Zeke as the rest of my family was. Occasionally, I caught him teasing Muloki about me, too, when they thought I wouldn't hear them. I always worried that this teasing would encourage Muloki to press me for more than the good friendship we had. But Muloki, though he flirted shamelessly with me, never asked for or expected anything more serious from me.

"He is with Pontus, little daughter."

I smiled at the affectionate way he addressed me.

"Thanks," I told him and set off in that direction, pushing and dodging my way through the throngs of people.

Melek was filled with refugees who were fleeing from Moroni's armies in the east. It was said that he was taking the eastern lands by the sea with a vengeance, and sometimes, especially when I was lonely, I wished I was there with Kenai and Jarom.

I stepped up behind Muloki, noticing his shoulders looked especially broad in his red tunic. The ends of his black hair curled lightly around his ears and the back of his neck. It was really a shame I could not love him, I thought.

He was completing a purchase. Pontus handed him a small wrapped package and they clasped arms.

"Hi, Muloki," I said. "Hello, Pontus."

I might have been mistaken, but I thought Muloki blushed. He tucked the package into his satchel and gave my hair a tug.

I punched him in the arm and turned to Pontus. "Show me the goods," I told him.

He grinned and pulled the cover off a tray he already had before him. He must have seen me coming. He knew I was not here to look at the jewelry he displayed.

I leaned forward and studied the elaborate knives and daggers on the tray.

"Looks like you got a good supply of obsidian," I noted. "This is not from our mountains."

"No," he agreed. "It is from the lands far to the north." He pointed to a large spearhead forged of steel. "This comes from across the sea. I was only able to afford this one."

"Do you have a buyer in mind?" He wouldn't have purchased something of this nature unless he did.

"Certainly. She is about so tall." He held his stout hand at the level of the top of my head. "Long hair. Brown eyes. A penchant for deadly weapons."

I laughed and glanced at Muloki who also showed his

amusement. I was not a prospective buyer for the spearhead. I had no need whatsoever for a steel spearhead. Besides, I preferred flint for spears.

"Do you think it would go well with this sarong?" I asked them, holding the steel up to my shoulder and posing for their opinion.

"Perfect. Very beautiful," said Muloki with a warm gaze.

"Quite, but I'll leave the pretty compliments to the young man," Pontus added with a wink.

I placed the spearhead back on the tray. "Did you sell those beautiful arrowheads?" I asked.

"Yes," Pontus said. "I sold them to an overconfident, swaggering young man who said he needed them to shoot rabbits."

I looked up at him. "If he wants rabbits, I hope you tried to sell him one of those snares too."

"I think he already has snares set," Pontus said, and I thought he was trying not to laugh.

I looked at him for a moment longer trying to figure out what was so funny. I glanced over my shoulder at Muloki to see if he had caught Pontus's joke, but he was looking across the square at a group of people. I followed his gaze. More refugees from the looks of it.

"I know her," I said suddenly. It was clear that we were looking at the same girl. She was the most beautiful in the bunch, standing a little apart from the others in a blue sarong that looked very much like the one she had held up to me on a similar market day.

"Thank you, Pontus," I said as I gripped Muloki's elbow and towed him across the square.

When we neared the people, I called out to the girl.

"Melia!"

Chapter 17

Melia turned when she heard her name, and when she saw me she burst into a relieved grin. I broke away from Muloki, and we flew into each other's arms.

"I hoped I would find you!" she exclaimed.

"Did you find your father?" I looked around. "Did you make it to Nephihah? How is your grandfather?"

"Grandfather died almost a year ago. I did go to Nephihah, but my father was not there, or I could not find him if he was."

"I'm sorry," I said. "But I'm so glad you've come. Mother is here and Micah. You remember Micah. He is married now, and you will love his wife as well."

Melia looked past me to Muloki. "I can't wait to see your mother," she said.

"Oh!" I turned and stepped aside. "This is Muloki, my..." I bit my lip. "My friend."

Muloki rested a hand on her shoulder and said, "Hello, Melia." He kept her gaze and let his hand linger on her shoulder.

"And is your Ezekiel here in Melek?" Melia asked brazenly. It was obvious that she wished to know the exact nature of my friendship with Muloki. How I had missed Melia's boldness!

I shook my head. "No. He is yet in the southlands. He has not been discharged from the army."

"I thought your army was voluntary."

"It is." I took a breath. "He chooses to stay."

Melia gave me a look of sympathy but turned her eyes back to Muloki. "And you do not fight with the army?" she challenged playfully.

He smiled at her, not at all shamed by her question. "I have served a great deal of time in the army and given much."

"All five of his brothers died."

Her eyes widened.

"Tell us what is happening in Nephihah," I begged her. "Kenai is there, and Jarom."

She giggled. "Jarom did not race his brother home to get to you first?"

"Melia!" I caught the look of interest on Muloki's face. He was too perceptive to miss it. He was not missing anything because of the language these days. "No. I think Kenai talked him out of it. They're together, I think, in Nephihah. But enough about that. What is happening there? Is it as they say?"

A shadow fell over her face. "What do they say?"

Muloki spoke before I could. "We have heard that the Lamanites flee before Moroni's army, that he forces them all from the land. That he raises the Title of Liberty wherever he goes and persuades his countrymen to take up the cause of freedom."

Melia smiled wanly. "Yes, I think that is the way of it."

I looked deeply into her eyes. "You can stay with Mother and me. And Darius. He's home now too. Come, let's go find Mother. She's here in the market."

After Melia said a farewell to those with whom she had

traveled, we found a quieter path and made our way to Kalem's tables. Muloki and I flanked Melia, and she told us how she had petitioned Helaman for several units of the striplings to escort her and some others to Nephihah after her grandfather had died.

"I looked there for months with no luck. Soldiers and civilians from all the neighboring cities were pouring through the gates in fear of the Nephite armies that marched through the land. And the more people that came, the more difficult it was to look for him. I had almost determined to come here to Melek to find you when one morning we woke up and the Nephite army was inside the city walls!"

"You weren't hurt...or anything?" Muloki asked. He was a Lamanite warrior, and of course his mind would go to the atrocities soldiers often did to women. He must have seen vicious things. Perhaps he had even done some himself, though I couldn't imagine it.

"No. Moroni's army was fierce and terrible, but only to the soldiers there. To the women and children they were as gentle as lambs."

I laughed. "I won't tell them you said that."

She smiled at that. "They gave us the option to come to Melek," she went on, "and I didn't even have to think about it before I agreed. The terms did not matter."

"What were the terms?" Muloki wanted to know.

But we had arrived at Kalem's tables.

"Mother!" I said. "Look who I have found!"

Mother hurried around the table to hug Melia as I had. "It is so good to know you're safe!" Mother said.

"Leah! I've missed you both so much!" They stepped back and regarded each other with grins, but then Melia's gaze slipped past Mother to Kalem and she stilled. Her only movement was the smile that fell slowly from her face. For a moment it was as if she was unable to move, but then she shook herself free of whatever troubled her and gave Mother a weak smile.

Slowly she stepped out of Mother's arms and approached

Kalem, who was by then regarding her just as curiously as she regarded him.

"Are you Kalem?" she asked him in her bold way.

He gave a nod, and I saw tears form at the corners of his eyes.

I caught Mother's eye. Could this possibly be what it looked to be?

I looked back to Kalem and Melia. They stood still, staring at each other, both with unreadable expressions, for long moments. Finally, Kalem's bottom lip began to tremble and he looked as though he might break down in sobs.

But he held them back and said softly, "You look just like your mother."

Melia smiled at last, a small tentative smile. "No. She said I looked like you."

Muloki nudged me, and I looked up at him. "Did you know?" he mouthed.

I shook my head. How could I have?

Darius had never met Melia, so he was slightly less amazed at the happenstance than Mother and I were. But for a boy who had once craved Kalem's attention so much for himself, he was content to let Melia have it all during the evening meal.

"Mother died years ago, and I went to live with Grandfather," Melia explained while we ate.

"When did you start looking for me?" Kalem asked as he handed his empty dish to Mother, and his eyes followed her as she took it inside the hut.

"Almost immediately."

"And your grandfather agreed to this?" I noticed Kalem was careful not to speak Zeram's name aloud. Speaking the name of the dead would not be polite.

"It was his idea. He felt Mother had overreacted and been unfair." She blushed a little. "I took longer to warm to the idea."

"I only wonder that you did at all," Kalem replied, genuinely humbled.

"Grandfather explained how he thought Mother had been unfair. He even said it was his fault, giving her whatever she wanted all the time."

Kalem nodded slowly, lost in his past.

"We started in Zarahemla and spent a lot of time there searching for you and learning the languages. I took to them quite well, because of my youth, Grandfather said. And Grandfather had of course been schooled in languages when he was young. Finally, someone told us the people of Ammon lived in the land of Jershon. But when we went there, you had all moved to make room for the Nephite armies. We came to Melek next and learned that you had traveled with the striplings, so we set off to search the cities in the south."

"You haven't had a very good life," Kalem said morosely.

"Oh, Grandfather was wonderful to me. He taught me so many things during our travels. When I was little, he played games with me as we walked from place to place. He was determined to set things right. I always knew that, and I always respected him for it. I've had a good life, Father." Melia said his name tentatively, trying it out. She clasped his hand in both of hers. "Let your heart be at ease about that."

I knew how his guilt had plagued him, how he had not expected to ever gain his daughter's forgiveness.

I left them alone and took the rest of the dishes I had cleaned with the coals inside the hut where I found Mother talking to Muloki. They glanced at me but kept talking, knowing I didn't understand a word they said. It was strange that they spoke in the old Lamanite language because Muloki could both speak and understand Nephite quite well by then. I wondered, naturally, what they were discussing, but giving up eavesdropping as hopeless, I just put the dishes away and turned to leave again.

My sling caught on a hook near the door, the one we used to tie back the mat when it was too warm inside the hut. I untangled it, but when I went to replace it at my belt, I paused.

It was my first slingshot, the one Seth had given me on that long ago day when Helaman had let me join the army. Gideon had stepped forward to spar with me. Micah had introduced me to Seth. And Seth had given me the sling.

Stepping back into the recesses of the hut, I brought it to my nose. The smell of the leather brought back so many memories. I thought of my first battle with the sling—retreating from the army at Antiparah, leading them away, turning to face them.

Was there anything as noble as that yet to come? Had I any adventures left? When I looked to the future, I felt bleak inside. If Zeke didn't marry me, I probably would not marry at all. What man would take on a feisty, man-killing warrior like me for a wife? For the mother of his children? I had heard the things they called me, even here in the village. And what else was left to a girl who did not marry and bear children? The future stretched out endlessly empty.

Muloki seemed less interested in marriage as he got to know me better, and Zeke had not even bothered to come home to me yet. He had not so much as written a letter or sent a message to me.

Gideon had wanted to make some kind of statement with that unwise and embarrassing kiss in the street, but in the end, he hadn't wanted to marry me either. He must have been so relieved to have gotten away, to have escaped to the army, and I had let him do it so easily.

How I wished I could go back to the army too—the only place I felt I truly belonged.

"You miss it," Muloki said from behind me.

I turned and realized Mother had gone, and we were alone. Strange that Mother had left us alone like that, but I felt the sling in my hand and knew why she had gone.

"Yeah," I said. "I miss all of it. The training, the fighting, boring guard duty, marches, patrols, my unit." I looked up at him morosely. "Do you ever miss it?"

He considered. "In some ways."

I nodded. There were certain parts I would not miss either.

"It's not so much that I miss the war. It's more that I don't feel I belong here at home."

"What do you mean? You have a wonderful home. A family that loves you. Friends." He grinned and put his fist to his chest. "Me."

"I know."

He sobered and studied my face. "You have the heart of a warrior."

Not the heart of a homemaker. But there was so much more to it. I didn't belong anywhere.

"That girl you met at the gate of Antiparah," I said quietly to Muloki. "The one who lied to you and had a hidden dagger strapped to her leg—she was the real me." I pointed one of my fingers to myself and jabbed it into my chest. "So much more real than this one."

Muloki took a stool at the table and said calmly, "I think you're wrong."

I shook my head. "I'm kidding myself here." I gestured to the inside of the hut, the domesticity of it all. "This is the lie."

"You should seek the guidance of the Spirit."

I rolled my eyes at him. "Do you think that thought has never occurred to me? I ask in prayer all the time what I should do. I get no answer."

"Perhaps you are asking the wrong question."

I started to protest, but his words sank in, and I stopped.

"Or perhaps you think too much," he went on.

"What? I don't have anything to do but think."

"While you milk the goat. While you grind the maize. Tend the garden, sweep, weave, cook, carry water, launder clothing—"

"Stop! Yes!" I laughed.

He stood and went to my hammock. He crouched and

gathered all of my weapons, carrying them to the table with his large hands and dropping them with a clatter. "Stop doing these things that do not challenge you, that leave your mind to wander."

"But I'm supposed to cook and sweep and weave." I eyed the weapons wistfully.

"So do them. And then do what you love." He motioned to the weapons. "Your problem is this. You want to be doing all the proper things all the time so that when Zeke strides into the village he will see you doing them. He will see the girl he wants you to be."

Curse his perceptiveness! He was right. I didn't even have to acknowledge it.

"But what else is there for me? Zeke is the only man who wants me, and I'm not even sure about that anymore. You know he's stationed in Judea now."

When he just looked questioningly at me, I sighed and said, "That's where Eve lives."

Muloki chuckled. "Every man wants you. These men keep their distance because you claim to love Zeke."

I looked at him doubtfully.

"There are many men who want a warrior for the mother of their children. But nobody wants a wife who loves another man." He stepped closer to me. "You wear this like a shield."

At least he was speaking my language now, but I frowned. Wore what like a shield?

"What do you mean?"

"I will show you." He moved closer to me, his eyes intent on mine. "If you put your shield down, something like this might happen."

In the soft light from the low fire in the stove, Muloki leaned down and rubbed his cheek into my hair. I felt him brush a kiss there. Then I felt him take my slingshot from my hand and slip it into the belt at my waist, threading the rawhide through it with nimble fingers. It weighed heavy there because this belt was made for fashion, to match my sarong, not for combat.

He leaned down and kissed my neck, drawing tingles up and down my arms, and all I could do was close my eyes. I should have moved away, but I felt the hard handle of my axe as he placed it into my hand. He moved his fingers up my arms, wove them into my hair, and placed his last kiss on my lips. He didn't stop kissing me until a long, slow moment had passed.

At last he drew away and looked deeply into my eyes. He wasn't looking for acceptance of his kiss. He reached out to lift my dagger from the table and tied it onto my arm, pulling the rawhide thong tight so it pinched my skin with a familiar sting. He lifted my bow and laid it over my shoulder, just where I liked to wear it.

His eyes fell on my sword, sheathed in its leather, lying dormant on the table. He turned slightly toward it and unwrapped it. Holding it between us, firelight glinting off its beautiful obsidian, the shadows hiding the blood-soaked areas of the wood and highlighting the mysterious words inked in blue, Muloki said, "If you drop your shield, your dramatic, beautiful nature may shine like the moon again. If you drop this defense, you will have the freedom of motion to take an offensive stance."

I couldn't help smiling. I didn't know if what he said was true, but the way he said it was, at least for me. It was the first thing that had made sense to me since I had left Manti.

"If you drop this shield, you would have to admit—" He broke off, and his eyes slipped past me. I heard the mat at the door fall back. I turned but there was no one there.

"Darius," Muloki said. "He took one look and left."

And after Muloki said, "Think about this shield you carry," he left too.

The next morning, Darius went with Micah to purchase sheep, a small herd our families would share.

While they were gone, I went to see Cana who was still so happy she was glowing. She really was. A light shone around her face and her person, and everything she said made me smile. In a way, I wanted to be jealous of her happiness because surely it came from being at peace with who she was and where her life was headed. But I couldn't. She deserved happiness.

Micah did too, and I was sorry for what I had said to him.

I bid Cana goodbye and went to meet Micah and Darius in the pasture outside of town in the hills where they kept the sheep. I found them kneeling together mending one of the fences. I passed by several other small herds before I reached them, and by then they had noticed me, and Darius had made some excuse to leave.

I watched him walk away while Micah continued to work on the fence alone. After a moment of silence I said, "You chose fine sheep. They will give beautiful wool."

"Thank you. I think so too."

"I just saw Cana. She looks so happy."

"Mmm-hmm," he said around the rawhide lashings he had just clamped between his lips.

"I'm sorry for what I said. About Kenai. I didn't really mean it."

He took the rawhide from his mouth and lashed it tightly around two adjoining posts. "Yes you did. But it's okay."

"No it's not. I love you. It's not okay to be unkind to people you love."

He laughed. "It's not okay to be unkind to anyone."

"You're right, as always."

He cut off the unused portion of leather with his knife, one of Father's knives, like mine was. I stared at the top of his bent head, his hair shiny black in the sunshine, until he finished and stood. We began to walk toward Darius and the sheep.

He took a deep breath and let it out. "Do you really think I would be so heartless as to take no thought of Kenai's feelings? He is my brother. When Father died..."

He trailed off for a moment. I thought he was considering his words carefully, but I looked over and saw him swallow hard, attempting to push past a lump in his throat.

"When Father died, I became his father too, in a way. Do you think I don't know he enlisted in Moroni's army because of me? Because he couldn't face coming back here? If he dies there—"

"Micah," I said, but he waved me off and continued speaking.

"At first I had a feeling in my heart, when we were in Cumeni—starving, humble. I prayed a lot during that time—you know we all did—and the Spirit put the thought of marriage to Cana in my mind. I had never considered it before, though I can't think why now, and so I pushed the idea aside many times."

"Oh," I said. I wished he had told me that before, but I could see it was very special to him and why he would have wanted to keep it to himself. There were things in his life, especially as we grew older, that were not his sister's business. I wished I could have realized that sooner.

"Finally, the impression was so strong, that I sought out Kenai and discussed it with him. I knew a little of how he felt. I had seen them together as you had." I wished someone had told me that too. "His disappointment showed, but he agreed I should act on the prompting. So I did. I talked to Hemni, as I already told you, but I also talked to Cana. I couldn't imagine being married to her if she was in love with my brother. I had to know it from her."

We neared Darius. "I'm sorry," I said. "I didn't know all that."

"Let's just move on," he said quietly.

"You forgive me then?"

He looked down at me. "Before you even knew you were sorry."

Chapter 18

That afternoon I winced as I held the rawhide between my teeth and cinched the knot tight above my bicep. I slid my blade into its scabbard and strapped on the rest of my weapons—the bow, the quiver of arrows, the axe, the sling, the sword—and I went to the falls.

The trek through the trees was familiar. I passed the turnoff to the old training ground, the place Muloki had called humble. I remembered this with a light heart. In fact, the closer I got to the falls, the lighter my heart got. I could hear the rushing water before I emerged from the trees, but I passed through the mists and dropped most of my gear in the meadow beyond.

I went to the tree into which I had learned to throw my axe. It had grown, and the scar had healed over.

But it was still there.

I traced it with my fingers much the way I had traced Muloki's scar—the way that had put my mother into such a panic. I smiled at the memory of it. I had been more interested in the battle wound than I had been in Muloki.

I pulled in a deep breath and took my axe from my belt. Bouncing it a little in my hand, refamiliarizing myself with its weight and feel, I positioned my grip, and another memory surfaced.

Hold it here at the end of the hilt. Feel that?

For the first time in a long time, I did.

I moved back from the tree, first the twenty paces Gideon had taught me to throw from, then ten more.

I turned, and I threw.

The blade lodged into the tree with a hard thunk and in the quiet that followed, in the soft intake of my breath, I knew I had been dying at home in the village. I had let myself wilt like a moonflower in the heat of the morning.

I went to fetch the blade from the tree and saw that I had opened the old scar.

Again, showoff.

Satisfied, I moved back ten more paces for my next throw.

When I went home for the evening meal, my heart was light, and I knew I would not stop going to the falls to practice with my weapons.

"You look happy tonight," Mother said during the evening meal.

"I am happy," I said on a shrug and smothered a grin.

The next morning I did my household chores, but instead of staying in our courtyard to weave with Mother through the afternoon, I suggested she seek out some of her friends instead. I felt her eyes follow me as I ducked through the mat at the door with my weapons, but risking her disapproval anyway, I dropped them with a clatter and began to strap them on. I took a deep breath, but when I turned to her, I caught the glimpse of her smile as she tightened the threads of the pattern she worked on her loom. Filled with pleasure, I made the trek back to my own training ground.

The third morning, I didn't walk to the meadow. I ran.

Though I was weighed down with my weapons, I ran with wild abandon. I hopped over limbs, bounced off of rocks. I was fast and light. I was free. Nothing could make me stop, and nothing could catch me.

So it was strange when I felt eyes watching me from the trees as I dropped my gear near the river and knelt for a drink of the clear, cold water. I shook the water off my hand and wiped my mouth with the back of my arm as I leaned back on my heels and glanced around.

I didn't feel that prickle on my neck. No warning from the Spirit. The only thing I felt was the light touch of silent eyes.

I set up my targets near the trees and counted off my paces until I was farther away than I had ever been before. I took my axe from my belt—not the useless belt that matched my sarong, but the thick woven one Reb had made me—and I jostled it into position in my palm. I turned, and I threw it hard at the tree.

When I inspected the mark it had made, I saw that I had deepened the groove I had opened two mornings before. The old scar was almost obscured by the new damage.

I felt Gideon's presence as sure as I felt the breeze lift my hair off my neck. There was no way to be in this place without thinking of him.

I yanked my axe from the tree and threw until my arm ached. Each time when the axe left my hand, I knew it would hit my mark.

This training for nothing was ridiculous, but it felt right. My mind was clear, my heart was light, and my future did not look so bleak and pointless. Even my appetite was heartier.

If I had to be lonely, I wanted to do it here in the mists at the base of the waterfall where I could be honest with at least myself. Here in this meadow where I had so many memories that were good.

And only a few that weren't.

Suddenly, I dropped to the ground, rolled to the side,

sighted, and shot an arrow at my target. Again and again I did it until I had shot from a number of different angles.

I wished Pontus hadn't sold those fine arrowheads. All the arrows in my quiver were quite worn. Perhaps I would run to the place I had found the obsidian, gather the pieces to make more, and ask Kalem or maybe Muloki to help me do it. The army had taken a lot of the obsidian, but surely there were a few shards left for me.

Yes. I would sit with Mother—she could weave, and I would hammer arrowheads.

I could just see her face.

I ran all the drills I remembered from training with the army, and I did the extra exercises Gideon had taught me, the ones to increase my strength. I was surprised at how my muscles had atrophied and also pleased to find it did not take long to strengthen them again.

I stopped when evening began to fall, and I knelt near the river again for a drink. I had nearly forgotten about the silent eyes, but I felt them much heavier than I had before. Someone or something was here in the meadow.

My mind went back to the golden mountain lion I had seen on the hunt. I had looked up to see him staring at me. I had followed him and irrevocably taken his life. I had never seen a lion here, but it was not impossible.

I stood panting from exertion for a moment, hands at my waist, looking around. I pretended to be looking at the sky, the waterfall, the distant horizon, but I was searching the woods for a sign of another presence.

I hadn't really expected to find one, but I did, and my heart began to pound.

I slowly made my way closer, gathering my weapons as I went. The silent eyes were assuredly watching me now.

I thought I imagined the flowers gently bobbing in the water. But they were really there. A piece of rough bark was caught up in some reeds at the edge of the river, and on it floated three beautiful moonflowers. The large white blossoms had barely begun to open in the early evening.

And they had been freshly plucked from their vines.

"Gideon." His name stuck in my throat. I glanced up expecting to see him, and when he did not appear, I searched the woods again. I wanted to call out to him, to bid him to show himself, but I knew Gideon, and I knew if he wanted to show himself he would be standing before me already. I didn't know why he stayed away, but I could respect his wishes even when mine were so very different.

So instead of calling out, I knelt, took one beautiful bloom from the bark, wove the stem into my black hair, and sent the others floating downstream.

When I entered our courtyard, Mother and Darius were waiting for me.

"Where have you been? We're going to be late for the evening meal."

I was not late getting back. I looked over my shoulder at Dinah's. Even if we were eating with Hemni and Dinah and their girls tonight, I still was not late for the evening meal. Our mothers were very consistent with mealtimes.

Catching my glance, Mother said, "We're going to Kalem's. Melia is cooking."

If that was the case, then we did have to leave immediately.

"Alright," I said. "Just let me put my gear away." My gear consisted solely of weapons, something both Mother and Darius noticed.

Melia was beaming when we arrived. And then she was busily serving us food.

Mother got up to help her, but I stayed put on my stool in the yard. Somewhere, Kalem had acquired more stools for this night.

I looked around. Suddenly, this looked more like a celebration than merely another evening meal.

"What's going on?" I whispered to Darius.

He shrugged, but Muloki overheard and gave me a wink.

I could see that Mother was agitated and obviously wished to assure Melia she had done well. So I too made sure to compliment Melia on her cooking. It was different than Mother's, but good, and I asked her for her recipes.

I helped clean up the dishes, taking them to rinse in a small stream that ran nearby. When I arrived back at Kalem's, I saw that Micah and Cana had arrived. Cana sat near Darius, while Micah talked with Kalem a distance away.

"I didn't know you were coming," I said to Cana as I sat next to her.

"We wanted to be here earlier, but we were eating with my family. They've received a letter from Jarom."

"Is he well?"

"He seemed to be."

Kalem cleared his throat and we all looked at him. Micah stood at Cana's side with a hand on her shoulder. Darius leaned forward resting his elbows on his knees. Mother stood and went to stand beside Kalem.

"I'm glad you've all come," Kalem said simply, taking a moment to look each of us in the eye. "I have all the people I love here tonight. I am a blessed man. I have been reunited with my Melia at last. In Muloki I have found the son I never had. And for many years, I have considered the rest of you my family." He paused, and then he deliberately took Mother's hand in his own. "And now Leah has agreed to make it all official."

I looked up at Micah. He already knew. I glanced at Cana, but she was as surprised as I was. Darius jumped to his feet.

"Finally!" he exclaimed.

My eyes found Muloki's. He sat across from me. He let his happiness for Kalem show, but he looked at me with a thoughtful gaze.

Then he turned his eyes to Melia.

I saw them warm, but his lips were set in a frown. I knew

what was happening. He was choosing between us. And I knew that in the end he would choose Melia, because I pushed everyone away.

I stood and went to hug my mother. "You will be happy," I told her.

As the evening went on, I watched Mother and Kalem hold hands after so many years of not touching at all.

I watched Melia and Muloki work together, smiling, to finish the evening chores. Muloki slept outside now and worked all day away from the hut, but they both lived there with Kalem. It wouldn't be long.

I watched Cana gently and so easily getting Micah to do what she wanted him to do.

I stayed as long as I could stand it, and then I said, "Dare, you want to walk me home?"

He did, and we told everyone we would see them later.

"Did that feel weird to you?" he asked.

I knew exactly what he meant, and I laughed with the relief of being away. "Yes. It seems you forgot to bring yourself a girl."

"Well, I did think of bringing Mui..." he said with a grin.

"Oh, no," I giggled. "You musn't steal your brother's girl."

We both sobered at that.

"No," he said quietly. "But it has all worked out for the best. Micah and Cana are happy."

But Kenai wasn't.

"Cana said her family had a letter from Jarom today."

He brightened. "Yes. An embassy came in to Melek with letters and packages from Nephihah."

"Did you get a chance to read their letter?"

"No, but I read my own." He reached into his satchel and pulled out a fold of thick flax paper. "Here."

I took it and read it as we walked. "He sounds wonderful," I said with relief. Darius watched me closely. As I read to the end, I began to feel my face heat, and when I had finished, I folded it over quickly and handed it back.

Darius reached out, let his hand hover near it, but did not take the letter from me.

"What's going on?" he asked after he had studied me for a moment. "Is there something going on between you and Jarom?" At last he took the letter and replaced it into his satchel.

"Nothing's going on," I insisted. "Only that Jarom wishes for something between us," I added, deciding to be honest. Jarom had written it into Darius's letter anyway, and Darius was closer than a brother to him. There was no point in trying to hide it, not anymore. "At least, that's what he wished for before I left Manti."

Darius sighed. "I was afraid of that."

"You knew?"

"I noticed things. I think it troubled him greatly. I'm surprised you knew."

"He told me. Otherwise, I wouldn't have. I didn't notice anything."

"No," he scoffed. "I guess you wouldn't."

I ignored his rude comment. "What am I to do about it? It appears as though his feelings have not changed, and that they have in fact deepened."

"Could you return them?"

"No," I said softly. "Never."

"Because of Zeke?"

"Because I am a person of honor. It would be too cruel. I love Jarom as I love you, but there cannot be more."

"I know," he said.

Dusk was falling over the forest. I heard an owl in the trees, a wolf in the distance.

"Do you really love him as you love me?" Darius asked after a time.

"No," I admitted. "But it could never be enough."

He heaved a burdened sigh and changed the subject. "What have you been doing in the forest with your weapons? Not hunting. I never see you bring home meat."

I glanced at him. "Just practicing. Training."

"For what?"

"For nothing. It's dumb. A waste of time." I sighed deeply. "But it is the only time I feel like myself, Dare."

"Oh, I understand," he agreed readily. "I feel the same way."

"You do?"

"Sure. That was our whole life for a long time. Raising sheep and watering the fields is not exactly what I want to do either."

"What *do* you want to do?" I asked, realizing I had never actually put much thought to his ambitions.

He shrugged. "It doesn't matter. But I should have guessed you were feeling this way too. I mean, look at you—you can't even walk through the forest without feeling you need someone with you. Habits like that don't just go away."

I hadn't recognized it, but he was right. Walking through the forest wasn't even enjoyable anymore because I always felt like something was missing.

But when I ran, light and free, I experienced the old joy.

In that moment, I realized why Gideon had given me the ball. I thought of the countless hours we had spent kicking the ball with our unit, joking and laughing together. And with a sudden warmness in my heart, I thought of the times he and I had played alone, keeping the ball aloft between us while we talked, smiled helplessly, and fell in love.

Men are that they might have joy.

I took the ball from my satchel and ran my thumb over the soft leather.

"What do you have there?" Dare asked.

I gave a prayer of thanks in my heart and tossed the ball high into the air. When it came down again, I hit it with my elbow to my brother, who enthusiastically returned hit for hit.

When morning came, I stepped out of the hut into the

silver dawn. Clouds hung low on the horizon. They were dark but beautiful and full of life-giving water.

I milked Mui, but I placed a loose rope over Abigail's neck and walked her over to Chloe's. I had talked to Mother about giving her back, and she agreed we didn't need two milk goats.

"Chloe!" I called outside their gate.

When she came through the mat at the door, I saw her look at Abigail and then at me in confusion.

"She misses you," I said. "She won't give sweet milk to me." I patted Abigail's head, knelt down and handed the rope over to Chloe.

Her eyes widened and she threw her arms around me, almost knocking me over with her joy.

"Oh, thank you Ket-ah!"

"You are welcome, little Kanina." I hugged her back, squeezing her so tight she squealed with laughter.

Isabel came out of the hut then, and she gave a teasing little grimace when she saw that the goat was back. "Good morning," she said politely to me as Chloe led the goat into the yard.

Hemni and Dinah came from the hut, talking busily about the day ahead. When Hemni had tousled Chloe's hair, winked at me, and patted the goat, he walked out through the gate to go to his tannery for the day. Isabel followed him.

I caught Dinah's eye. Isabel was thirteen, and she put in long days sometimes with Hemni. Dinah sighed, exasperated.

"She reminds me of you," she said, adding a smile to the sigh. I couldn't tell if it was a compliment or not.

I looked to where Hemni and Isabel were disappearing into the trees.

"Zeke ought to like that," I said. "At Cumeni, after he fainted, the first thing he said when he became conscious was that one of me was bad enough."

She laughed at this. "One of you is hardly enough," she said. "The world needs more girls like you and Isabel."

"Girls who do a man's work?" I asked, frankly surprised at her opinion.

She tilted her head. "Well, no. Not exactly, I guess. Girls who follow their hearts. Girls who obey the Spirit. Follow their own path. Girls who do not waste their talents simply because someone says it is not right or insists they can't do it."

"I wish you would have gotten that idea through to your son," I said with a little smile.

"Oh, you know Zeke has his own mind and heart. He is a good son. Immovable, stubborn—those can be such good qualities."

I gave a little snort.

"If they are not met with such stalwart resistance," she conceded.

I studied her face. Dinah had kind eyes, lined with many years of laughter, brimming with many years of hardship. She looked at me with faith and love.

I sighed and asked plaintively, "Dinah, do you wish very much for me to marry Zeke?"

She pressed my arm and led me to sit in the courtyard. "I wish very much for you to follow your heart. Does it lead you to Zeke?"

"I do love Zeke," I told her. "Very much."

"Well, I know that, dear." She patted my hand and left her hand resting on mine. "You must ask yourself if you can live without Zeke. Can you be happy without him?" She looked to where Hemni had disappeared into the trees. "I once felt as you do."

I turned my hand into hers and clasped it. I couldn't imagine her being conflicted about marrying Hemni. He was so steady, so honest, so hard-working, filled with goodness, and was very handsome besides. He loved her and their children beyond measure.

"It was very much the same as for you. He was the son of my father's friend. At the time, I felt my decision was rushed. In the end, my father made it for me because I could not. But I trusted him, and I trusted Hemni. And I trusted that they did not want me to be unhappy. Neither of them wanted my heart to be in turmoil."

My eyes shot to hers. She smiled. "And after a time, it wasn't."

"You make it sound so easy."

She laughed. "If you didn't love Zeke so much, you wouldn't be so troubled. You are trying to think of a way out of the marriage that won't cause him pain. It's just not possible. So you tell yourself you will marry him, and it's no wonder you look at me with confusion in these sad eyes."

My heart jumped into my throat. "Dinah," I whispered.

She gave me a grave look. "Even if I had not witnessed Gid kiss you at your gate, did you think your mother would not have told me about him?"

I looked down into my lap, my face hot as coals.

She put her arm around me, encircling me in her warm understanding. "It can be noble to do as your family wishes, my dear, but be honest with yourself and realize that is why you have done it. It takes strength to follow that path." She squeezed my shoulders. "But it takes as much strength or more to follow a new path, to blindly step where the Lord leads you."

"I'm not sure I understand."

"Sometimes, the fiercest battles in life are not fought on the battlefield. They are fought inside the heart."

I put my arms around her and hugged her. "Thank you, Dinah. I will think on this."

She took a deep breath. "Do more than think," she advised. "You have decided in your mind to choose my son, and I see that you have nothing but turmoil in your heart." She paused and tried to hide her sadness. "Choose differently, and hear what the Spirit tells you then."

Chapter 19

I was standing at the top of the falls when I saw a band of Nephite soldiers come in on the West Road. This was not an unusual sight. A great many of the striplings had come home when Micah and Darius had, and I still frequently saw soldiers coming and going.

I thought I recognized the loping gait of the leader of this band of men, and so I ran down to the meadow, strapped on my weapons, and darted through the thick vegetation toward the West Road. I came out ahead of them and waited above the road in the evergreen leaves. My heart filled with excitement as they came around the bend and I could see them clearly.

I slid down the hill on my feet, a skill I had learned while building the embankment in Judea, and began to walk toward them on the road.

About two units of men approached me, a wide grin forming on their leader's face.

"I didn't expect a welcoming committee," called Kenai.

When he spoke, I broke into a run. I reached him, and he

picked me up and swung me around like a child.

It was strange, but I barely registered it at the time. We normally weren't any more affectionate with each another than light teasing. Kenai had gotten taller, and hard, and new scars marked his arms, his temple, and a scary one bisected his throat.

I noticed this all at a glance while I registered the other men stopping too and pulling up their water skins.

"Are we close then?" one of the men asked.

"Another hour by the road," someone else answered, and I knew his voice.

I turned and saw Jarom making his way up through the loose ranks.

I was stunned at how much he had changed. He hardly resembled Zeke at all now. He hardly resembled himself. He had cropped his hair very short, and it stuck out in a way that was adorable. But that was the only thing adorable about him. He had developed the muscles I had always sought for myself. He had grown several inches taller, which made his leathern kilt look shorter. He had become broader through the chest and thicker in the arms. He was seventeen, but he was full grown. Like Kenai, he had new scars and his eyes had seen more, much more, than mine had.

The men were calling to Kenai, whistling, telling him his girl was pretty. And they were much less polite than I expected them to be.

Jarom stood looking me over, drinking me in with his eyes, arms folded over his huge chest. He laughed. "Keturah is the captain's sister!" he called back over his shoulder. "She is *my* girl!" And he picked me up and kissed me, brief but hard and full on the mouth in front of two units of cheering soldiers.

When Jarom set me down, I slapped his face, much to the amusement of the men. But I couldn't resist the laughter in his eyes, and my mouth twisted up into a smile despite myself.

I offered to lead them up through the trees and Kenai looked longingly toward them, but in the end decided to continue on the road. So I traveled with them, flanked by Kenai and Jarom and felt more comfortable than I had in all the time I had been home—well over a year now.

"Are you home for Mother's wedding? Will you be going back? Have you been stationed at Nephihah all this time? Was Captain Moroni there? What is he like?"

"Whoa, Ket," Kenai laughed. "One question at a time."

I took a breath. "Are you here to stay?"

He and Jarom exchanged a glance. "Yes," he said.

"Captain." Someone had come up beside Kenai as we walked. I leaned forward to peer around my brother and groaned out loud when I saw who it was.

"Allow me to greet your sister," Mahonri said with a glint in his eye that looked more like a sneer.

Kenai drew his knife with a flourish and cast a meaningful look at Jarom. "The next man who greets my sister dies."

Barks of laughter, guffaws, and challenges went up through the trees, but I noticed Kenai did not sheathe his knife. These were not the same boys I had gone to war with, boys who relied on the prophet and on the Spirit implicitly. These were men who had fought in the ranks of the regular Nephite army.

When the soldiers settled back into their own conversations, Kenai asked, "How is Mother?"

"Happy."

"I'm happy for her too. She's had enough grief."

"Much of it caused by you when you joined Moroni's army."

"Do not start talking about who has caused Mother the most grief."

He had a point.

"We should both be tied up and shot with our own bows," I conceded.

"I'll load the arrows," Jarom offered.

"You've caused your own Mother grief," I told him.

"Nah," he said. "She's got the girls to keep her company. She doubtless barely notices I've been gone."

My eyes shot to his. "I hope you don't believe that," I said.

He shrugged and grabbed my hand.

This Jarom was very little like the Jarom with the brooding eyes and slow smile I had left in Manti. The brooding was still there but hidden by these strange smiles that did not ring true. This was a wall, one he did not seem to be letting down. Whether he was protecting himself from my reaction to his arrival home or from something else, I didn't know, but I would not wall him out. I would be honest with him.

I tried to let go, to shake his hand away, but he held on tight, teasing me.

I couldn't help but laugh a little. "Jarom!" I said. "I should tell you right now that I'm in love with someone else. There can be none of this," I held our hands up, "between us."

He dropped my hand and placed his over his heart. "You wound me," he said dramatically. But then he leaned in closer and said, "But we don't need love to kiss in the moonlight."

Kenai cleared his throat. "Don't make me skin you alive."

Jarom spared barely a glance for my brother as he snaked an arm around me, inappropriately cupping my waist with his hand. I gave a little yelp, and he drew me to a stop so he could place his other arm around me and pull me much too close to him.

But he had caught my arm between us. I threw it up and jammed the heel of my palm into his nose, causing it to bleed instantly.

A little blood would not set back a seasoned soldier like Jarom for long, even if I had broken his nose—which I hadn't—so I punched him in the stomach and proceeded to drop him to the ground.

The men around us fell silent.

I had my blade at Jarom's neck.

"No need to skin him, Kenai," I said. "I'll do it myself."

Jarom stared up at me with fire in his eyes and deep red blood slowly seeping from his nose. "You're perfect," he said.

I tried not to show how his comment pleased me. I touched the sharp edge of the blade to his skin. "Your mother would have my hide if I skinned you before she can cook you a welcome meal, but I think you do need a shave."

He reached a hand up and rubbed it over his stubbled cheek. "Captain, call off your sister."

Kenai gave a huff of amusement. He moved off down the road, and the others followed their captain. "Can't you control your own girl?" he called back over his shoulder.

I glanced up at Kenai's retreating back, which was a mistake. No sooner had I done so than Jarom kicked himself up and reversed our positions. He held both my wrists above my head with one strong hand.

I stared up into his face, calmly allowing him to pin me down. There was no point in struggling. There was no way for me to get up unless he permitted it. We'd wrestled in dog piles with my brothers many times over the years, and when he had been younger and smaller, I had been able to hold my own at times. But not now.

"I mean it, Jarom. Friendship is all I can offer you."

"Is friendship all you feel for me?"

I swallowed. There was no way to answer that question. "We've been apart so long we're practically strangers."

He nodded agreement, but said, "You haven't changed. You still fight first and talk later. You still have no idea what you do to a man."

"And how would a boy like you know?"

His eyes flashed with hurt.

I swallowed again. "Let me up," I said.

He immediately moved, got to his feet, and held out a hand, which I took. We started after the company of men, who were moving along the road with all their gear rattling softly around them.

I handed Jarom a folded bandage from my satchel for his nose. "Friendship it will be then, Ket," he said as he absently dabbed at the small amount of blood there. "Only, will you keep your mind open to the possibility of more?"

"That's the first thing you've said that makes sense," I said. "I may be the same, but you have changed."

He slowly let out a deep breath. "I know."

"Kenai has too," I said.

"Kenai has too," he agreed. "Don't judge us, though, Ket."

I laughed a little. "Don't forget that I've been to war myself. I've seen what you've seen."

He stopped walking, and I drew to a stop too, turning to face him.

"You haven't." His brown eyes became intense. "You'll get along with both of us better, especially Kenai, if you realize that now."

I searched his eyes, wishing I knew what he meant, and I did him the courtesy of not asking more questions.

"Darius will be glad to see you," I said as I turned to walk again. "He's getting pretty tired of hanging out with me."

"I'll be glad to see him too. Has he found a girl yet?"

"Are girls all you think about? And no, now that you mention it, he has not been looking for a girl."

"Wise man. You girls are all trouble."

"I thought you'd *never* realize that." I heaved a melodramatic sigh while I wondered silently who else he was talking about.

"Well I didn't say *you* wouldn't be worth the trouble."

"Ha. Every other man I know has decided I am not worth the trouble. Save yourself the hassle and find a better girl. There are many better girls than me."

He brushed my hand, but didn't take it. "I hope you don't believe that."

That startled me. I did believe it. I considered myself basically unmarriageable and figured any man that Micah wrangled into marrying me would be settling for a very poor wife in exchange for the novelty of having a warrior launder his tunics.

"Don't settle on me, Jarom. That's all."

"I was right. You haven't changed."

But he was wrong. I had.

The people of the village were already out on the street greeting Kenai. The rest of the men had gone on to the city or other towns and villages where their own families lived.

Mother was still hugging him, and Dinah was waiting anxiously near her elbow, probably to demand of Kenai where her second son was.

When she saw Jarom walk into the village whole, healthy, and smiling, she placed her hand over her mouth and her face crumpled—her whole body crumpled—into tears of relief.

Jarom stepped to her and folded her into his arms. "Ah, mama, don't cry now," I heard him say into her hair. I moved away to give them their moment of reunion.

Micah and Darius were working, so as Mother drew Kenai into the courtyard and offered him food, I said I would go fetch them home.

I stopped to get Kalem, Melia, and Muloki on my way back. Kalem and Muloki were hauling their goods into the lean-to on the back of the hut. It was full, so I knew they would be setting out in the morning for other markets.

"Mother wishes you all to come for the evening meal tonight to celebrate Kenai's homecoming."

Kalem's face lit as if it were his own son returning.

"What can I bring?" asked Melia. "Bread? I have some made."

"That would be perfect, thank you."

Melia made the most wonderful bread from wheat and other grains. I couldn't believe I had gone my whole life eating only corn cakes.

"I'll hurry with the inventory," Muloki said, and I

watched as he returned to the merchant's cart at the back of the courtyard.

"Do you travel as far as Judea to market?" I asked Kalem.

"Not usually," he said. "Their trade comes in on the South Road, but I have been to their market on occasion. Why?"

I shrugged the question away, but he had to know. I still had not heard from Zeke. He was so obviously avoiding me and the family obligations he would have when he returned home. Kalem gave me an encouraging smile, but it faded when he saw my eyes turn to Muloki.

I joined Muloki at the cart. He was making tally marks on a scroll, but he set it down and tossed me an apple with a grin.

"Thanks," I said as I caught it. "Listen." I stepped closer. "Kenai watched you at the gate of Antiparah for days. Weeks. He was the one who asked me to go in. He may recognize you."

"Kenai was your commander that day?" he asked.

"Yes."

"I cannot wait to meet the man who would do this to his sister."

Muloki felt the same way about it as Gideon and Micah had—he didn't like it.

I touched his scarred arm. "I agreed. I obeyed his command and received miracles in return. I met you. You have come here and found a new family, new friends, the Gospel. You have fallen in love."

He glanced at Melia, busily gathering things to take to the village, though I could see he tried to stop himself from doing it by looking down.

"Do not think harshly of Kenai. You will see that he loves me. I considered it a high honor that he esteemed me capable of that mission." Then I added more softly, "You have not hurt me. I wish you all the happiness with your Melia that an old warrior can find."

He flashed me his grin, the one that still melted my knees and, if I was being honest with myself, probably always would.

I cleared my throat. "Kenai might not remember you. If he doesn't, I don't think we should bring it up." Everyone else knew about Antiparah, but somehow I didn't think Kenai would see Muloki as everyone else did.

Muloki nodded, and I turned to leave.

"Keturah," he said, his accent still heavy. "I will never do ill to the man who made it possible for me to find the Gospel." His eyes went again to Melia. *And love.* He didn't say that. He didn't need to.

"See you in a while," I said. I waved to the others and left.

My three brothers sat together in the courtyard while Mother and Cana bustled about.

I could see Dinah and her girls bustling about their own yard. It saddened me a little that Cana's first priority was to her husband's family. This was a joyous day for her own family too, after all. No one would have begrudged her helping her own mother, but Cana was very proper in all things. That was one of the things I envied most about her.

But her eagerness to serve in this way and the ease and practice with which she did it took the pressure off of me to do it. I felt both relief and shame for this.

When Kalem, Melia and Muloki came through the gate, I sensed Kenai's tension almost immediately, though I couldn't say if it was from recognition or from something else entirely.

I couldn't describe what was different in Kenai's personality, but it was something. Whatever Jarom had been alluding to—that thing, or things, they had both seen that I had not—it had changed them both. They wore their disillusionment as prominently as they wore their weapons. Their eyes had a bleakness in them I wasn't sure the absence of fighting and the love of their families could easily wash away.

I thought of my sprained ankle dangling in the headwaters of the Sidon River and how it had taken so long for the pain to ease. Surely God could heal their hearts in time.

But for now, Kenai wore an expression I was sure they

both would have been wearing if Jarom had been beside him. The Lamanites had been the enemy on the battlefield for more than five long years, and here the enemy stood before us in our own courtyard.

Kenai slowly stood and regarded Muloki.

Muloki regarded him back.

Mother, oblivious to the undercurrents of entrenched suspicion, performed all the introductions.

Instead of reaching out to politely clasp arms, Kenai stepped forward and threw a punch at Muloki's face.

"Control yourself, soldier!" Kalem barked out before Kenai made contact. And he surely would have because Muloki made no move to dodge or counter the punch.

Kenai instantly pulled his arm back, but stood shaking with rage in the midst of us all.

I had seen this before, and of course Kalem had too—men who could not stop fighting when the fighting was done. I had seen men who curled into small balls, whispered for their mothers, and refused to fight even before the fighting had begun. And I had seen various degrees of both of these extremes.

Every stripling was stalwart, brave, faithful, and firm in his belief that God would deliver him. But just as none of them had escaped physical wounds, none of them had escaped the mental effects of battle.

Darius still slept on his sword, and I felt uncomfortable without a companion in the woods. I was only at peace with a weapon in my hand, but had nightmares every night of slitting defenseless throats on the Cumeni crossroad.

Kenai threw punches at Lamanites.

It was the same thing.

"Come on, son," Kalem said. "Your mother has prepared a wonderful meal for you." He tenderly took Kenai by the shoulders and led him to a stool at the far end of the yard where Kenai sat and put his head in his hands without looking at anybody.

Chapter 20

Mother and Kalem were married on a misty day in between bursts of rain showers. Some of the village women thought this was a bad omen. They whispered it behind their hands, as they had once whispered about me, while we waited for the men of the wedding party to come for us.

But the rain, the smell of it and the gray clouds, reminded me of the drizzly evening I had spent in the Judean guard tower with Gideon. On rainy days, I felt wistful longing, and I felt it heavily on that one as I watched my mother be wed.

When the high priest addressed Mother by her full name and title, Leah of Middoni, Daughter of Helam, Wife of Rabbanah, she glanced guiltily at her four children who stood in various degrees of confusion around the canopy.

Glancing at my brothers, I could see that Micah knew, or had at least suspected.

Those gates he remembered Father leaving through had not been small garden gates like we had in the village, and I thought his memories were probably making more sense to him.

But I could see neither Kenai nor Darius knew who Father was or what that made us.

After the ceremony, Micah gave Cana a kiss before she went to serve the food to the guests, and the four of us drew aside together.

"Did I hear that right?" Kenai asked Micah as he visibly tried to ignore the kiss. "Rabbanah? The powerful and great king?"

"You did," I said. "I heard Kalem talking about it once."

"Eavesdropping?" Darius asked.

I shrugged.

"But why did she never tell us this?" asked Micah. "Why didn't you?"

It wasn't that I hadn't wanted to. I hadn't known how to. I shrugged again. "How was I to bring it up? I didn't even know if it was true. But I have thought on it, and I think it was a part of Mother's life that no longer existed, a life she had forsaken completely. I think it pained her a great deal to speak of Father."

"But, if this is to be believed, Micah is the heir to the throne of the Lamanites, and he lives in a hut in a tiny village," Kenai protested.

"Would it have changed anything?" I countered. "Would we have acted differently if we had known?"

"Yes!" Kenai insisted. "I'd have acted...better."

"How long have you known?" Micah asked.

"How long have you? I could see on your face that it wasn't a surprise."

"I didn't know." But then he grimaced. "I have many unexplained memories, that's all. Memories I have never put words to."

Micah had been six when Father died, Kenai barely five. Kenai was frowning now in an effort to recall something of the past, but Darius was like me, with no way of remembering the Land of Middoni, royal courts, or Father.

"That explains my steel jaguar shield," said Darius.

"And my full body armor," Micah added with an unexpected note of humor.

I looked to Mother and Kalem where they were receiving well-wishers. She caught my eye and grimaced in a kind of apology, but I gave her an encouraging smile and a little wave. I had long since made my peace with her silence on this matter. She had a reason, just as we all had reasons for the choices we made, and we would hear it later.

I turned back to my brothers. "Kalem's army went to battle specifically to remove the king from power. They did not like that Father had joined the Church of God."

"You should have told us," said Kenai, hands on his hips, staring at me.

I looked down. "I should have, and I'm sorry."

"Let us give Mother her joyous day without pressing her," Micah decided for us. "Let her tell us about our heritage when she feels the time is right, in her own time and her own way."

My brothers and I looked toward Mother, and we all agreed.

Over the next days, I took Kenai with me to the falls several times, thinking he might find a measure of peace there like I did, but he seemed to be more at ease working in the corn fields, and so after the morning meal at home, we would part company for the whole of the day.

On my first day alone again, instead of going to the falls, I went to the place of obsidian. It was abundant and I knelt among the broken shards and gathered what I needed quickly.

But I didn't leave.

I stayed on my knees, and I silently told God what I had decided to do. I had prayed so many times about this, but where I had felt confusion before, a whorl of turmoil and indecision, there remained nothing but stillness in my heart.

The only thing left to do was act on it.

I found Micah in the hills with his sheep. He was sitting on a small outcropping of rock and writing, probably poetry, on a tablet of thick flax paper.

I climbed the outcropping and sat beside him.

I looked out over the land. Lush and green, it was covered with trees and beautiful plants of all kinds. Perhaps some would see only a beautiful landscape. Perhaps Micah saw food for his sheep. I always saw medicines, the potential to heal and ease pain.

But that day I saw only a long ago battle. I saw Zeke standing firm between Muloki and me—his dark blood streaming onto the ground, in excruciating pain, perilously faint, ready to fight to the death for me, prepared to die before he let anything hurt me. I relived it over and over.

I stared forward, seeing only that moment in my mind. "I don't want to marry Zeke," I said hoarsely without looking at my brother.

He didn't say anything, but I felt him watching me, watching the tears silently trail down my face. They flooded from my eyes. I didn't blink them back. I didn't wipe them away. I owed Zeke my tears at least.

"But I will respect your wishes. I will marry him if you desire it, and I will be a happy bride and spend the rest of my life striving to be a good wife to him."

I got up to go, but I turned back after a few paces and looked Micah in the eye for the first time, though my chin trembled.

"I never lied to you," I said, and my voice broke. "I love him—" I choked on a breath but made myself say the whole truth. "So dearly."

I walked to the old training ground. The beans and squash were almost ready to harvest again. I walked through the field and noticed that the old farmer kept it up well. No weeds threatened to choke out the plants. No debris clogged the furrows, and water would move freely through the field.

It *was* humble there.

I took the nearly invisible path to the meadow, and when

I got there I dropped my satchel and all my gear into the long grasses and waded into the pool at the base of the falls. I stepped under the cascade of water and let it drench me, let it wash away my tears.

Later I sat on the bank, letting the rays of the sun keep my wet skin warm.

Telling Zeke would be easy compared to telling Micah had been. If Zeke had been anyone else, I would have refused to marry him. I loved Gideon. But Zeke had meant too much to me, and I to him.

I don't want to marry Zeke.

Had I actually said the words? They were bitter and hurtful and truer than any I had ever said.

The only thing that stopped me from leaving immediately for Judea was Micah. I had told him I would marry Zeke if he asked it of me, and I had meant it. I would make good on my words. He was my elder brother, and I would yield to his wishes.

When at last I returned to the village, damp and vulnerable, I saw Micah talking to Hemni. Making official arrangements or dissolving the expectation of them?

He spoke to Mother and Kalem too. Because they were married, he could rightly allow Kalem to take responsibility for me and my well-being and my marriage, but I knew he wouldn't. I could see he worried over my welfare a great deal, and I had been cruel and petty to accuse him of wishing his responsibilities away.

The only person he didn't talk to was me. In fact, I thought he was avoiding me. I didn't see him for days afterward, and when I finally did see him, he didn't mention Zeke or my marriage or my failings. Several weeks went by and no one mentioned Zeke.

On a market day that dawned with clear skies, I went with Mother to the main square of Melek. I left Mother at Kalem's tables and walked through the market with Melia.

Shopping in the market with Melia was a different

experience than shopping with Cana or even Mother. It bemused me to see her fawn over all the beautiful things. Melia had been born into the upper class and her mother and grandparents had spoiled her, always given her anything she wanted. Even now, though Kalem was not rich, he was not poor either, and he indulged many of her desires in the market.

Muloki, too, enjoyed purchasing gifts, and Melia was the recipient of many of his whims.

When we stopped at Pontus's tables, he grinned broadly and directed Melia's attention to his new stock of bracelets. He liked showing blades to me, but he loved selling jewelry to Melia. I had to smile. Neither one of them had any idea their tastes were extravagant.

"Did you get any more of those arrowheads, the obsidian ones?" I asked him when Melia was busily admiring the jade and silver jewelry.

Pontus shook his head. "But I do have some made from steel."

Steel arrowheads? "Let me see."

He directed me to the opposite end of the table, and stood with me for a moment until Melia called to him.

I waved him away and picked up one of the arrowheads to examine it.

It certainly was sharp. The straight edges angled toward a small point at the tip. I set it down and picked up another that had a serrated edge and then another that had a hooked barb on the side.

I glanced up when Kenai appeared at my side.

"That barb prevents the arrow from being easily pulled from its victim," he said after he had inspected it in my hand for a few moments.

I knew that.

"Clever," he went on. "But not very original. That's the very essence of war. You can't get it out of you, and if you do, it leaves you damaged."

"I know," I said. "I miss it, even though it was so terrible."

"I don't miss it," he said. "But I'll never forget it."

"I won't either." Although, for me, unlike for Kenai, it had been the most magnificent time of my life, and I sometimes felt there was nothing left for me to look forward to.

But my mind often went to the moonflowers I had found floating in the river. I had only seen them that once.

I reminded myself how Gideon had not intervened when my unit teased and persecuted me. He had stood back and let me fight my own battles. To make me strong. To make me sure of myself. And I thought with tentative hope that maybe there could be something left for me. Maybe I could win this battle in my heart.

Kenai and I both noticed when Muloki came up beside Melia and rested a hand at her waist. She looked up at him with sparkling eyes. She had been so disillusioned when we had met, and it was good to see her happy now. I was glad that she had found her father at long last, and from the looks of her and Muloki lately, she had found her husband as well.

"Doesn't that make you mad?" Kenai asked quietly, his eyes already back on the weapons before us.

"No," I said, surprised that his thoughts had gone in a completely different direction than mine had.

"He came here to find you because he thought he was in love with you, and now he's in love with her."

I shook my head. "He came here because he felt the Spirit when he met me, and it compelled him to find the gospel and a new life here."

Kenai grunted.

"You don't like him."

He snorted. "Am I so transparent?"

"I like him a great deal. So does everyone else."

"Yeah, well no one else, including you, watched him for weeks in Antiparah. Ket, why do you think I sent you in on a day he was at the gate? He liked the pretty girls, and I knew he'd overlook your foreign dress and speech because of it."

"You know that what a soldier does in war does not indicate how he would act in real life."

"No, but it marks his character."

I thought of how Muloki had lost his five brothers in the war, and of what effect that might have on a man. When we were subjected to great trials, we either humbled ourselves or became hard-hearted. Muloki had been humbled enough to feel the Spirit I carried with me as I walked past him. Of Muloki and Kenai, it surprised me which one had hardened his heart.

I glanced at Muloki and lowered my voice. "And God can change the hearts of those who will let Him."

Kenai made no reply.

Instead, he reached into his satchel and withdrew some coins. "Get me the barbed one," he said and dropped the coins into my hand. He left before I could say anything, and I watched as he shouldered his way through the crowds.

I made the purchase and tucked the arrowhead into my own satchel. As I walked along with Muloki and Melia and pretended to admire her new bracelet, I thought about my brother and how he was aching and broken.

I wished I could help him, but I knew that I couldn't. I prayed that God would send him someone who could.

When I returned home from the market, I found Kenai in his hammock staring at the thatched roof of the dim hut.

"Here," I said and handed over the arrowhead I had purchased for him, very aware that the reason he hadn't made the purchase himself was because he didn't want to talk to Pontus. He didn't want to talk to anyone anymore.

"Thanks," he said, taking it from me without looking at me or the arrowhead.

"I'm going to the falls. Do you want to go?"

"No thanks," he replied blandly.

"We could go hunting instead."

"No."

"Kenai, I really think..."

He looked at me then, and it was worse than when he hadn't looked at me.

"Okay," I acquiesced, and I left him alone.

As I ran through the forest dodging limbs and branches, I wondered how long I could keep going out to work with my weapons. Surely soon Micah would tell me he had made arrangements with Hemni, and when Zeke came home, I would have neither the time nor the freedom to practice.

But Micah hadn't said anything. I seldom saw him, and when I did see him, he looked like he might approach me with news, but he always turned and walked away instead.

When I came into the meadow, I was surprised to see Muloki sitting on the log above the falls, because I had left him with Melia in the market just an hour before. I smiled and waved to him. He motioned me up, but I laughed and shook my head.

"No!" I called. I wasn't falling for that again.

"I won't push you in!" he called back down to me.

I hesitated, but after dropping my gear on the bank of the river, I climbed up and balanced along the log to sit next to him. I gave him a warning glance.

"I promise," he repeated, his accent melting my heart and sealing the deal.

When I was settled, he handed me a wrapped package.

"What's this?" I asked.

He might have turned a little red. "I bought them for you a while back and never had the right moment to give them to you. And then I met Melia." He paused uncomfortably. "And, well, I wanted you to have them anyway." He gestured to the package. "Open it."

I untied the twine that bound the little bundle and pulled back the cloth wrapping.

Obsidian arrowheads.

I sold them to an overconfident, swaggering young man who said he needed them to shoot rabbits.

"Leah said you gave most of your arrows away, and she knows you've been using the few you have. I'll attach them to shafts for you."

I could do that, but not as well as he could. I nodded, my eyes still on the beautiful arrowheads, my thoughts on all they might have meant.

If you let your shield down, something like this might happen.

"Thank you," I said. "I love them."

"I knew you would."

The gift was not a beautiful bracelet like Melia's, but it meant so much more because it wasn't. I wrapped the arrowheads back up.

"Where is Melia?" I asked him.

"She has gone to weave with the women. She makes friends easily." The note of pride in his voice made me smile.

"One of her many talents," I agreed. "She made friends with me, and I was a soldier of the conquering army."

"Could it be that you make friends easily too?" he asked.

"More like push friends away."

He frowned. "You are still too much alone."

Being alone was not my problem. Loneliness was my problem, and I didn't want to talk to Muloki about how lonely I was. I waved his comment off.

"It's better that way. I make people uncomfortable. They think I'm strange, which I am. They don't know what to say to me, and we always end up having miscommunications. It's just better when I keep to myself."

"Is there no one you can talk to?"

"Is that why you're here? To talk about my lack of friends?"

He crossed his arms. "Yes."

My eyes met his, but I shook my head again slowly. "Let's not talk about that. Tell me, what is this I hear about your betrothal? When will it become official?"

I could see he did not want to change the subject, but he said, "We will have the ceremony next month when the weather is better. We did not want to encroach upon Kalem and Leah's enjoyment of their own marriage."

I nodded. "How long will your betrothal last?"

"We are determined to wait the full year," he said.

"Mother and Kalem did not wait half that long."

"No. But they both have homes and property, household possessions. They didn't need time to acquire these things."

The conversation trailed off. It was funny but when Muloki was not flirting with me, it seemed we didn't have much to say to each other.

"Keturah, I'm worried about you," Muloki said after a long silence.

"Me? But I'm fine, Muloki."

He shook his head. "You should be betrothed. It is your brother's responsibility to see that this happens for you. I do not think he is fulfilling his duty to you."

"Oh, Muloki, that's sweet, but I'm sure Micah is having a difficult time finding someone who—"

"Do not speak that way about yourself!"

I felt my eyes widen at the harshness in his voice. "I only meant that Micah—"

"And do not make excuses for your brother."

"I don't even want to marry, Muloki. I'll be so bad at it. I don't think I could ever be happy keeping a home for some man."

He turned to me in surprise. "Some man? Your husband will not be just some man. And even if Micah married you to someone you didn't love, you would come to love him in time. You will keep a home for a man you love. It is a way you will show him that you love him, and your distaste for it will make that much stronger the testament of your love for him."

He bent a little to catch my eye. "Hmm?" he asked.

"I guess so." Why did he have to learn Nephite so well?

"It's like with fighting," he continued. "Those men who

hate fighting must give so much more of themselves in war than those who enjoy it. Take Kenai."

"Kenai—"

"Hates fighting. He has given so much of himself away, he has lost himself."

"And that's just the problem!" I exclaimed. "I will lose myself if I—"

"That's not what I'm saying at all." He shook his head. "Those who lose their lives for God's sake will find their lives."

"But it wouldn't be for God's sake. It would be for Micah's, and Zeke's, and everybody's but my own."

His eyes narrowed. "Is there no honor then in raising up a righteous family?"

"Well, yes, but—"

"Raising a righteous family is not done for God's sake?"

He had me there. I twisted my lips into a frown.

"What man could you do this for?"

"Excuse me?"

"Whose home could you keep with your love? Who do you love enough? Zeke?"

I looked away again.

"Not Zeke then." I could hear a smile in his voice. "Hmm. Not Jarom."

I couldn't help a smile at his gentle teasing, but only because I was sure he wouldn't see it with my face turned.

"Leah told me of your true love."

I slowly turned toward him. What had Mother said to him?

His smile sparkled in his eyes. "Ah, I see she was right. You have given your heart, but not to your Ezekiel."

Melia must have been talking about it too. She was the only one who called Zeke my Ezekiel.

"Is everyone talking about me like this?" I complained.

"Everyone but the two men who should be."

"He's gone." That was the first time in the year I had been

home that I had admitted there was someone besides Zeke in my heart. Though, apparently, everyone knew it anyway.

"I will go get him for you. Kenai says he is in Judea now."

Even Kenai?

I laughed nervously. "No. Don't do that."

If anyone went for him, it should be me.

"It will be easy. I will bring him here so we can settle it."

"It's not your job to settle it," I pointed out.

"But Kalem has married your mother, and when I marry Kalem's daughter, I will be your brother. So you see, it is my job to settle it."

I laughed. "Well, it would not be easy. He wants to be in the army. He doesn't want to come here, and he obviously doesn't want me. You'd have to fight him."

He grinned. "I would gladly fight him for you."

I shrugged. "You'd lose."

Whether it was more absurd to think that Muloki would fight Gideon and drag him here for me, or that he would lose to Gideon, I wasn't sure, but we both burst into laughter, and in the next instant I noticed someone standing on the bank.

"Hello, Ket."

Chapter 21

It didn't matter that I grimaced at how our conversation must have sounded. When I looked up at him, he wasn't even looking at me.

He was exchanging a look with Muloki as if he was trying to place where he had seen him before, and a big part of me hoped he didn't figure it out.

He was the only other person who would possibly recognize Muloki from the battle of Cumeni.

"Zeke!" I exclaimed.

He turned his attention to me and smiled.

"When did you get back?"

"This morning. Midday." He couldn't contain another suspicious glance at Muloki. "Have you been here all day?"

"No. Sit," I invited. As he stepped out onto the log, I said, "I was shopping in the market with my friend Melia, Muloki's betrothed." I gestured to Muloki by way of informal introduction.

Zeke relaxed a little, but I could see he was still uneasy

about Muloki's presence. He was obviously Lamanite—the age of a soldier. I could see his mind piecing the clues together.

"You remember Melia from Manti. She is Kalem's daughter."

"Oh, yes, I heard about that. Congratulations," he said to Muloki.

Muloki nodded as he got up to leave.

"You don't have to—"

"Yes," he said simply. "You have much to discuss with your Ezekiel."

Zeke watched him go, and before Muloki was even out of sight through the thick trees, Zeke asked with steady calm, "Keturah, do you know who that is?"

"Yes," I said. "But no one else does. Only the three of us know."

He took that in for a moment. "What is he doing here?" he asked. "And why are you friends with him?"

Zeke knew I had breached the gate of Antiparah, but I told him everything again, even adding how Muloki had flirted with me at the gate and come to Melek to court me.

He was mad at Kenai all over again for asking me to walk into the enemy stronghold, but I held firm that it had been an honor.

"Don't give Kenai trouble about it. He is..." How to put it? "Not the same. And besides, it was a long time ago. It was a decision he made—had to make—and it was not the wrong one."

"Yeah, I've talked to him. He's different."

Kenai had known Zeke was back in the village and hadn't told me?

"You're not going to get mad? You're not going to lecture me for walking into Antiparah or reprimand me for befriending the enemy?"

He looked at me with a kindness in his eyes I remembered from long ago. Despite my suspicion that Micah had sent for him, it was good to see him.

"It reflects poorly on me that you think any of those things might happen," he said.

"I didn't mean, I just meant... It's been that way for a while, between us..."

"Since I started courting you and pursuing something you were not comfortable with."

Oh, how I wished I was comfortable with it. I looked at my old friend, his hair the color of black ash and his eyes dark, warm, and familiar. I looked at his strong shoulders and the new lines around his lips. I looked at him with all my regret in my eyes.

He got to his feet, balancing easily on the log over the water. "Come on," he said with a sad smile. "Walk with me."

I hated that I was the cause of the sadness in his smile, but I got to my feet and followed him away from the river. We walked through the meadow silently side by side as we had many times before, but we didn't talk or accomplish any of the things that needed to be said. After a while, Zeke bent and picked a pink flower for me, which I took and thanked him.

He cleared his throat and said, "In Manti, when I told you Micah and Cana were to be married, you were so upset. Remember?"

"Yes, I remember."

"You cried."

I hummed softly. It was true.

"And I said you could talk to me about the reason why, even if you thought it would hurt me."

"Yes, Zeke, but I didn't know what you meant."

"Do you know now?"

"Oh, Zeke," I protested.

"You cried because you thought..."

"Zeke."

"You thought..."

I sighed and closed my eyes. "I thought Cana was marrying someone she didn't love."

"Because?"

"Because she thought she had to, because she thought her family wanted it, because Micah asked her first, and because she didn't know if Kenai would," I finally blurted out.

"Thank you," Zeke said.

"For?"

"For being honest with me. For always being honest with me. You've always known, and I never listened to you."

"Zeke, what are you talking about?"

He took a deep breath and turned to face me, drawing me to a stop. "You and I, mostly I, have been trying to make this work for a long time now."

"Zeke, you're scaring me. What are you saying?"

"What you've been saying all along."

I searched his face.

"There was a time when you lied to yourself about your feelings for me," he went on. "And heaven help me, I let you."

"But I've never lied to you." I grimaced and qualified that statement. "Except about coming here sometimes. But I've never lied about how I felt for you."

"Of course you haven't, Ket. You've always done your best, and I've made it so hard for you. You were right. Love is not jealous, as I have been. If I had truly loved you, I'd have been as noble as Seth and Lib and half the stripling army, and I wouldn't have allowed my jealousy to affect your life and your decisions, to dampen your spirit, or make you sad for one single moment."

"But you were just protecting me. You had an understanding with Micah and my family, and with me, and you had every right—even a responsibility—to tell me how to act."

He laughed a little. "Neither of us would ever rationalize lying to another, but we are both good at lying to ourselves."

Suddenly, I laughed a little too.

Soon we had circled the meadow. I checked the sky. It would be time to start toward home soon. Dinah probably had a feast prepared for the return of her eldest son.

"Should we start back home?" I asked.

Zeke checked the sky too and rubbed the back of his neck. "Not just yet. I want to be very clear."

"Clear about what?"

"About you and me, Ket." He paused for a moment, took a deep breath, and went on. "When I saw how it hurt you to think of Cana marrying someone she did not love—just the thought of it—all I could think was how it would break your heart if it were *you* who married without love. I couldn't do that to you."

I frowned. "But I do love you, Zeke."

"You wouldn't be marrying me because of love," he said as his sad eyes gazed stoically into the distance. He smiled a little, though. "I know you love me. It makes it so much harder, doesn't it?" His voice was gentle and held a note of finality.

"To let it go, you mean?" I asked with my heart in my throat.

He cupped my cheek with his hand and swept my hair back with his long fingers. "To let it go," he affirmed. "I should have come here and said this long before now."

"Why didn't you?" I had been lonely and confused for a long time. I could have used his help to sort it all out, but I hadn't been ready for it, and I knew it.

Zeke shrugged. "I thought with Gid gone, you might come to your senses, realize you loved me or something."

I took a breath.

Then my heart started to pound.

"What about our families? What about—"

He shook his head. "No," he said softly. "We will not marry for them. There has never been anything official between us, not even a promise. And we are lucky."

I raised an eyebrow.

"We both have loving and understanding families."

"That's true," I said, wondering exactly what Micah had told him to bring him here. He had come to the village to end this. That was clear.

"I will tell everyone tonight so there will be no false hopes or vain expectations. I have already spoken with Micah."

The words were hard for him to say, but he meant them, and I thought I loved him more in that moment when he was letting me go than I had loved him in all the past years.

"Will you...go to Eve?" I asked. I didn't want him to, but that was unfair. I wanted him to deny that he had even thought of it.

He let out a breath and ran a big hand through his long, loose hair. "I saw her on market days," he admitted. "But I didn't really care for her that way. Her father suggested a union once, but I declined."

"Oh," I said. "You should introduce her to Jarom."

He burst into laughter. "I did once! "It was a disaster." His voice softened. "I think he really liked her."

"Ah," I said. "And he thought you liked her."

"Something like that."

"Are you here to stay? Are you going back to Judea?"

He slowly shook his head. "I will not be going back to Judea, but I have made other commitments with the army."

"You have?" My surprise showed. Zeke had served in Helaman's army out of duty, not desire. The fact that he would willingly continue now that the striplings had been disbanded really caught me off guard.

"Keturah, when I marry, I want to be in love." He caught my eye. "And I want my wife to be in love with me, really in love with no reservations. I haven't found that woman yet. I just can't see it any other way. My parents are in love, and that's what I've always expected for myself."

I thought of Dinah, how she had been so unsure of her feelings when she married Zeke's father.

"I do love you, Zeke," I said, dratted tears brimming at my eyes.

"But not enough," he said quietly. He took me into his arms. They had become hard and strong during the war but they enveloped me so gently. "And you know I love you," he whispered into my hair. When he pulled away he bent to kiss me.

I was old enough by then and had been kissed enough times that kissing was no longer something to be experienced, but something to be shared. And though I loved Zeke, he was not the man I wanted to share my kisses with.

But in the same moment I turned my face away from him, Zeke stopped himself. After a pause, he placed his kiss on my forehead like Micah always did.

He turned toward the village. "Walk with me?" he asked, his hand outstretched.

I looked at his hand and slowly shook my head. "No."

He held my gaze for a moment. Then he gave a quick nod and left, his long strides putting the distance between us.

I stood for a time watching him until he disappeared into the trees. I was experiencing so many emotions I wasn't sure what to feel first. Relief won out, and I fell to my knees and thanked my Lord in a brief but heartfelt prayer. I stayed on my knees until the tears were dried from my face.

"That from Zeke?"

I looked up from the flower in my hand. Why hadn't I heard him? I looked around, suddenly aware that a great deal of time had passed. Evening was falling fast.

He was the third man I had met in the meadow that day, none of them the one I wanted most to see.

"You missed the celebration meal," he said, taking a knee beside me. "For my amazing elder brother."

I ignored the slight contempt in his voice. "I lost track of time."

"I see that."

"What are you doing here?" I had never been here with Jarom, even in the company of our siblings.

"Everyone was worried."

"Don't you mean disappointed?"

He laughed.

"So you heard."

"Why do you think I came?"

I rolled my eyes.

"I told them I'd come find you, save you from the deep, dark forest."

"It's going to be very dark if we don't get moving. Let me just get my gear."

I hadn't even used it.

I made my way to where I had dropped my weapons on the bank of the river that afternoon before climbing up to talk with Muloki. I knelt and strapped everything on, ready to carry, ready to fight. When I rose, Jarom was standing much too close to me.

I tilted my neck to look into his face. He had definitely gotten taller.

"How about that kiss in the moonlight?" he said in a seductive whisper.

I glanced at the sky. "There's no moonlight."

"An insignificant detail," he insisted softly.

I looked him in the eye for a moment and then took a step back.

He took a step forward, crowding me with his body. "I'm not that little kid anymore, Keturah."

"An insignificant detail," I said, wincing at the flicker of pain that passed through his eyes.

"What is this, then?" he asked. He held the stone I had given him in Manti, just a smooth stone I had taken from my bag on the spur of the moment. I hadn't planned it, hadn't meant anything by it.

He had said it was a stone waiting to be slung. And he had given me a broken stone he had salvaged from the wreckage of a battle.

"You still have the obsidian shard. I won't believe you if you tell me you don't."

"I do," I said. I reached into the pouch in which I kept my

slinging stones and felt for it. I had taken it out many times and fingered the rough edges. I withdrew it then and held it out on my hand for him to see. "But I told you that stone was not a promise."

"And you told Zeke you wouldn't marry him."

I shook my head. "He didn't ask me to marry him."

He looked at me doubtfully. "If he didn't, then he is a bigger fool than I thought. Would you have said yes?"

"I would have honored my brother if *he* had asked it of me. But no, Jarom, I would not have told Zeke yes. My heart is given elsewhere."

He looked at me with dawning understanding on his face.

"I told you on the West Road, that first day you came back. Don't pretend you didn't know."

"I guess I thought you meant Zeke. I chose to ignore it." He finally took a step away from me.

"We all do that. Like I pretend you don't have a girl in every city you've been stationed in."

His brief grimace turned into a mischievous smile.

"Please," I said with teasing exasperation. "I've been in the army. I've known a thousand men like you."

I saw the flicker of pain again.

As apology settled in my eyes, we heard the sudden and close call of the margay, and both our heads snapped toward the sound.

The shrill call was a signal my brothers and I used to communicate, to spread warnings or to indicate we were close by and didn't want an arrow in the neck when we came through the trees. Zeke and Jarom had long ago adopted it, and during my time in the army, my unit had adopted it as well.

We scanned the area thoroughly, but though we watched for someone, nobody came through the trees.

We looked at each other. A warning call then.

By silent agreement, Jarom led out, and I dropped the pink flower I had been holding into the long meadow grasses as we slipped into the forest. Jarom had learned stealth from Kenai, whose skills I had learned to trust completely, and I followed him willingly toward the place from which the warning call had come. But when we got there, we didn't find anyone.

"There!" I whispered and pointed to the barely noticeable broken stem on a large evergreen leaf. It was an obvious trail and we would have to track it.

As we painstakingly followed the trail, which had been clearly set, we circled around toward the West Road, but the trail ended several hundred paces short of it. We cast around in all directions, even behind us, but we couldn't find the way to go in the coming darkness.

Frustrated, I sounded the margay and we both waited in silence, listening for a return. After a moment, we heard it in the distance beyond the West Road. What was going on, and who was out there?

"Run for the striplings," I whispered. There were enough striplings in the village and the surrounding villages to form a small patrol.

"No. I'm not leaving you here."

"Just go. I'll move toward the margay's call in case whoever it is needs help. You can run faster than me, and I can shoot better than you."

He snorted, but he turned and ran silently and swiftly back through the trees without another word.

That was one thing I did love about Jarom. He never questioned my ability to fight, and as he had claimed that morning in Cumeni, he would never try to suppress it.

I turned to face the unknown. I sent up a prayer and stepped into the falling darkness where the Lord led me.

I started toward the road, but I heard movement in the underbrush, and I immediately dropped into it myself, years of training making it second nature. A heavy feeling came over me, and I had felt it so many times I knew what danger lay out there in the forest without having to see it for myself.

Lamanites.

It was dark enough by then that I felt safe rising to see what I would be facing. To anyone watching, I would appear to be a mere shadow in the dim forest.

Unfortunately, my enemies appeared to be merely shadows too. When I lifted my head above the level of the underbrush, I saw that there were a lot of them. I counted quickly. Probably fifty dark shadows floated through the gray twilight.

I couldn't shoot them all.

I waited for them to pass. When I was about to make a move to pursue them, a thick hand clamped over my mouth.

"Kanina."

The word was so quiet as to be almost indiscernible from the light brush of the breeze through the leaves. If there hadn't been a hand over my mouth, I'd have thought I imagined it.

I gave a slight nod, indicating I would neither struggle nor make noise. But when he moved his hand, I whispered one word.

His name.

"You've had a busy day," he said softly.

Was that jealousy? Anger? Had he been spying on me?

"So have you. What's going on? Where are those men going?"

"I followed them beyond the West Road. They were leaving, but they decided to return."

"Where were they going? Return for what?"

"Captives."

I turned my head slightly. "Captives for what?"

"Women, Keturah!" he burst out harshly, like I was too dim to understand. "Women and children," he added more softly.

"But, how do you—"

"I know what I heard."

"I trust you." I waited a moment. "Are you alone?"

"Are you?" he shot back.

"Jarom left to get the others."

He snorted. "Well, he can only warn them. I think the men are headed to your village."

Mother. Dinah. Cana. My heart dropped into my stomach. Isabel. Sarai. Chloe.

I jerked upright. "We have to get there!"

"That goes without saying."

I thought of his mother and wondered that we were still there having this conversation, one of us bitter, the other frantic, and both of us confused in very different ways.

"Follow me," he said as he moved slowly into a crouching position.

When he was satisfied that all the men had passed us, he motioned me to follow him. We moved as quickly as we could through the dark forest. This wasn't a new experience. We had done this many times together.

When we neared the village, I passed him and took the lead. I knew Jarom had gotten here in time to warn the villagers because they weren't in the village. I led Gideon toward the small stream in the little hollow deep in the forest behind Hemni and Dinah's.

He stopped me with a touch on my arm and questioned me with his eyes.

"I trust you," I said. "Do you trust me?"

He gave one decisive nod, and we continued on.

I sounded the margay as I approached and was relieved when I heard the immediate answer.

It was eerily familiar when I met Kalem near the stream to exchange information. But this time, I allowed Gideon to do the talking while I looked around to make sure everyone I loved was there.

"Where is Isabel?" I broke in.

Kalem looked at us gravely. "She went alone to the tannery after the evening meal."

Gideon and I glanced at each other.

"The boys have all gone to look for her."

I hurried over to Hemni, who had to turn away from Isabel in her hour of need, who was bound by his oath to resist the temptation to fight for his daughter.

Sometimes daughters had to do the fighting for themselves.

"I will find her," I vowed to him.

His eyes glittered in the moonlight with unshed tears. "I know you will," he said. "You must. I could not bear to lose two daughters in one evening."

We stared into each other's eyes, and I knew that whether or not he agreed with the decision Zeke and I had come to, he would support us in it.

I thought then of the fathers on the training ground so many years before. How they had instructed their sons, given them all the knowledge they had, demonstrated the movements of the weapons, drawn diagrams in the dirt of the corn field. They had done everything short of taking a weapon into their own hands to provide their sons with all they would need to win the battles ahead.

And then the fathers had trusted their children and let them go.

I thought of my own father. We had been so young when he had given up his life, just little children. But had leaving us alone on this earth really been so different than what Hemni had done by taking that oath?

My father, the king, had sent us into the world with all he had to offer, with what he deemed to be of most value to us in life's battles—his testimony.

Mother had given us his shields and weapons—the Holy Spirit, the word of God.

And faith.

As soon as Gideon and I were back in the trees I grabbed for his hand and pulled him to a stop.

"Let us send up a prayer," I insisted.

My insistence wasn't necessary for he dropped to his knees instantly. I followed him, and he uttered the words.

Then we were on our feet and running again. We circumvented the village, choosing instead to run straight for the tannery. We heard calls and jeers before we arrived. They were so loud that even though I sounded the margay again, I was sure nobody heard it.

The light from the moon was dim, but the clouds moved then, and Gideon and I were able to get a better look at what was happening.

The Lamanite men had bundles and pallets of things they had looted from the village and probably other surrounding settlements. Perhaps there were even some captives, but it was much too dark to tell for sure. The bundles and captives would make their travel slow. They did not anticipate being followed.

They knew the people of Ammon would not contest them, but did they not know the sons of Ammon were home from the wars?

I was sure Jarom had been able to gather no more than ten men from the villages. Gideon and I made twelve. The odds were not in our favor, but then, they never had been.

As the Lamanites started to depart with their stolen goods, it became quiet at the tannery, and we could do nothing but watch. Gideon and I fell in behind the enemy. We followed them past the village and on toward the West Road.

Were they really so bold as to think they would march out of here right on the main road?

We heard an owl and Gideon instantly pulled me to a stop next to a large kuyche tree.

"No, that's Kenai. He uses the owl sometimes when the margay has been compromised."

Gideon answered the call and we stayed where we were, standing so close we could feel each other's breath. Slowly Gideon let his hand run down my slick hair from my crown to my shoulder. It seemed to be an absent-minded action because his every other sense was in use listening and seeing into the night.

But I knew that Gideon did not do things absent-mindedly.

We heard the owl moments before Kenai appeared out of the darkness with Jarom, Zeke, and my brothers. Muloki was with them and Mahonri and Jonas from the neighboring village of Antum. But I was surprised when Lamech, who scowled at me, and Enos, who gave me a subdued smile, emerged from the dark forest with a man who looked so much like Gideon—broad shoulders, chestnut colored hair that fell to his shoulders, inscrutable expression—they were surely brothers.

Jashon.

He looked from Gideon to me and scrutinized me as curiously as I scrutinized him. When he looked back to Gideon, I noticed the slight raise of his eyebrow.

Four chief captains, the lost heir to the Lamanite throne, Teancum's personal guard, five lethally trained assassins, a fierce Lamanite warrior, and a fourteen-year old kid with an attitude.

I almost laughed when I wondered who would emerge as the leader that night.

"They've got fifteen captives," Zeke told us. "Isabel is among them."

Chapter 22

"But I didn't see any captives! Only provisions. They only took provisions."

I looked to Gideon to confirm what I had seen.

"The prisoners were gagged and bound, Keturah," he informed me softly.

"Some of the little ones were on pallets," added Kenai. But he laughed just a little. "Isabel fought like a wildcat."

Little ones? "Why didn't you stop them?" I demanded. He had obviously been close enough to see.

"We were only three against fifty at that time. They didn't intend the captives immediate harm. Better to wait until we gathered our men and surprise them when we have the advantage."

"When they are sleeping," Gideon added as he caught my eye.

And suddenly I knew what Kenai and Gideon were both planning.

It had been the one thing I had done in the army that had

really bothered me. Killing men while they slept, when they had no defense against me, did not sit well with me. I guessed I was like Kalem that way. He had killed my father when he was unarmed and defenseless, and his guilt had harrowed him for many years.

I thought of the men I had killed on the Cumeni crossroad so our army could get into Cumeni to lay the siege. The deaths haunted me still, and I could finally understand why our parents had made such a powerful oath against shedding blood. That was something I had never been able to understand before that night and had, admittedly, resented a great deal.

I swallowed hard and listened closely as the men made their plans.

We had a time to wait, and I lay on the ground as close to invisible as possible between Kenai and Darius. We had followed the Lamanites until they stopped to make camp late in the second watch. We lay in small groups a short distance away from them, spread out until we had them nearly surrounded. We could only hope that they were too tired to harass their prisoners tonight. If they attempted to, we would shoot into the shadows and pray our eyes were as keen as we needed them to be.

Waiting in the darkness was torture. It was not worse than the sheer terror the captives must have been feeling, but it was torture nonetheless.

I thought of Isabel fighting for her freedom like a wildcat, like the margay whose call we used as a warning. Dinah had said the world needed more girls like us.

Isabel, nearing fifteen now, was almost as old as I had been when I marched away to war. It was time for Hemni to start thinking about a betrothal for her. Another year or two and then a year-long betrothal. I smiled into the darkness. I had a feeling Isabel would be putting up a bigger fight than I had.

Finally, the wind shifted and the breeze would no longer carry our whispers to the enemies, so I turned to Kenai.

"You saw them take Isabel?" I asked in a low tone.

He didn't take his eyes off the still shadows in the distance to speak to me. "Yeah. But she practically walked out with them willingly."

"But you said she fought like a wildcat."

I saw the hint of a smile on his lips. "She fought to free the other girls. When she finally admitted she couldn't, she went willingly. I think," he paused and shook his head. "I know she figured that if she went, she could free them later."

"She could have gotten away?"

"They pushed her away. They didn't want to take her. She was too much trouble."

"She's just a little girl," I said.

"A little girl who carries a tanning knife," Darius broke in.

"What?"

"I think she's been watching you for a long time, Ket."

It had never occurred to me that other young girls might be looking to me as an example. I cringed. I was such a poor one. Girls should look to women like Cana and Mother, but not to me.

I gripped my own knife and turned back to the enemy camp. I felt suddenly responsible for Isabel. I would get her out of this. I would.

All thirteen of us lay silent and absolutely alert for several hours. The third watch had nearly passed, and it was deep in the dead of the night when I finally heard Kenai let out a slow breath.

In the next instant he was up and stealing into the camp. I heard the low call of the owl. My heart pounded. He was so broken inside and still so brave.

He was moving quickly, but his feet were silent and the wind was still with us. There were three sentries still awake, each one facing one of the two small fires that glowed. We had been watching long enough to know there were no other sentries beyond the firelight. If there had been, Kenai would have taken them out long ago.

Jarom and Gideon emerged from the darkness at the same moment and none of them hesitated when they reached the small circle of firelight, just kept moving crouched low until they were on their men. In the next instant the sentries were dead.

I had been watching my shadows for hours. I knew what positions they lay in, how often they rolled over, how very close they were to the thankfully sleeping and unharmed captives. Probably they planned to sell these women or give them to their superiors, the purchase price of honor.

As if there was honor in what they did.

And with that thought in my head, I got up in the same moment as Darius and all the others and sprinted for the circle of men.

I kept my focus on the men I was to kill. These men were not innocent. They were nothing like the guard on the Cumeni Road. They had faces. They had crimes.

Just as I was about to cross from the darkness into the firelight, one of the Lamanites called out to his brethren. He had awakened, and he sounded the alarm.

This did not alter our course of action. There would be no retreat. There would be no quarter given. We would not wait for a better time to fight, like Isabel had had to do. Unlike Isabel, we were completely prepared to save ourselves and others.

Three of my men were slow to wake so I was able to get them with my dagger. I drew my sword to fight another. When he was down, I glanced around and saw a huge man bearing down on Zeke. I stashed my sword and positioned my bow in the same movement of my arm with the precision and speed I had gained from years of practice, drew an arrow, and in the next moment met Zeke's eyes across the camp as his opponent fell at his feet.

But there was no more time than that before another enemy was upon me.

I dropped my bow over my head and felt it fall comfortably into place on my shoulder. I pulled my axe from my belt in time to block the enemy's. I kicked him and broke my axe free from his when he stumbled. I swung hard and wild—almost too wild. I was so furious with this man, with all of them. How dare they destroy our peace? Right here in our home. How *dare* they?

"Kanina." Gideon's steadying voice was all it took to bring me back into control. I took more time with my next two swings and was rewarded with blood.

Panting, I turned to thank Gideon, but he was gone. I found him engaged in a fight across the fire from me. How had he gotten there so quickly?

My mind went back to the meadow and all the times I had felt him there with me. But I fought free of the memories and rounded to fight the real enemy.

But there was no one. They were all dead or still fighting. They would be dead soon. We would not leave wounded, and we could not take prisoners.

I looked around at my brothers, all twelve of them. But I counted again. Ten, eleven, twelve.

Thirteen.

I stared in amazement as Isabel stood strong and proud over her fallen enemy.

Kenai noticed her too and approached her with care. He was right to do so. There was no telling what emotional state she was in. But it was clear she was okay—relieved and scared, but okay—when she didn't attack Kenai and instead fell into his arms and let him comfort her.

I watched them for a moment, standing in the firelight together, the shadows and light flickering around them as they embraced. Maybe, I thought, she could comfort him too.

From the corner of my eye, I saw the man Isabel had fought was not dead. He had propped himself up enough to aim an arrow—not at the couple standing over him, but at Gideon, who stood victorious near the main fire, hands on hips, surveying our success.

My sling was on my belt and I grabbed it and loaded it in almost the same second. I barely noticed I had loaded Jarom's jagged stone, the last remnant of the war, into the sling before I had slung it at the man.

The man jerked and slumped back to the earth, instantly dead from two projectiles—mine, that landed in his heart and another that landed simultaneously in his eye.

I turned to scan the camp for the other slingman and saw Jarom standing still poised in position with his sling swinging from his hand.

He caught my eye, glanced at Gideon, and gave me a slight nod. Then he grinned, winked roguishly, and blew me a kiss before turning to the others.

I turned too and found Jashon studying me carefully. He stood with Lamech who was describing something to him, probably his part in the battle.

Don't fall in love with me, I thought ridiculously as I replaced my sling on my belt and wiped my axe down with a rag, remembering what Gideon had once said about yielding to his elder brother. I couldn't contain a small smile that made Jashon narrow his eyes.

He watched me until Enos clapped him on the shoulder and motioned to the captives.

We woke the poor things and untied them. Some had slept through the battle, and some had lain awake. I hoped they had all used the good sense to close their eyes to it.

Many of them were still frightened and cowered from their protectors. The men were being so gentle, even trying first to loosen the bonds before showing their knives to the children if the bonds had to be cut. But I realized the captives did not know half of these men, so I stepped forward.

"These men are Helaman's striplings," I told the women. "They will not harm you."

In all, there were seven women and eight children, mostly girls, that had been captured, and I knew most of them. No wonder Isabel had fought so hard—these were her friends, girls she went to church with, women she looked up to.

We didn't especially want to bury the Lamanites, but we didn't want anyone coming across the grisly scene either, so we took the time to dig a wide, shallow grave with two shovels we found among the dead. The men took turns digging while Isabel and I helped the women tend to the frightened children. Gideon's kinsmen had traveling food in their packs, and we gave it to the captives along with water to drink.

Jashon brought me the offering of food. "Here," he said. "For the children."

"Thank you." I glanced over my shoulder to where they sat and the women soothed them with soft songs, calming words, and gentle touches. "I think they will appreciate it."

I started toward them, but Jashon called me back. "Keturah."

He didn't say anything for a moment. I was almost ready to just turn away again when he said, "I can see now why we have traveled all this way."

He turned abruptly and returned to Enos, who gave me a nod, and Lamech, who sent me a scowl.

It was past dawn when we arrived back in the village, but no one there had slept. People from other villages had gathered too.

The captives returned to their families, all of them weeping with relief.

The thirteen of us stood back, observing the reunions. I looked around at the others. Micah went into Cana's waiting arms. They really were sweet together. Kenai walked past them with a curt nod and Darius followed him toward our home where I could see Mother waited anxiously at the gate with Kalem, who held her back with a steadying arm.

Zeke and Jarom stood near each other, but a telling distance separated them. I hated the thought that I had come between them. I knew their strained relationship went beyond me, though. They stood identical in their stances but so different in every other way. I thought Jarom had deliberately changed every physical aspect of himself that he could to set himself apart from his brother.

I watched sadly as they glanced at each other and by tacit agreement walked home together, escorting Isabel between them, gently pushing through the emotional crowd on the road.

Muloki had likely been at Mother's fire with Kalem and Melia when Jarom had run in with the warning. Mahonri and Jonas lived in the neighboring village, and I guessed someone could have run for them when they were needed. But what were Gideon and his kinsmen doing here in the village?

As I was wondering this, my eye caught Gideon's. He stood a short distance away with his kinsmen. It had been over a year since I had come home, and not one day had passed that I hadn't thought of this man. Seasons had passed. I knew I had changed, and I wondered in what ways he had changed. It was strange to see him so real and so close after all that time.

And yet, somehow, it was like all that time had not passed and we had never been apart.

His gaze was unreadable. That had not changed. I could not tell what he was thinking as we stared at each other in the early part of day, when the air was soft and the light was diffused by the mists.

Someone stepped between us, and I looked up to focus on the face of Mahonri. He was looking me over as he had done that first day I had met him in the hills outside of Antiparah, the way that had made me dislike him.

"Good work last night," he said. "You really have a way with men."

I brandished my knife. "Would you like to experience it first hand?"

He laughed and put out his arm between us.

I stared at it for a moment, and then I clasped arms with him. His respect was the respect of a man I did not like, but maybe I would try to see past my first impression of him. Just because I did not like a person did not mean he was unlikeable.

Mahonri was surly, but he was loyal, honorable, faithful, and willing to do what had to be done—all good reasons to modify my opinion of him.

When he and Jonas moved out for home, I turned my eyes back to Gideon.

But he was gone.

I searched the crowded village road for him, for any of his kinsmen. They were all gone, and once again, I stood alone.

But I was not alone. The Holy Spirit stood beside me. I knew he had guided me through the night, just as I knew he had guided me in the past years.

I walked down the village road until I got to Hemni and Dinah's.

I found Chloe in the yard milking Abigail.

"Chloe," I called over the fence.

She looked over her shoulder. "Hi, Keturah."

"Will you milk Mui for me and tell my mother I have gone for a walk?"

Her eyes lit up. "Alright," she said. But then she looked toward the woods. "Are you sure you should go out there alone?"

"It is safe," I said.

Because I had made it safe.

She nodded, and I walked on into the trees, weapons and all.

Whatever Gideon and his brothers and cousin were doing in Melek, they were obviously not here to see me. He had come here before and left me the flowers, but he had not come to stay.

As I walked, my heart was breaking all over again, but this time I wasn't consoling myself with the thought of Zeke. This time there was nothing to console me, nothing that could. This time I would allow myself to grieve as Gideon walked away from me.

I could have gone to the meadow, sat above the falls and let my tears fall into the water below me, let them be swept away by the love of God. But instead my feet carried me to a place I had only been twice before.

I had knelt there thinking of molten rock flowing like a slow river, a miraculous impossibility, and I had met Gideon. I had knelt there among the broken shards and confessed to my Father that Gideon was the man I loved.

I knelt there now, a place that held only memories of Gideon and was not tainted with feelings for others. This was the place I could feel close to him. This was the place I would grieve for him, and I would take from it the stone for the weapons I would use to continue fighting as he had taught me to do.

I stared at the deep brown earth in front of me for a long time, trying not to remember it was the color of Gideon's eyes. But I gradually began looking around at the beauty that abounded in this place. The foliage and underbrush grew up around the rock formations. It was clear that rock had been mined from the obsidian beds, but the plants had grown up around them again, crawling over them and cascading down the edges of small ledges. I noticed plants Mother used for healing, too.

And I noticed a vine of moonflowers near me. I reached out to take one. I wanted to bring it to my nose, to weave it into my hair, to remember.

To remember a discarded white flower among the black stones, Gideon on one knee reaching for it. Lying back in the beds of moonflowers, opening my eyes to see unchecked love in Gideon's face. A parting token tenderly given before Gideon led hundreds of men to Zarahemla.

Three white flowers floating in the river in our meadow.

I heard the grasses behind me part and I stilled, my hand poised to touch the flower.

He stood for long, silent, charged moments—the only man who could possibly be standing in this place with me. I could hear him breathe. I could feel his heart beat.

I withdrew my hand slowly from the flower, leaving it where it was.

"Are you married?" he asked gruffly.

I did not turn, but shook my head.

"Are you betrothed?"

I shook it again.

Silence.

"Good," he said at last.

And there was silence again.

The breeze fluttered through the vine of moonflowers. It lifted my hair off my neck, and I gathered it and swept it over my shoulder.

"Do you not speak?" he asked. Was that a smile in his voice?

I smiled, too, at the ground in front of me. "I choose to whom I will speak," I said softly.

"And you do not choose to speak to this warrior?"

I shrugged.

The long grasses shifted again as he moved closer to me. He went to a knee behind me and I could feel the warmth of his body, though he did not touch me.

"Are you so indifferent to me?" he asked so quietly it was like the wind that swept across my bare neck, and I shivered. But it wasn't the wind, I realized, as he stroked my neck again with the back of his knuckles.

"Don't be angry," he said.

"I'm not angry."

I reached back and took his hand. It was rough and hard and dry as I remembered. I brought it around to my lips and smoothed them over the rough places and the scars.

He allowed it and after a few moments touched my cheek and turned my face to his. Without another word, he kissed me, warm lips moving over mine in slow caresses, and tears were seeping from my closed eyes before he was done.

I felt him move, reach forward, and when I opened my eyes he held the moonflower in front of me.

"Do you know what I like about this flower?" he asked.

I gave my head a small shake.

"It is different from all the other flowers because it only blooms at night. You have to be looking for it to see it. You have to be lucky to catch it while it blooms." He lowered his lips to my ear. "But when you do, it is the most beautiful thing in the heavens or the earth."

I took the flower.

Gideon stood and came around to stand before me. I looked up, and he held out his hand for me.

And I took that too.

Chapter 23

I put my arms around his neck when he pulled me into a tight embrace. I felt his hard hands at my waist, sliding to my back, tucking me close to him—where we both knew now that I belonged.

"I love you, Keturah. Since the first day I met you here, you've had my heart."

I closed my eyes. My heart was blazing with heat, but I was calm, and I felt powerfully in that moment that my will and Gideon's will and God's will were one.

"My family has traveled here with me. We've come to negotiate the betrothal contracts. Will you agree to this? To a betrothal?" He pulled back enough to look into my face to determine my reaction.

Could he be so unsure?

I let him search my gaze. "I am sorry you are not sure already of my answer. I fear I have let my actions lie, if you do not know the feelings of my heart."

"Become my wife," he said, a small smile touching his

lips, and it was not a question. It was a conviction.

"Yes," I said, and it was not an answer.

He eased his hold on me and turned me toward the village. Hand in hand we walked toward it.

"I was hoping you would consider living at the farm near my parents. You don't know the measure of comfort it would give me if you were there to protect them."

I loved the idea of being needed for the talents I possessed. It might make the housework bearable. "But where will you be?"

"I'm committed to working as a guard for Helaman, but I've arranged with him to work one fortnight of each month in Zarahemla, or perhaps traveling with him wherever he may desire to preach. There is much work to be done. He must reestablish the church in all the lands of the people of Nephi. A great many of the priesthood leaders have been slain in the wars and scattered to other areas."

I nodded.

"Zeke has agreed to work the other fortnight of each month so I may be with you."

Hot tears stung at my eyes. I quickly whisked them away before they could fall. "That was kind of him. Where will your brothers be? Not at the farm?"

"They will come and go as they please. I don't know where life will take them, but I know none of them want to farm." He paused. "Lib, Ethanim, Zach, Noah, Reb—they all live in the nearby town. You would be near them. Would you like that?"

"I would love that."

"I also thought, if you prefer, we could acquire a home in Zarahemla. But it is crowded there in the city, and I thought you would miss your forest."

"You were right," I agreed. "I would miss it very much."

"I also thought, well, I would rather raise our children on the farm."

I bit my lip and nodded.

As we walked back toward the village together, I asked him, "When did you decide to come back?"

"A few weeks ago I woke in the night to a feeling, an overwhelming feeling, to come for you. I was still upset. Jealous, hurt, and angry. I didn't understand why this could not be. But I came. I made it here in two days."

A few weeks ago. I remembered the night Muloki had talked to me about letting down my shield. I had come to a decision that night, deep in the second watch, long after my family had fallen asleep. The following morning I had strapped on my weapons and gone to the meadow. Two mornings later, I had felt Gideon's presence there and found the flowers.

Could it be that Gideon had felt the impression from the Holy Ghost in virtually the same moment I had decided not to marry Zeke?

"And you watched me in the meadow."

He flushed a little and nodded.

"And you left me the flowers."

"Yes."

"But why did you not show yourself? Come to visit?"

"I thought you were probably married. I felt so foolish even coming at all."

Could it really have been so simple as making the right choice? Had the Spirit been keeping Gideon from me until I made the choice not to marry Zeke? Could the use of my agency really affect others in this way?

"And when did you determine I wasn't married?"

"When Micah came to find me."

"Micah!"

"I had been back in Judea for a week. He talked with me, and then I think he summoned Zeke also."

I thought Micah was avoiding me after I had told him my decision, but he had gone to Judea.

"What did he say?"

A slight smile touched his lips. "That is between us men."

I smacked him in the chest, but he did not say anything further on the matter.

"But just now, when you asked me if I was married..."

"I wanted to hear it from you."

I nodded. There were things I wanted to hear from him, too.

"We determined not to tell you until I could make arrangements with my family, with Helaman, and with the army."

"But that was weeks ago."

"I'm sorry it took so long."

It had taken me over a year to come to the right decision. I guessed a few weeks wasn't really so long to wait.

"And when Muloki came—"

"Muloki!" I covered my mouth with my hand, but mostly to hide my smile. "He didn't! What did he do?"

Gideon cast me a sideways glance. "He requested my presence in Melek."

Just yesterday Muloki had suggested this, and I thought he had been joking. But he had already done it, the weasel.

"What did he say?"

"It was not anything he said, but he was very persuasive."

"Oh, Gideon." I couldn't help a small giggle that escaped as he rubbed his jaw.

"Zeke traveled with us from Judea—Enos, Lamech, and me— but we stopped in my village to get my parents, and Zeke continued on alone. I was surprised to find Jashon at home."

I had talked to both Muloki and Zeke at the falls yesterday, and they had both known Gideon was here in the village and what he was here for.

I was too filled with joy to be upset with them.

"You look very much like Jashon. I can see why Lamech's differences are so obvious."

Gideon made a sound of agreement.

I looked up at him, still hardly believing he was there,

hardly believing he had come seeking a betrothal. I slipped my hand into his to assure myself he was real.

"You actually traveled with Zeke?" I asked.

He nodded. "He loves you, Ket."

"He was my best friend for a long time," I said on a sigh.

"Not any longer?"

"No. Not for a long time now."

"Zeke had just one request of me—after he reminded me how many men would kill me if I ever made you cry."

I thought back to a few minutes ago when the tenderness and wonder of his kiss had made me cry. But to be fair, he had brushed the tears away with his big, rough thumbs.

"I don't suppose he realized you could only die once, and that I could take care of it myself."

Gideon laughed and hooked an arm around my neck. His voice was husky in my ear when he said, "Try it."

When we neared the village, I turned to him. "Gideon, what was it Zeke asked of you?"

"He wanted me to take you to see Helaman about your sword."

"Ah, yes. Helaman once said he could interpret the writings on it if I brought it to him in Zarahemla."

Gideon looked at me strangely, frowning a little. He drew me to a stop, and then he reached over my shoulder and withdrew my sword from its scabbard.

I suddenly realized. "You've always known, haven't you?"

I hadn't come across a language yet that Gideon didn't know and understand.

He looked at it, my sword, once so purely beautiful. Now it was scarred from many battles, discolored, stained, chipped in places. But the flint tip always scrubbed up white, and purple still gleamed from the obsidian blades. Its paint in red and orange, green and yellow had weathered well. And the words in royal blue, a mystery to me, were still prominent and even darkened by the blood I had shed with the power the Lord had given my arm in times of need. Beneath it all, beneath the adornments and sharp edges, the natural, golden colored wood still shone.

Gideon fingered the lettering. “I didn’t realize others couldn’t read this,” he said quietly.

“You’re the only one,” I replied with the reverence that was overtaking my heart. I looked from the sword to the face of the man I loved. “What does it say?” I asked him.

He looked at me for a moment, then replaced the sword in its sheath on my back. I felt its weight, familiar and comfortable, as he dropped it in.

“It says *Daughter of the King*.”

He lifted my chin and placed a kiss on my lips. Then he turned, took my hand, and began to walk toward my home where our families waited for us to return.

Please enjoy the first chapter of

The *Spy* of Cumeni

Chapter 1

I stole through the darkness next to Keturah, hardly believing what I had just done.

It wasn't anything Keturah and the others hadn't done, I assured myself as I pulled in a slow breath. And it wasn't anything that hadn't needed to be done.

I looked from Keturah to where my brothers glided quietly through the night ahead of us. It struck me that Zeke and Jarom had been doing this kind of thing for nearly six years—since they had joined with Helaman's army and gone to war.

I had only been eight years old. They had been gone so long, I hardly knew them now. We were almost like strangers. Jarom had been home for a few months, but Zeke had just returned yesterday.

I cast a secret glance to my other side, where Kenai walked protectively near me. Kenai was our closest neighbor and Zeke's best friend. He had been Jarom's captain in the army, and I had heard Jarom talking to Father about him.

"Kenai is still at war inside himself," he had said, and

Father had frowned deeply and put a hand on Jarom's shoulder without looking at him.

I wondered what had happened to Kenai that made him the way he was—sad all the time, not eating, not interested in anything, violent at random times, melancholy. I wondered if time would heal his heart.

And mostly, I wondered why he had held me so tenderly after I had stabbed that terrible Lamanite man.

I wasn't discreet enough when I glanced at Kenai—I must have been staring—because he caught my eye in the moonlight. He didn't smile at me, not even a little, just kept walking on. But he glanced at me now and then. I could feel it.

Or maybe I imagined it. It *had* been a long night.

The twilight had already begun to wane into darkness when I decided I had better hurry home. Alone at my father's tannery, I had been stretching some skins so they could dry overnight, though to be honest, that had only been an excuse to be gone from home. I started for the village and was moving swiftly through the trees when three men appeared on the trail before me. I knew immediately by their strange clothing and their shaved heads they were not the kind of men I knew in the village. I had never seen a Lamanite, but they fit the descriptions I had heard.

One of them, the one I had just stabbed in the gut with my tanning knife, had grabbed me and dragged me back to the clearing near the tannery, where many men had begun to gather, some holding struggling girls or women whose bruises were already showing.

My eyes shot around to the other captives in the clearing. I knew all of them. Some were tied. Some were gagged and staring at me with terrified eyes. A child began screaming for her mother.

Something in that cry set me off. Like Keturah, who had joined Helaman's army when she was just fifteen and gone away to war, I wanted to fight anyone who sought to steal my people's freedom. But Keturah fought for peace, and I was more interested in fighting for justice.

I kept a tanning knife strapped around my waist, but when the man had grabbed me, I hadn't been able to get to it. I had wanted to slash at him, to wound him and make him sorry he had ever left his Lamanite lands, to make him sorry he had ever touched me. It wasn't really a practical place to keep the knife, but it felt secure and reassuring tied there.

While I had been tied up and marched through the trees, I realized that being unable to reach my knife had been a piece of luck. I hadn't used the knife, so they hadn't known I carried it. And while they slept, I had been able to slip it out and cut through my bonds.

Zeke and Jarom were talking in low tones ahead of us, but Zeke turned around after a while and focused on me in the darkness.

"You okay?" he asked.

"I'm perfectly fine," I said.

Jarom turned back too, and I saw him roll his eyes at my snippy comment before he turned them to take a long hard look at Kenai, probably, I thought, to determine how he was holding up.

Jarom had been through all the battles with Kenai, even up through the most recent they had fought under Moroni's command in Nephihah, and I knew he worried about him—like he thought Kenai would do something reckless or dangerous at any moment, maybe harm himself or someone else. Since they had been home, I had seen Jarom surreptitiously watching Kenai. And secretly, I thought this watchfulness was the reason Jarom had gone with Kenai to Nephihah instead of coming home. I only wondered why it hadn't been Zeke who went with him.

Zeke turned to Keturah then, and by his dismissive glance, I knew she was the reason he hadn't gone with Kenai. She had to be. I didn't know it then, but in the days that followed, I noticed a rift between Zeke and Kenai. How could Zeke be friends with the brother of the woman who had rejected him?

Zeke looked her over briefly and just turned forward again like it wasn't his duty to ask after her welfare, like it wasn't his privilege to know she was okay, like he wasn't her intended husband.

Before the war, he would have demanded to know whether or not she was okay, babied and coddled her until she stomped off offended and mad at him. But something had happened between them. Earlier that night at his homecoming celebration, Zeke had announced to both our families that he would not pursue Keturah's hand in a betrothal. He said they had come to the decision mutually, but Keturah had let him face everyone alone—she hadn't even dared to show up.

This is what I had gone to the tannery to think over while I stretched and worked my hides. I produced the softest hides in Melek, even Father couldn't make them as soft, and everyone wanted them. But that night, my work was only an excuse to get away and think.

Zeke and Keturah had been basically promised to one another since childhood. Everyone, themselves included, had expected them to marry. And one day, today, Zeke just announced that they weren't going to.

It was so unfair.

I had to do everything my parents said, so why didn't Zeke?

It wasn't that I felt Keturah should have to marry my brother if she didn't want to. I was heartily against that. But she was *supposed* to want to. All the other girls in the village wanted to. She was refusing him just because she could. She was spoiled and selfish and heartless, and most importantly, she got everything her way, and I never did.

Except, well, there was the tannery.

When Zeke and Jarom had left for the war with Helaman's army, I had only been eight years old. But the next day Father said, "Isabel, I could use your help at the tannery."

I sat in our yard milking the goats that long ago morning. I had to milk, Sachemai, and to make matters worse, I now had to milk Mui, Keturah's goat, while she was away with the army. I liked that her family had entrusted me with this responsibility, but I hated milking the goats.

"Steady now," I said to Sachemai as I patted her side. But she wasn't steady, or I wasn't, and what milk I had gotten went everywhere.

Chloe giggled.

I ground my teeth. I sat and stared at the mess and the stupid goat that was now cropping the grasses at the edge of the yard.

I might have started to cry if Father hadn't come from the hut then, surveyed the scene, and decided he had too much work to accomplish alone.

That one moment, that one statement from him had changed my life.

Or at least it had changed my chores. After that day, Sarai and Chloe cared for and milked the goats, and I went with Father to the tannery.

It turned out that he actually did need my help at the tannery. He had too many orders he couldn't fill without help, because he had given almost every scrap of leather he had to the militia for scabbards, tents, legging pants and kilts, satchels and so forth.

It smelled at the tannery—that was my first impression. And I was sure I smelled of dead animal carcass when I went home that evening because Father and my brothers always did. Zeke had always gone immediately to bathe in the creek, even when it was cold, because he hated the smell of it. Secretly, I thought he didn't want Keturah to smell it on him. Father and Jarom had never seemed to care quite as much. We girls and Mother made a lot of soap, an extra chore, all because Zeke wanted to impress Keturah.

And that brought me back around to being upset with them both. All that soap making for nothing!

The sun was dawning and the light was increasing. I glanced around. We had come quite a ways while my mind had been wandering. At the pace we were traveling, we would be home in the village in a quarter of an hour. I had thought the younger children might hold us back, but they were all understandably eager to get home.

Keturah moved ahead to talk to Muloki. She slugged him in the arm and he laughed heartily.

My brothers still walked side by side ahead of me, but they weren't doing much talking. I couldn't put my finger on why, but it seemed there was a rift between them too, possibly bigger than the one between Zeke and Kenai. When Zeke had arrived home in the village, he had exchanged a hard look with Jarom, even while Mother embraced him. They seemed to have studiously ignored each other since then except in Mother's presence, and then they acted normal, even joking with each other like the best of friends. But if I was any judge, they weren't.

Most of the other captives travelled at the front of the group led by the man called Jashon and his brother, who Keturah was even now staring at as she walked beside Muloki and tried to appear interested in what he was saying to her.

I watched her closely for a time. How was it that she had gained her freedom, earned her freedom from marriage, and yet she clearly pined after this strange warrior when she was supposed to be pining after my brother?

"You think she's crazy," Kenai broke into my thoughts.

"Oh," I said, surprised. He had noticed I was staring at his sister. I blushed at the thought of him noticing anything about me. "No...I..."

"He's asked for her hand, you know," he said over my pathetic stammering. He put a finger to his lips. "It is a secret. She doesn't know yet."

"Oh," I said again. "Will she accept, do you think?"

"Without a doubt," he said. "But that doesn't matter. Micah has already done so on her behalf."

This sparked my temper. It didn't matter? Micah had already accepted on her behalf? I did not think women should be given in marriage, as was the custom. I thought a woman should give herself.

"That is absolute nonsense! It is so infuriatingly belittling when men—"

Kenai broke in with a chuckle, the first I had heard from him in the weeks since he had been home.

"What's so funny?" I asked, annoyed.

"Those were a lot of big words for a little girl like you."

My jaw went slack, and then I stuck out a foot and tripped him.

He stumbled and looked back first in confusion and then in amusement to where I had stopped and drawn my knife, ready for a fight.

I was a little girl, but how dare he call me one!

He chuckled again, low in his chest. "Put that knife away, or I'll take it from you," he warned calmly. And I might have, except that he added with what looked like a deliberate smirk, "That knife is not a play thing like your dolls."

Oh how I wanted to hurt him in that moment. I didn't move, but not because I didn't want to. I was holding my ground. I would never cut him with the knife, but after what had just happened, after being bound and abducted, I felt safer holding it. I would never use it on him, but I wanted to make a point. I was not little. I was not helpless.

"Come on now," he said. "Put it away."

By now, the others were a distance ahead of us and no one, it appeared, had noticed we were missing. Some rescue mission, I thought as I watched my brothers move on down the road with the others.

Why couldn't my brothers be as protective of me as Keturah's were of her?

Not that I would particularly want that.

And of course they thought Kenai was protecting me. They knew I did not need protection from Kenai.

Suddenly, I was on my back in the dirt, staring up into Kenai's face and he had taken my knife from me.

"I warned you," he said quietly.

"Give me my knife back," I said with irritation.

He smiled. "You're not old enough to play with this knife."

I struggled, trying to get up, trying to retrieve my knife from his hand where he held it just out of my reach.

Kenai forced me to stop wiggling by allowing more of the weight from his chest to rest on me. My panic must have shown in my face because he went very still and then quickly withdrew until he knelt up on his heels at my side. I didn't move, and he stared down at me.

"Sorry, Isabel," he said uncomfortably and handed me my blade with the hilt extended toward me. He wouldn't look me in the eye. He glanced up ahead, got to his feet, and offered me a hand. I grudgingly took it.

When I was standing, I put my knife into its scabbard, which I had tied around my waist after the fighting had stopped—this time on the outside of my sarong. I sent him a disgusted look, but I said, "It's okay. You're trained to act."

"Yeah, trained to act," he said under his breath. "Come on." And he started off after the others.

I walked after him for a few steps and then caught up and walked beside him, still wondering what had happened.

When the group ahead of us walked into the village, Kenai and I heard the relieved cheer go up. Nobody noticed we walked in together minutes behind everyone else.

Kenai put a light hand on my back and led me to where Zeke and Jarom stood surveying the many reunions. He punched Jarom in the arm—a kind of wordless greeting they used, and perhaps, that morning, it was a transferring of responsibility for me. He didn't look at or speak to me, and I tried not to watch him as he joined his younger brother, Darius, and they made their way home together through the crowd. But I failed.

Zeke stood with his hands on his hips and looked down at me. "I thought I was done with strong-willed women," he said.

It wasn't a compliment.

Jarom smirked, but I disregarded both of them, put my chin in the air and set off for home, where I could see Mother on her toes trying to spot us. Father stood behind her with his hands on her shoulders looking just as anxious.

I felt Zeke and Jarom fall in on both sides of me as I wove through the crowds of people, but I didn't look at either one of them. I thought it would be best if I just ignored them, but halfway home I thought *why not?* So I slipped my foot out and tripped Zeke. When he stumbled, Jarom laughed. But while he was preoccupied laughing at Zeke, I tripped Jarom too, and then I ran ahead of them into my Mother's arms. By the time my brothers reached home, tired and annoyed, I was safely ensconced in my Father's protective embrace.

No. Not protective. Father could protect me from spiders or the rain or perhaps a wild boar, but he could not protect me from Lamanites, or really from men in general. Because of an oath he made long ago, he could not protect me from what had happened that night.

I thought of the man who had come courting Cana long ago—long before Micah, Keturah's oldest brother, had come home from the war to ask Father for her hand. Zareth had seemed so nice at first, but when Father had seen his true nature once in the city, something he would not even discuss with us, he had flatly refused to let the man have any contact with Cana, or any of us girls for that matter.

I guessed there were ways he could protect me, I thought as I looked up at him.

But I wasn't so dumb as to think that parents could

protect their children from everything.

Take Kenai, for instance. He was alive and healthy and whole, but something had gotten the best of him, and no amount of his mother's faith had been able to stop it from happening. Everyone said so behind his back, though I knew nobody meant to be unkind. They wanted to help him, but nobody knew how. I wanted to help him too.

I looked back over my shoulder as I stepped from Father's arms. Darius and Kenai were talking to their mother, Leah, just a few paces away. They both glanced at me, and I looked away embarrassed.

Zeke and Jarom's bratty little sister—that's what they saw.

"Isabel, you need to take someone with you when you go to the tannery," Zeke said to me. "Keturah took someone with her everywhere during the war, and it always kept her safe."

"And Keturah's supposed to be my model of behavior?" I asked skeptically. If I remembered anything about my brother, I remembered that. He hated the way Keturah acted. Loved her. Hated her actions.

He sighed.

"Besides," I said, "I remember a raid that happened right here in this village. Home is not necessarily safe either. Face it, you wasted six years of your life and it's no safer here than it was before you left."

"Isabel!" exclaimed my mother.

I just gave everyone a scowl and walked into the hut.

"How long has she been like this?" I heard Zeke ask in a low voice. "But as much as I hate to admit it, she is right. Wickedness abounds, even here in Melek."

"She shouldn't resist our protection," added Jarom.

A fine time to get protective, I thought as I remembered Kenai's chest pressing down on mine, his eyes searching for something in my face, his sudden movement away when he found it.

Chloe's voice brought me out of my memory. She was talking to someone in the yard. Going to the side door, I listened. It was Keturah. She was going alone into the woods.

I didn't know what Zeke was talking about. Keturah hadn't been accompanied by a guard everywhere she went. Not Keturah. She had been home from the war for over a year and here at home I never saw her with anybody. Not even other women, let alone guards, unless you counted Muloki, but even that had stopped now that Melia had come to live in the village. The whole idea was ridiculous. Improbable. Impossible. I wondered why Zeke would even dream up something so preposterous. Did he want to be the one to accompany me everywhere? That was a laugh.

I gathered up all the things I would need for the work day—my lunch, my tools. I didn't like to leave my tools at the tannery unattended overnight. Father had given them to me. They were mine, and I didn't want to lose them. The previous night had been a fine example that even in the land of Melek we were not without crime.

The people of Ammon were good people, but they were not above succumbing to temptation. And lately, in the past few years, many refugees from all different kinds of foreign places had been arriving in Melek for the asylum our Nephite government offered here. And we had to just accept them and all their different customs, even different religious beliefs and value systems.

Hence, I carried my tools with me.

When I stepped into the courtyard ready to go to work my whole family stopped talking and stared at me. After a moment, Mother offered everyone breakfast, which no one accepted.

Chloe was at work milking the goat. Why shouldn't I go to work?

Well, of course I knew why. I had been kidnapped from the tannery not twelve hours ago. I had been awake and traveling all night. But it was daylight now, and I wouldn't be alone. Besides, did they think I could go to sleep after stabbing a man—a Lamanite!—with my knife?

I felt my knife tied securely to my waist, and I squeezed my eyes shut so I would not cry. I was not going to sit around all day sucking my thumb and looking to be coddled.

About the Author

Misty Moncur wanted to be Indiana Jones when she grew up. Instead she became an author and has her adventures at home. In her jammies. With her imagination. And pens that she keeps running dry.

Misty lives near a very salty lake in Utah with her husband and two children, where they cuddle up in the evenings and read their Kindles. Well, she does anyway.

Made in the USA
Charleston, SC
26 January 2016